The Transformation of Gloria Weidman

Ren Benson

For my aunt, Gloria

Prologue

Dean took a deep breath of the crisp morning air. He got up every morning at exactly six and made his breakfast. After a quick, dry piece of toast, coffee in hand, he'd amble down the sloped back lawn and step onto his boat dock in his slippers and robe, staring out at the rising mist from the lake. There was rarely anyone else up and about at this time of day – the solitude suited him. He noticed the grass was getting a bit high. Maybe that chunky kid from down the street would offer to mow for him again. He was getting older and the stigma of being a widower made him the target of sudden kindnesses. A casserole here, a lawn mown there. Nothing he wouldn't have done himself in better times.

He glanced at his watch, the frail hands of it barely visible in the sepia light of dawn. Almost six thirty, and it was Sunday. For a number of years, at exactly six thirty in the morning, every Sunday, Rusty Fry would buzz past Dean's dock, burning fuel and oxygen as he sped by in his cigarette boat – breaking several laws, including the speed limit – spraying Dean in a misty rainbow of exhausted lake water laced with oil. The first time it happened, Dean suspected it was a miscalculation, a drunken lark. But instead of screaming curses, Dean simply raised his coffee cup and shouted, "See ya later, ya slick bastard."

Three years later, it was practically a comedy routine, perfected by years of mutual cooperation. Dean noodled over various insults to shout to his elusive neighbor this morning. *Something* cocksucker - maybe *dumb* or *stupid* - was high on the list of potential candidates. Outside of this bizarre weekly ritual, Dean had no contact with Rusty, who was quite a few years younger. Who wasn't, these days? The receded hairline and pot belly of his nemesis put him at maybe late fifties, sixty, tops? He knew Rusty worked in a neighboring town, a bigger one, not this small one on the lake. Was it Tyler? Or Longview? Did something with taxidermy, or was it bail bonds? Something lucrative. The cherry red boat was a beauty.

Normally, as the semi-stranger passed, he'd speed up and whip the tail of the long speedboat around, slicing it perfectly to the southeast, narrowly avoiding a collision with the dock. Rusty would finish by pumping the engine, stirring up several large waves, lifting what appeared to be a permanent beer from his lap as a salutation, punch the gas and speed off until the next Sunday. Not the classiest of exchanges. But it was something to do, some routine, not too up close and personal, yet *somewhat social*, and that amount of contact suited 'em both just fine.

Dean heard a distant buzz and scrunched his eyes, peering into the fog over the water. There he was, like clockwork. The red of the sleek, shiny fiberglass boat appeared on the water line, drawing closer, faster and faster. The boat rushed forward, moving out of the fog, weaving a bit unsteadily as it accelerated. Dean stood, transfixed on the dock, watching the speedboat move faster and faster, the space between the dock and boat shrinking exponentially with time. Dean thought, as the boat failed to arc into a slice upon its approach and smashed into the pier, *he should really slow down.* The speedboat launched into the air, careening sideways as it went airborne, sailing past Dean's wide eyes as he remained rooted to the spot, remarkably unscathed by the explosion of decking and fiberglass.

He saw Rusty's hands clasping the steering wheel - the

ever present, silver can wedged between his generous thighs - sunglasses still dangling from the stub of his neck. There was no head! The boat sailed like an unwieldy dart into the aluminum siding of Dean's boat house with a crunch, forcing its front end through a weak piece of metal which groaned as it was pierced and collapsed, the mangled red boat slowly sinking into the bashed frame of Dean's weathered pontoon.

Stupid cocksucker it was.

Chapter 1

Life, if you're lucky, is long and strange. Gloria once heard this mantra from a raspy-voiced, shaggy-haired *guru* at a squalid sit-in for women's rights when she was seventeen. Her best friend Dee was *going through a phase* and dragged Gloria there to meet *like-minded freethinkers*. It was a small, sweaty, hairy crowd. She'd listened raptly, her young mind soaking it in. These exciting, radical thoughts. The notion that one person *could, would* change the world. The smell of damp polyester and righteousness. That's what it felt like then. Not so much that *she* might change the world, but maybe *someone around her*, someone *more organized*, someone *more tenacious*, someone not planning on marrying and having a family *and* career. Someone sitting to her right or left, their smeared eyeliner and unwashed clothes a testament to their feminine strength, their eyes riveted to the simultaneously old-young face of the exotic man speaking. *That* someone would change the world. And she'd be nearby, watching triumphantly, reporting it or talking about it on the evening news.

And here she was almost fifty years later, straining to overhear the officers' discussion a few stools down while shutting out the stream of chatter to her right. Dee didn't seem to notice and went on with her tale of woe regarding one of her four interchangeable children who shared no less than three fathers, seven ex-spouses (two of those incarcerated), nine grandchildren (with two active child custody disputes) and inconsistent employment sprinkled throughout the mix.

"No goddamn head. I'm telling you. That drunk

motherfucker took it off on a net. Ain't never finding it. Don't know why they waste their time searching for it."

"Damn shame," Dale commented, placing beers in front of the two men, one still sporting his blue uniform.

"I thought he was a private dick?"

"Weren't nothing private about it," another patron slurred.

Everyone within earshot laughed. Gloria made a discreet note in her small notebook, scribbling furiously with a tiny pencil she requested earlier, no doubt stolen from the mini golf place up the road.

Dale turned back, grabbing the drink from Tiny's hand, placing it in front of Gloria as requested. The guy in the booth, the young one with the book, quietly ordered it for her, his voice low and confident, hooded green eyes, honest looking sort if not unusually younger than his general clientele. Dale had never seen this kid before. Maybe he was visiting family or a college student from up the road. They wandered in from time to time. This one seemed harmless enough, though he deemed it an odd thing for a young man to do. Tipped well, at least. Manners to spare.

"From the gentleman in the booth," Dale winked as he slid a second amaretto sour in front of her. The drink already in Gloria's hand was almost full. She looked dubiously at the glass Dale placed in front of her while tilting his head in the direction of the corner booth.

Well, what have we here, Gloria inelegantly craned her head around spotting a fairly handsome, *very young* man with floppy, dark brown hair that fell to his shoulders unevenly, his heavy-lidded eyes intently focused on a paperback book, one knee folded up on the seat cushion. He sat alone. Comfortably alone. Out of place here, she thought, pinching her lips together. He must have felt her bewildered gaze burning a hole through the top of his head because he looked up, raised his tumbler of scotch and went back to his book with a smile. Or was that a smirk? That was definitely a smirk.

She spun back around in her seat, sliding the drink back to Dale. "You tell that *ass*…butt…face, no thanks. I don't appreciate being made fun of," Gloria was discombobulated. She eyed the drink on the bar and the half full drink in her hand, weighing the cost ratio to the psychiatric toll and decided it wasn't worth it. Pulling her purse up from the floor, she gathered her reading glasses back up, placed her phone into a side pocket and slapped a twenty down to pay for her drink.

"Oh, he's cute, Glory, just take the damn drink. Don't look a gift horse in its pouty mouth!" Dee nudged her, rolling her eyes. Dee, her oldest friend in the world, always there to encourage her to take the cheapest way out of every situation. They couldn't be more opposite. As Dee gloriously descended into a bawdy, lusty autumn of life, defiantly comfortable with her Rubenesque stature, a self-loving cherub with endless confidence born from an endless supply of willing paramours, Gloria could feel her once supple body drying up into a husk of elderly gristle. Had she really reached a phase of life that invited ironic ridicule from hipsters? Not if she could help it. She had half a mind to march over and give that young thug a piece of her well-preserved mind.

"You aren't leaving?" Dee cried. She pulled Gloria back down. Dee, making efficient strides on her third pina colada, was in no hurry to move her generous form from the warm, worn barstool. "I'm tired," Gloria waved her off, stuffing her notebook into her oversized purse which she pulled to her chest like a shield. She wanted to turn around and shoot the young man a dirty look but couldn't face his knowing smirk again.

Dale returned after sliding a particularly intoxicated police officer another beer, shaking his white head ruefully, "I don't think the man meant insult, Glory." He frowned, pushing the twenty back to her, thinking maybe he should have refused the kid, "No charge, honey."

Dee waved sullenly as Gloria struggled off the bar stool, hitching her baggy capris back into place with a defiant tug.

"Thanks, Dale," Gloria took the twenty back, slipping it into one of her many pockets. Her eyes watered as she exited the bar. Halfway home another car flashed their headlights, and she realized she'd driven the five miles home with her lights off, distracted by murderous thoughts. She blamed Dale, mostly. *What* was he thinking? When that *boy* asked him to pass a poor, lonely, post middle-aged woman a drink to *mock* her, he *should* have told him to *fuck off*, like a gentleman.

When she was twelve and Dee was thirteen, they'd been helplessly besotted by seventeen-year-old Dale's long, flowing hair. Her older brother, Karl, ran around with him in high school, before they both joined the army. As impressionable young girls, she and Dee did everything they could to hang out with Karl and Dale and their high school friends – stealing beer from their parents, drinking in someone's barn or boathouse, sneaking into high school parties.

Since then, Dee had been married four times. Most recently *to* Dale. That sad liaison took place well over twenty-five years ago and only lasted nine months, right up until they both realized they hated the other one's children so much it wasn't worth the fading passion and parted as friends. One might think that would make things at one of the few bars in town awkward, but it wasn't. And sometimes, their shared history earned them free drinks.

Chapter 2

Scanning the local paper the next morning, the crumbs from her English muffin dotting the grainy, horrific photos of the Rusty Fry crime scene they were currently calling *an accident*, Gloria flipped to the most recent target of her misplaced ire, *Ask the Editor*. She crowed aloud as she spotted her last missive to said editor - a scathing review of one of his articles - the right wing, misogynistic ravings of a small minded, small statured man. But that was *just her opinion* to the editor. Seeing her words, sharp as they were in black and white, stirred her. This was the day to get moving on her research and start writing, instead of just telling her students how *they* could write.

A small-town murder mystery…those seemed to be in fashion in modern publishing, she mused. Perhaps something a bit curious and supernatural. The victim a taxidermist/private investigator/werewolf hunter. There's your whimsy, she snorted.

Go time. After one more cup of coffee.

Can you pick me up Car broke agin

She glanced down at her phone. It was her nephew Terry, again. Misspelling again, again. Where was autocorrect when you needed it? And where was that when she was starting out? Did it really matter, though? Terry wasn't a scholar. He was just a groundskeeper at the Community Center where she taught. It didn't matter if he could spell.

Terry was her brother Karl's youngest, most disappointing, progeny. While the other four Weidman children rose to such vaulted ranks as air force captain, high school principal, tanning salon owner and one homemaker home-schooling a brood of fair-haired geniuses, poor Terry seemed to zig at every zag, usually ending up in a ditch somewhere. Or on probation. At times, both.

Currently, he was the town's lone marijuana distributor. With the family name, it might be considered destiny. Terry naively assumed no one in the family knew about his side job. No one spoke about it, but they all knew. In fact, Gloria was half tempted to ask for herself. No one seemed to remember, but she'd partaken from time to time as a rebellious, happening teenager and was quite the hip young adult through the late seventies until she went through her first divorce, lost her pot dealer in the process and switched to wine. But wine got boring as you got older and had to drink less. She knew her cousins Betty and Woody were current clients. It was rather obvious when they all wandered off for a *brisk walk* after Thanksgiving gatherings and came back reeking of weed and perfume.

Terry tended to text his aunt only when he was in need. His mother, Linda, had no patience for her youngest. His father Karl was simply a dick. And his old, Aunt Gloria was local now – she was retired – she *also* loathed his father, feeling Karl was unnecessarily hard on the whimsical young man. Of course, the whimsical young man in question *was* thirty-two now. But he'd long been her favorite. And, the longer she lived, the more she realized it didn't really matter what you did, it was how you did it. Terry did everything joyfully.

Gloria glanced at her watch. What else did she have to do? Rusty Fry's funeral, which she planned to attend even though she'd never met the man, wasn't until tomorrow afternoon. Her daily run to Brookshires grocery for fresh vegetables was flexible, although past three it turned into a madhouse. Mom wasn't expecting her to visit today. The only thing she'd planned was more research and staring at an empty page trying to force herself to start an outline.

Where u at? She texted back, picturing a future full of young people who simply clicked and hooted - their interactive video clothing constantly updating with various emojis to signify what they felt or wanted. Or what offended them. Perhaps to be supplied by their more verbal, robotic personal servants.

The point, he answered. Ah, he was frolfing again. Was that it? Frisbee golfing. It looked stupid. And probably was, but he‘d been whole hog on it for years, organizing (loosely, it *was* Terry we were talking about) an East Texas league that played other tiny, one-horse towns – or, as Gloria liked to say in moments of feigned ignorance – one *whore* towns. Was that a good title for her book? *Missing Heads in a One Whore Town*. Maybe?

She drove to the park near the point leisurely, annoying the cars behind her with undisguised glee. The Point at the lake which, depending on what tornadoes wrought that year, either boasted tall, soaring pine trees or denuded destruction. Gloria liked living near the lake, but never *on* the lake. She never understood the allure. It was a tornado magnet, flood risk and friend to fauna and snakes of all kinds. And there were rumors of giant catfish haunting the woody bottoms of the man-made lake. She'd even heard, in the past two days, the giant catfish theory floated as a suspect in the *beheading* of Rusty Fry. Considerate of the bottom-dwelling fish to decapitate him *and* put him back in his boat, she thought. Idiots.

Terry gave a hopeless wave as she pulled into the small, grassy parking lot. His rusting Camry was the only car there. A friend stood deferentially away. Which made more sense, now that she thought about it. How would one frolf alone? What Gloria never understood was where the golf balls came into play?

Both men were dressed in frumpy, sweat-stained, oversized t-shirts atop baggy, ripped khaki shorts, and ball caps. The official uniform of the sport, obviously. Terry hopped in her idling car, motioning his young companion to follow suit.

"Thanks, Aunt Glory," Terry gave her a sweaty, impish smile as he folded his lanky frame into her aging Cadillac. He gestured to the guest in the back seat, "You remember my friend, Henry? He was with me last time this happened. I don't know what's wrong with that piece of shit. Sorry. I gotta get it into the shop soon. Tomorrow."

Gloria shrugged. Terry's car was obviously in steep decline. The shop could only do so much. The vehicle in question was at least fifteen years old. And, for thirteen of those fifteen years, Terry had been nickel-and-diming it back together while it steadily fell apart under his abuse. She turned with a smile to greet his friend, but the smile died on her lips. It was *the guy*. The *jerk* from the bar. Only, as she thought this, she realized *he* wasn't the jerk.

He grinned sheepishly at her, scrunching up his eyes as if amused by the situation. "You don't remember me, do you?" he surmised. "You picked us up a few weeks ago, in Bullard, after the tournament. I thought that might be the case the other night."

Terry looked on in confusion until Henry casually explained, "I ran into your aunt at Flossy's the other night. But I don't think she remembered me."

Recognition rushed her now. She felt like a complete assbutt. And she prided herself on being of the non-asshole variety, in general. Her face burned red as she craned her head around to look the young man in the eye, "Oh, no!"

He threw his hands up good-naturedly, "Don't worry about it. I've been told I'm not that memorable."

Gloria frowned. How could she forget such an open smile? She remembered now. He was about ten years younger than Terry

- his skin still smooth, unwrinkled, unblemished – twenty-three at most, probably younger. He had striking green eyes. How had she not noticed *that* the other night? He was average height. A little pale and furry, but he wasn't completely unremarkable. His face was gentle and lively, his hair a bit long. She just had no reason *to* remember him. It wasn't like they were to run in the same social circles. Or any type of circle.

"I didn't mean to scare you the other night," the young man admitted in a low voice.

Terry glanced between his friend and his aunt with furrowed brow.

Gloria laughed and waved her hand, "No, you didn't. I thought-" She pursed her lips, stopping herself from repeating the idiotic thought he had been trying to hit on her, "Never mind what I thought. It's my fault. I'm an asshole."

"You're not an asshole," Henry laughed. He had a nice, rich laugh that made him seem more mature, more graceful somehow, cramped in the back of her car beside several sacks of to-be-donated clothes.

"Your well-mannered friend tried to be a gentleman and buy me a drink the other night and I blew him off," Gloria finally explained to Terry. Gloria put the car in reverse, glancing in her rearview mirror at the serene young man, "Where to, boys? And Henry, I'm truly sorry. I will gladly accept a beverage from you the next time we cross paths at Flossy's! My deepest apologies. I'll remember you next time. Senior moment."

Of course he wasn't trying to pick up a *mature*, mysterious woman at the bar. He was trying to be polite to his friend's elderly auntie.

"You can just drop us both at Terry's. I can walk home from there," Henry offered, glancing out the window as they pulled onto the blacktop road that rimmed the lake. Dark, aggressive clouds threatened to the north and the air was heavy and electric.

Terry lived in a small house Karl and Linda purchased for him as a fixer upper several years ago. Karl owned several rental properties throughout town, in addition to the gas station/barbeque/hamburger grill from which he'd made his fortune and reputation as a big man in the tiny town. Of course, Terry hadn't fixed anything three years in and the house listed to one side, covered in vines and overgrown bushes with its eroding porch and roof. It was a fairly short, silent drive.

As Gloria pulled up the beaten blacktop driveway, she turned her head, "Henry, I can take you home, too. Where do you live?"

He hitched his head east, "I rent a cabin off Southpoint. Near the piers."

"I can take you," Gloria decided. It was the least she could do after spurning his generosity the other night. Although, the longer she thought about it, it was still an odd thing for a young man to do.

"You sure?" Henry squinted up at the setting sun. "'Cause I don't mind walking. It's not too far."

"Don't be an idiot," Gloria sighed. "It's at least a mile. You'll get run over. Come on, I don't mind. Least I can do for being so rude."

Standing patiently by the open window witnessing the negotiation, Terry shrugged, scratching his small pot belly as he waved laconically, "See ya, man. Thanks Aunt Glory."

"No problem, kid," she smiled fondly at him.

Henry slid into the front seat, studying Gloria from underneath long, dark lashes. Gloria had turned her radio on low when she stopped to pick them up and the music was just a suppressed hum in the background as they drove.

"So, Henry, where are your people?" He looked startled she'd spoken.

"Your parents?" Gloria went on. "Siblings? Where do you hail from?"

"Oh, uh, I'm an orphan. No people per se," he smiled calmly as he said this so she didn't know if he was joking or if it was a pain just far enough in the past he could speak of it without emotion. "I'm from all over, you know. Just vagabonding around the south for a few years. Here and there, doing whatever interests me."

"Wow," Gloria laughed, "that is the most generic background I think I've ever heard. The man from nowhere and no one, traveling the world alone."

"Yeah, you got it," he smiled shyly.

"You must be very young, I mean – shouldn't you be in college?" She was fishing. She was so bad at judging age as she got older.

She glanced out the corner of her eye to see him think for a moment before shrugging and responding. "I'll be four hundred and forty-eight. This year."

Gloria laughed out loud despite herself, "Well, Henry, that makes us peers."

She squinted her eyes, reading the old, rusting street signs as she pulled into a small enclave and drove up a winding one-lane blacktop road. At the foot of the road sat the cabin, a lone light shining from one of the windows. "Sorry again about the other night. My memory isn't that great," Gloria babbled self-consciously while the young man slid from her passenger seat.

He leaned down to peer at her before he slammed the door shut, "Thanks again, Gloria. See ya around." He waved without turning back, sprinting inside just as the sky shook with thunder and plump, warm raindrops began falling with distinctive ploops on the cracking orange earth.

Chapter 3

"Mine is the blessing of the Lord."

"Amen," Gloria repeated under her breath, studying the netted and hatted backs of heads from her position under the perimeter of the green tent. She didn't want to draw any attention to herself, nor have to explain she shared no connection whatsoever with the deceased other than morbid curiosity. If asked, she could easily blend in with the throng of friends and associates, claim she'd known Rusty through work, hired him to follow a husband, knew him in college, consulted with him on capturing a werewolf. All possible retorts if asked. If nothing else, it allowed Gloria to drive to a neighboring town and admire their verdant body farm. She, herself, couldn't imagine anything else in death more stifling than remaining in one place.

It seemed rather morbid, now that she was here. To come out of misguided interest to a man's last moments above ground – a place of ritual and solitude and the droning Baptist preacher, who'd already presumably spoken at length of Rusty's virtues and rewards in heaven at the church, now actually singing his praises as the casket lowered into the freshly turned dirt with a squeak, then an awkward moaning noise from the gears which clicked to a halt, moaned once more and continued its rotation rather clumsily down and down.

Three similar looking women - wan, long-faced and craggy skinned, a hodgepodge of grey-toned teeth, the owners' heads topped with long, bleached hair that flowed past their shoulders

- wheezed and cried together, taking turns consoling one another before another member of their trio would be overcome with grief and the comforting began anew. Sisters, perhaps? Gloria covertly glanced at her phone, checking the time. Who knew research was *such* a time suck? Had it been too much to hope to spot just one of several ex-wives, children or long-time associates she could plumb for actual information?

"Friend or family?" a deep, lilting voice whispered in her ear, close enough she could feel the rush of breath against her neck.

A chill ran up her spine. Not the bad kind. Everyone around her rose, mingling as a few lingered over the open grave, mixing and talking as they squinted into the sun, moving from their seats under the tent to the overgrown grass of the cemetery. The minute she heard the voice, she knew it was the strange young man from the Point. Henry. She turned, the corners of her eyes crinkling against the glare, yet her pace didn't slacken as she walked away from the mourners. He rushed to keep up.

"Henry? Well, what do you know?"

He wasn't dressed in a suit. He sported pointed cowboy boots peeking from under the hem of his pressed jeans; a short sleeve, button-down shirt with a western design emblazoned across the front and a worn, grey sports coat folded over his right arm. Completely acceptable funeral garb in a farm town. He probably didn't own very much, Gloria reflected, thinking of their brief discussion.

She smiled to lighten the mood, retroactively answering his question, "Old friend. Hadn't seen him in years and years. I just felt compelled to come, share my condolences."

"You didn't know the guy either, huh?" Henry teased her, prying the truth from her wide-eyed protest.

"Admit it," he smiled. "It's cool. I'm nosy too."

“Can I admit something even stranger,” Gloria confided as they walked down the pebbled path to the small parking enclave together.

Henry’s eyes lit up conspiratorially at the suggestion, “I’d love it if you did.”

“I think this guy was *killed.* And not by catfish. And I’m not even sure it’s the first murder. There have been *a couple* of mysterious accidents lately,” Gloria glanced around as she made this revelation in hushed tones. She didn’t know why she decided to confess to this particular young man, but something about his honest eyes made her want to tell the truth. She had the strangest feeling around Henry. Like he was an old friend.

“Right on,” Henry nodded in agreement, leaving the silence to hang between them, inviting her to continue, “so there’s a killer?”

“How do we know it’s not you?” Gloria added with a glint of humor in her eyes.

“You just never know, do you?” Henry wiggled his eyebrows in mock menace, pacing himself beside her. “Are you a detective on the side? I thought Terry said you were teaching now. But you’re a writer, yes? Wait, are you writing a new book?”

It struck her later that he’d bothered to ask her nephew about her past. Gloria shook her head ruefully, lying to herself as much as Henry, “No, probably not, just nosy too, I guess. And yes, I was once considered a writer, but *that* was a lifetime ago and now I just teach others to write.”

“I dig it,” Henry added. Gloria slowed her pace, staring up at him suspiciously. He went on, “You know, *I* was a late reader and writer, but I’ve always enjoyed both equally.”

“Then you should come by my class sometime. It’s just community center stuff. To keep busy. Keep the creative juices from atrophying." Stop. Babbling. Gloria willed herself.

"Oh, yeah?" He nodded. "Who knows, maybe I'll drop by sometime."

He reached around her, effortlessly opening her door like a practiced gentleman, ushering her to sit. He did this so smoothly Gloria didn't realize what happened until she was pulling away, her sweat-dampened hair fluttering in the blast of the air conditioning.

He hadn't really answered any of her questions, though. Had he? And he hadn't allowed her to ask anyone else any questions. What a strange young man. Before this week, she didn't know he existed, and now she'd seen him three times in four days.

Chapter 4

Gloria's class was about forty minutes into its too-brief hour when she heard the door creak open in the back of the room. It wasn't a very large space – what was once used as a Sunday school room of a defunct church. Baptist naturally, this *was* East Texas. Now born again as classroom B for the regional Community Center. Henry slunk into an empty seat. Not a desk. There were no desks in community classes, just random chairs in a cluster of eight - three of which usually remained empty.

Gloria had just briefed the cluster of eight on first person approaches for their new assignment - choosing a random character and writing from that perspective. The story was to be about anything of their choice, outlining a few famous examples she knew would hit home with her students; *Twilight*, *The Great Gatsby* (the print version) and *A Tale of Two Cities*. She tried not to lose her train of thought, merely nodding and smiling as Henry sauntered in and made himself at home.

"How long?" her eldest student, a graying man of sixty something, asked. Memoir writer, she assumed.

"As long as you'd like. I say shoot for a couple of pages. But if the mood hits you then by all means, continue," Gloria swept her hands out. The students got no credit and dubious instruction, yet they outpaced the college students she once taught in terms of dedication and interest any day.

"And it's about *my* life?" a dubious younger writer repeated slowly.

"No, *you* are the *I* of *your story*. It doesn't have to be you." Gloria struggled to explain, "First person, remember? You could write from the perspective of an old woman like me. Of the girl sitting next to you. The guy in the car on the road out there. Any life, any person you can imagine dropping into…any story you can tell from a first-person perspective." Gloria spun around to the portable whiteboard she'd dragged in her first week teaching, pointing to the simple diagram she'd drawn to illustrate her lesson. "I'm not sure *what* about *this* is confusing, but I look forward to reading all of your work next Thursday. Same time." It would be interesting to see what was turned in at this rate.

As she hoped, he lingered behind the other students filing out the door casting baleful, suspicious glances at Henry as they exited before congregating on the sidewalk between the center and the parking lot.

"Didn't expect this, did ya?" he winked at her.

"How did you…?" she cocked her head in question.

"You mentioned it the other day at the funeral. And I thought I always wanted to learn from a master. So, here I am." Gloria didn't know how to reply.

"When we love, we love hard and crazy. That leaves no room for the small and the weak."

It was an odd pick-up line to hear from the lips of a very young man and took her an embarrassing second to realize he was quoting a line from her third book back to her. So, he had read the book! She paused as he opened the exit door, shading her eyes as they adjusted to the setting sun, the sky pink and purple beyond a black horizon of trees bordering the old church's property line.

Gloria laughed, "You may be the only person of your generation to ever read that book."

"Was it a true story?" Henry asked.

"No, not really," Gloria supplied smoothly. She'd answered the question often enough in the years after that book was published. "It was just an amalgam of people and events. It was about loss. And I did lose my brother. But not in Vietnam like the book. In Germany - in an accident while he was drunk on base. Motorcycle accident. The rest of it – the German brothers – little things like that, just stories about my family I was raised hearing. But no, the only truthful part of that book was the emotion invested in it. I was struggling with so many things, going through another divorce, trying to find my way. I always found comfort in writing, so off I wrote. Poured everything into that book. But no one loved it like I did. And that's a shame." She caught herself and stopped. Her second husband told her often in their short union she talked too much about herself, her projects, the assignments she'd taken on for various publications over the years. She'd grown self-conscious about going on too long, boring her audience. *The world isn't your classroom*, Phillip would tell her, *stop lecturing everyone* and putting them to sleep with the latest book idea you'll never complete. She didn't blame him, per se. But she'd punished him by stopping altogether. Then, he wasn't even married to an author anymore, just a woman with little ambition and an even smaller idea of how to make a living outside of her marriage.

When they reached her car, Henry again reached smoothly around her, opening the door and ushering Gloria to settle herself inside. He protectively scanned the perimeter with his eyes.

"Good class," Henry joked. "Next one, I'll be on time."

"Oh," Gloria was surprised for the second time since his unannounced entrance. "You're coming back? That's great! You know you don't have to actually turn anything in? You can just audit the class, if you'd like. It's not like anyone is getting a grade here."

"I totally plan on turning in my homework next week, just like every student. I've always wanted to learn to write," he assured her. "I'll see you next week, teach!"

With that, her door snapped gently closed.

What…in the hell, she thought, clicking on the ignition. Was she crazy or had Henry found a way to walk her to her car and disappear without a word about himself yet again?

Chapter 5

"Can I have a word?" the facility director mouthed as Gloria breezed past the front desk of the assisted living facility. Her heart sank. Dammit. What now? Pasting a wooden smile on her face, she turned, holding her bag of groceries in front of her chest.

"Beverly," Gloria sighed.

Beverly was a very uptight, very brittle woman of indeterminate age. She had coarse brown hair, sallow skin and a permanently clenched jaw. She shook Gloria's hand, encasing Gloria's fingers within her own small, feverish, rough ones, offering a look of shared sorrow.

Gloria had never known a person who worked so aggressively to be compassionate. Showing this compassion competently, pushing it onto the families of her clientele, seemed to pain her physically. Her face clenched as if she was constantly trying to squelch a gas pain. Which in turn made Gloria leery to touch her hands. It was too tempting to pull her finger.

"Gloria," Beverly Kent nodded, signaling Gloria over to the administrative hallway of the facility. She didn't lead Gloria into her office, which would signify even worse news - though being pulled to the side, away from the cheerful greetings of the lobby, was never a good sign.

"There's some things we need to discuss about Miss Dottie's continuing care," Beverly reported solemnly.

Miss Dottie was Gloria's mother, yet she always felt maternal in these meetings, as if Dottie were her mischievous child and not a grown, stubborn woman of force who in her prime wielded a belt on her children as nimbly as she'd run her staffing office for all those years. Miss Dottie wasn't going gracefully into her good night. Secretly, it pleased Gloria to see her mother fight nature. She planned on doing the same herself. Gloria nodded, her heart racing.

"She's been wetting her bed again," Beverly frowned, whispering, "and hiding the sheets from the staff. I'm sure she's just embarrassed, but we can't have that."

"Ok. Do you think a spanking will straighten her out? Or do you recommend I withhold her allowance?" Gloria deadpanned.

"And," Beverly winced delicately, "there's been some confusion. With the male staff. She's been…verbally harassing some of the orderlies. Asking for Wade. She won't let Mr. Hanover in to clean. Says he scares her now."

The mention of her father momentarily threw her. Ugh. Him again. The phantom. The *deserter*. The fuzzy memory. The destroyer of families. Why on Earth did Dottie continue to ask for that man? He left when Gloria was eight and never looked back, never called, never checked on any of them. Gloria shrugged. What could she say to these allegations? She was sure they were all true.

"She just seems like she's, that it might be time…for us to think about moving her upstairs to a room with more…help."

Her heart dropped. Gloria's mind went blank. The ominous *other* wing. From assisted to full care, specialized care. The *final* wing. The groceries suddenly grew very heavy in her arms. She shifted the weight of it.

"I'm sorry," Beverly stated gently, reaching out awkwardly to pat Gloria's shoulder, "she's a wonderful lady. I wish these things were easier."

Gloria bit back some tears and hefted the grocery sack

more securely in her arms, "It is what it is, right? But I don't think we're there *quite* yet, are we? She seems – aside from the occasional incontinence - okay, right? She seems okay?"

"We'll discuss more later. We have some time," Beverly smiled stiffly, stepping back to let Gloria pass.

Who had time? From what she could see from the oppressive grip of sadness she spied in every nook and cranny here, it didn't seem like anyone had much time. Gloria saw residents as young as herself drooling in some corner of the assisted living facility. She wasn't sure about the *living* part.

"But I'll talk to her about the sheets." Bitch, she thought. Just wash the sheets and let her have her dignity.

Beverly made a motion to dismiss Gloria, who fled gratefully back up the hall, across the quad to Dottie's apartment. She entered without knocking. She was there enough.

"Mom? I got your Dr Pepper," she shouted, dropping the groceries on the countertop, making her way quickly to the handi-capable bathroom. "Be right there."

She shut the door, grabbed a hand towel, shoved it over her mouth and cried dejectedly like a little girl. After a moment of abject self-pity, she wiped her face, washed it with cold water and exited with a forced smile, "How are you today, Mom?"

She bent and kissed Dottie's forehead. Dottie's gaze was riveted to the television watching one of her talk shows, something with doctors doling out ridiculous advice about sulfur enemas. Dottie smiled, patting Gloria's hand where it rested on her shoulder.

Gloria plopped down in the chair across from her and studied the rapidly shrinking woman. Had she always been taller than her mom? She remembered Dottie being seven foot tall when she was younger. And stocky. Stocky enough to put Gloria's father,

Wade, in a headlock at some point in their young married life. Stocky enough to whoop Karl when he joined the army without her permission. Stocky enough to live forever. Dottie ignored Gloria's gaze and watched her show.

"How are you today, Mom?" Gloria repeated more loudly, enunciating clearly.

"I'm wonderful," Dottie answered cheerfully without turning her head, "I saw your father, though. What an ass. But he is *still* so handsome."

Gloria's shoulders drooped, but she didn't correct Dottie. No doubt some handsome orderly or male nurse received an earful today.

Chapter 6

After she left the nursing home, her daily pilgrimage to the grocery store already complete, Gloria was at a loss at what to do with her time. She'd stayed busy for the better part of sixty years, but she hadn't re-acclimated very well to small town life. Aside from her weekly classes at the Community Center, she was bored out of her ever-loving mind. Was it wrong to wish for more than the occasional accidental beheading in town?

She ended up trolling through towering arches of gothic paperbacks at The Pea Picker, a local bookstore in the same strip mall as the grocery store. For a brief, shining moment, Gloria's first novel held a prized position on the racks of the ancient retailer. One full row of her only success. But alas, its time as a minor critic's darling, *a feminist fever dream* she remembered it being called, was short and quiet. Though she'd heard rumbles from an occasional student it had become a bit of a cult classic because of the angry, unapologetic female protagonist they held as a bit of an inspiration.

It was ironic, though. She hadn't meant to write that type of book. It felt like the book wrote itself. Her own words looked foreign to her now. She didn't recognize the confident, angsty woman who'd written *that* book. It certainly wasn't her anymore.

Two sharp raps on her window startled Gloria from her reverie. Dropping the books in her lap with a guilty blush, she looked up. It was Linda, her sister-in-law. Linda flashed a great pearly smile, her veneers waving like white flags in the sun at a parade, her unnaturally red hair lifted in one, shellacked wing floating on a light wind - the wispy hairs beneath the wing fuzzy and thin, like bird's down. Her jewel encrusted tennis bracelet threw off sparkles of reflected light, temporarily blinding Gloria as she forced a smile and activated the button to roll her window down. Ah, Linda Lester, homecoming queen of '74, *how cruel is time*, Gloria thought briefly, spitefully.

The window moaned petulantly, emitting a high pitch whine as it slid down. The exact sensation Gloria felt whenever she was forced to make small talk with Linda. She thought she spotted the back of Linda's head inside the bookstore, so she'd doubled back the other way, checked out silently using smiles and hand gestures and made it to her car without being forced to speak. Luckily, the young cashier, assuming Gloria was mute and deaf, gleefully launched into skilled American sign language. He seemed confused by her peace sign in response. If only she'd driven home before she stopped to smell the damn books.

"Linda!" Gloria trilled to her sister-in-law, "*What in the world* are you doing?"

Linda always spoke with her hands, as if conducting a secret concerto, "Runnin' errands. You know, right. Karl wouldn't even know where to begin to find his own ass after all these years. Forget about grocery shoppin'. He don't know where they keep anything at the Brookshires. You'd think the man couldn't read," Linda laughed at her joke.

Gloria was pretty sure, if memory served, Karl didn't read. Well, at least. Linda was probably closer to the truth than she realized. Yet somehow, remedial reading skills and all, Karl was the success in their family.

"How's everything?" Gloria nodded.

"Oh, great. Did Karl tell you? Missy's expecting again!

We're thrilled. This'll make four, can you believe? What a blessing and a miracle!" Missy's exhausted uterus probably felt differently about this miracle, Gloria thought. Linda went on, "Terry got a raise last month, but I think he's still dating that…older woman," this was whispered. "Lake trash," this was mouthed. "Your brother's garden is just spitting out tomatoes and jalapenos. You should come by and take some, we can only eat so much salsa. I know you love your dips, Gloria."

That part was true. Salsa, ranch dip, dipping while she danced, dating dipshits. Points for Linda.

"You hear about Rusty Fry's accident?"

Gloria nodded. It was a small town. She'd heard about nothing else in days.

"Did you hear about the other body they found by the Piers this morning?"

Now she was listening. That was where Henry lived.

"No – what? who?"

"Some woman…they don't know who. She ain't from here," Linda's eyes lit up with the realization she was giving Gloria fresh gossip.

Gloria experienced a mysterious, brief stab of relief.

Linda went on, "And they say her throat was slit. Ear to ear. Head almost detached. So now," here, Linda leaned conspiratorially closer to the window and lowered her voice, "they think maybe Rusty Fry's death wasn't an accident either."

Linda rocked back on her heels, smug as if she'd just disclosed the second shooter in JFK's assassination. Gloria played along, leaning in.

"How did you find all this out, Linda? This is crazy!"

"I know!" Linda's eyes lit up, "Karl told me. But don't tell nobody. He vowed to solve this crime before anyone finds out there might be-" Linda looked around to ensure no one was listening and mouthed the following word, "a killer."

Gloria stifled a laugh, "What's Karl gonna do, Linda? He's the mayor, not the sheriff."

More to the point, what did she think she was going to do?

"I know," Linda nodded in agreement, "I hope he doesn't get hurt."

"Surely not," Gloria raised her eyebrows in shock, "You tell him to watch himself. Too brave for his own good."

Linda nodded sternly. After a moment of awkward silence, she tilted her head, pressing her lips together in a gesture Gloria knew would precede the following question. "How's your mama doing?

"She's fine, I guess. Still a handful, but she's - you know - not getting any better, that's not how age works. Ya'll should get out there to say hello," Gloria admonished lightly, unable to help herself.

Linda looked guilty, masked it quickly and smiled, "Well, I better git." Jingling her bracelets again, she shrugged and took a step back.

Gloria started her car. That was usually the way the conversations ended. It worked for her. She smiled, backing out as Linda wiggled her fingers in a cheerful wave good-bye.

Chapter 7

Ann Delancy, PI - one of Gloria's favorite characters from the long-running Hardcourt crime thriller book series - would squat down, place a forearm across her thigh and stare stoically out over a crime scene, telling the nosy observers the crime scene itself would speak to her and tell her where to look for clues. Though she didn't think she could recover gracefully from a low, investigative squat, Gloria hoped loitering lazily over the site of this crime would do the same for her.

Though it was sweltering, the parking lot she rolled into near the Piers, an aptly named collection of long piers jutting out over the low water line of the lake, was deserted. There was a point in Texas each year when it was just too hot to go outside. And though one might think the lure of the refreshing lake would entice the bold, those with any sense stayed put in their air-conditioned homes. Once the sun set, you'd hear the lake come back to life. But during the late day heat, it was funereal, which Gloria found appropriate. Even the fish took a break, the lake appearing fallow and dead.

The gravel beneath her feet crunching, Gloria patrolled the perimeter of the parking lot, the lazy lines of heat rising from the black asphalt making her vision hazy. She perused the wood of the piers, staring at her toes while she walked, leery of any curious stains. She crouched down, squinting at the ground. Was that blood? No, just a bag of Cheetos, long buried. Not a clue. She tried to get into the mind of the victim. What that poor woman must have felt, she thought, scanning the water line.

"They found her over there," a familiar voice cried out.

She heard a dog bark at her side, her hand enveloped in the scratchy tongue of a large black and tan Rottweiler, a goofy look of accepting joy on his face as he lifted his forelegs and danced around her feet.

"Hey there," she cooed, scratching the friendly beast under his chin. Glancing up, she spied a slim shadow outlined in the bright light of the sun, pointing to a patch of dry grass beneath a few listing pine trees.

"You again?" Gloria tried to conceal her joy.

"I promise I'm not a stalker. At least not a very good one," he shrugged, walking forward so that the shadows fell from his face and she was able to see his smile. Henry was in flip flops, the same ripped khaki shorts from the day at the park and another worn t-shirt, this one said Class of '76 in distressed, faded ink. His longish hair was pulled back into a tiny ponytail, only visible when he turned his head to motion to the patch of trees. Ugh, she thought, the dreaded tiny ponytail.

The dog giddily sniffed at Gloria's feet, chasing a scent to the water line where he barked at the waves, pouncing on a stick floating too close to the water line.

"You heard about the latest murder, huh?" A dimple in his left cheek revealed itself as he teased her.

"I did. It's awful. I don't even know why I'm here," Gloria stammered.

Henry shrugged as if her answer was of no consequence to him. The dog, his paws wet, ran back up from the water line with the stick in his mouth. Henry knelt down, petting the dog's head while it nuzzled his leg affectionately, "Research?" He winked.

"What's his name?" Gloria motioned to his dog.

Henry looked down at it with a puzzled frown, shrugging, "I don't know."

"What do you mean you don't know?" Gloria laughed. "You mean you never asked or he never bothered to tell you?"

Henry smiled, "Let's say he belongs to a friend. I just take him out for walks here and there, when he needs it."

"And your friend didn't tell you his name?"

Henry thought for a moment, stroking the velvety top of the dog's head, "It's possible he's not aware I'm walking the dog."

So, the dog was stolen? For walks. Gloria wasn't sure how to respond. She'd only just met Henry but somehow, she wasn't surprised. He was out walking a dog that wasn't his and she was investigating a murder that had nothing to do with her as research for a book she'd likely never write.

Henry seemed to read her thoughts. He hitched his head toward the copse of trees, "They found her over there. Neck cracked. Head almost knocked completely off."

He followed Gloria as she wandered toward the site of the actual crime, her gaze scanning the ground.

"So, do you also investigate recreationally? Side gig? Or just for research?" he quipped.

Gloria blushed, "I don't even know why I came out here. Just nosy, I guess. Not enough to fill my mind anymore. And I've had writers block for over thirty years, there's that. I read about that first accident last fall – no head there as well, and the second. I told you all that. Then I heard about this one and I was weirdly inspired. So, I thought, maybe? I don't know?" Why had she confessed all of that, Gloria caught herself. *What was she doing?* He was just so easy to confide in. Like the dog, he didn't even care if you told him your name. "It's not often this town sees anything amusing. Or new, murder or no."

Henry glanced at the sky and then the dog, still chomping the stick to pieces with glee, "I better get him back."

"Sure," Gloria nodded. She was sad to see him go.

Henry whistled through his teeth and the dog bounded up the sloped incline, "See ya!"

"You, too," Gloria waved as the duo retreated over the hilly ditch and across the black top road. She watched as Henry's shadow grew smaller and smaller, the dog bouncing a few steps ahead of him, returning to his side when Henry whistled. That boy was an odd one, she thought.

Chapter 8

What am I doing here, Gloria asked herself once more. Just having a drink, she lied to herself. Again.

"Can I get you another, Glory?" Dale disturbed her frantic inner monologue.

She was really out of practice being out and about without acting like a dumbass and still wasn't sure what possessed her tonight. She glanced down at her half-finished amaretto sour, "Nah, I'm good."

"You think Dee's OK?" Dale broke in again, his eyes searching over Gloria's shoulder into the dark parking lot beyond the thick, sweating windows of the bar.

"You know, I'm sure she is. I just left her a message to meet me here, if she wanted. It was optional, last minute," Gloria trailed off, she felt exposed in her small lie. She wasn't sure why she'd felt a need.

"Oh," Dale's face relaxed, then twisted slightly in confusion. "I thought you said she was meeting you?"

"I thought I'd hear back from her by now," Gloria shrugged, placing a hand over her phone, "It's not often I get out on a school night."

"I only see you two times since you come home," Tiny commented, noisily placing a stack of clean drink glasses beneath the bar.

"I know. I'm a hermit, what can I say? I'm teaching again and Mom was-is a full-time job, for sure," Gloria prattled, winking at the giant, bald barback.

Dale nodded knowingly, "I'm glad she's doing alright. I know my mom loved that damn place. That Beverly Kent. She's the best, right?"

Gloria wrinkled her nose in distaste, remembering Beverly Kent's constipated, pity face. Dee was the one who'd suggested the assisted care home to Gloria when Dottie's illness was finally too much for her alone. She remembered how much Dale's mother enjoyed her days there.

"It's a nice place," Gloria confirmed with a fake smile.

Dale floated away, behind the bar, to another pocket of long-term patrons. This was so stupid, Gloria admonished herself, peering casually around the dark bar. She wasn't sure *why* she was there. She wasn't looking for company. She was just restless tonight. And it wasn't *why* - it was *who. Who* she'd hoped to see. She just wasn't sure *why*? Or *what* she was expecting. Sipping her drink faster, she convinced herself to leave before she looked even sillier. Obviously, she'd hoped to see *him*. And it really didn't make any sense.

She jumped up, backing out the front doors, adjusting her bra strap beneath the canvas strap of her purse as she waved to Dale and pointed to the twenty beneath her empty glass.

"Later, honey. I'll tell Dee she missed ya if she comes," Dale waved the white cloth he'd been using wipe down the bar.

"Well, she'll be confused," Gloria muttered to herself as the door swooshed closed, blocking the hum of the AC inside. She hadn't even called Dee, but the lie slipped from her mouth in a moment of social discomfort. She sat for a moment, her car cranking to life, the cool air sputtering into action and finished her internal monologue; a lengthy diatribe in which she shamed herself for being hopeful. Especially for the sight of a slightly delicate, *very young* man with whom she had nothing in common and who had only been respectful and nice to his friend's greying auntie. The car's engine shuddered and shook, choking to a stop. The air conditioning quit pumping with a huff and Gloria was left in sudden silence. She punched the ignition aggressively, pumping the gas. The engine rolled over several times but wouldn't catch.

"Motherfucker," she muttered, kicking open the door. She poured the contents of her purse on the hood of the car, under the weak shaft of illumination from Flossy's sole, unbroken parking lot light. She grabbed at the business cards littering the contents of her purse. The first was the chiropractor, not it. Ah, Beverly Kent's card – she'd gotten that treasure the day she and Dottie toured the retirement facility a year ago. Dottie seemed unsure of it at the time but as the next few weeks went by and she suffered two more falls, one of which resulted in a shattered wrist, she realized it was for the best. Where was her damn AAA card?

"Won't start?"

"Oh my God!" Gloria cried, her hands flying up to cover her throat. The soft, male voice startled her so violently, she jumped.

And peed a tiny bit.

"Seems to be going around," the voice went on. "Your car obviously caught whatever ails Terry's. Maybe there's a family gene?"

"A family gene for poor car maintenance, that's for sure," Gloria turned to face Henry, hands clutched to her chest. "You scared the shit out of me."

(Just the pee.)

"Sorry," Henry shrugged, a smile crinkling the corner of his eyes. He had a book tucked in his armpit. He pulled it out and shook out his arm. She noticed a small helmet dangling from the fingers that held the book.

"Reading and riding? Motorcycle?" Gloria motioned to the helmet and book. She hadn't heard him arrive.

"Harold Robbins," Henry admitted, holding up the worn paperback in his hand, "and a moped. I'm afraid my groovy motorcycle days are behind me."

Gloria agreed, "Yeah, you seem like more of a moped guy to me."

"Can I give you a lift?" he tilted his head to the green moped parked beneath the streetlight beside her car.

"Know anything about cars?" Gloria asked hopefully.

"I know they are complex mechanical creatures that boggle the mind. I know the more advanced they become, the less I can do with them. I know they hurt the environment," he pressed his lips together and raised his eyebrows mischievously as he finished.

"Well, it's been many years since I've ridden in anything open-air, but what the hell, mind giving me a ride home? I'll deal with this disaster tomorrow."

"No problem," he handed her the helmet which she fit it over her head, taking a moment to self-consciously pat her hair before donning - noting how very dry it had become with age and lamenting briefly the days when her hair was soft and silky and she wouldn't have thought twice about the possibility of her hair shaping itself to the helmet and remaining that way when she removed it, unaware.

Adjusting her purse to her left hip, Gloria slipped Henry's book inside of it when he handed it to her, his feet balancing the motorbike between them.

"Hold on," he instructed, pushing the ignition button. The moped started with a small kick and Gloria tightened her loose grip on Henry's shirt.

"You OK?" Henry turned his head.

"Yes, ready. I'm holding on," Gloria assured him, shouting unnecessarily as the helmet stunted her hearing.

The moped took off at a moderate speed, the zing zing zing of the engine filling the dark shadows of the tree-lined blacktop roads. For years living in the city, Gloria forgot how dark it got out here when the sun finally set. It was only eleven, but there weren't any cars about. In fact, there was a vacuum of sounds except for the throb of crickets as they puttered down the two-lane road. She'd forgotten how beautiful a truly dark backroad could be with a Brothers' Grimm-tree canopy framing the barrel of her sight.

"Where do you live?" Henry shouted over his shoulder. They'd been on the road for almost a mile and Gloria assumed he knew, like everyone else in town.

"At the top of thrill hill, you know it?" Gloria shouted as a gnat flew into her throat. She gagged silently.

"Lilly road? Yeah, which house?"

"The blue one," she sputtered.

Pulling up before her dark house, a sliver of the streetlight illuminating the gravel drive, Gloria wobbled unsteadily from the back of the scooter, hoisting her purse back across her shoulder as she pulled the helmet from her hair, covertly fluffing it out. The bike idling, Henry placed his feet to either side of the scooter, shaking his hair.

"Thank you," Gloria shouted over the zing of the running motor. Henry nodded as she turned to walk inside.

She heard the scooter's motor click off, the fall of Henry's footsteps behind her, "Gloria?"

Her hand stilled on the doorknob as she turned to face Henry. Rather shyly he asked, "Any chance you'd meet me for coffee sometime?"

Gloria tried to keep a straight face, replying casually, "Sure."

"How about Friday?"

"Alright, when and where?" Gloria heard her voice answer though she felt like she was floating outside of her own body. No need to pause like you might have other plans, she realized belatedly.

"Flossy's?" Henry raised his eyebrows in invitation. "Five okay?

"It's a…day." She'd *almost* called it a date, only swerving away from the term at the last moment when she returned to her body.

He threw his head back and laughed, winking playfully, "Ok, then. It's a *day*."

Chapter 9

Dee took another long sip of wine and eyed Gloria suspiciously.

"So, it was just like *Grease 2*?" Dee frowned, doubt and amusement swirling behind her eyes like smoke.

"Well, yes and no," Gloria struggled to explain. "I *certainly* didn't straddle him as we rode, we both know that's impossible with my lower back. And it *was* a moped we were on - not a motorcycle. I'm not insane. And there was no singing. But yeah, if I had to make a comparison."

Dee shook her head, barking a throaty laugh, "Ah, Glory! You're hysterical."

"I know," Gloria sipped her wine, lines of worry creasing her face. "It's weird, right. I mean, nothing happened. But Dee-" Dee arched her eyebrow in question. "He was already going the right direction, like he *knew* where I lived?" Gloria observed.

"Spooky," Dee confirmed. "Your stalker knew *approximately* where you live. The big blue house on the highest hill in a small town with only about ten streets. And your nephew sells him weed, you think. Or maybe just Frisbee frolks with him?"

"Frolfs," Gloria corrected, "Frisbee golfing. Yes, that's all I know about him. Except for his name. His whole name. It's Henry Wynter. Wynter *with a y*, he said. Can a name be sexy?"

"Tell me again! What happened when he dropped you off?"

"I was walking to the door and he said, *Gloria*," Gloria lowered her voice slightly to imitate Henry's, "would you have coffee with me sometime?"

"And this doesn't strike you as the least bit odd for a young man?" Dee prompted.

"Maybe," Gloria bit her lip. "But it didn't feel odd."

"And *how* did *it* feel?" Dee stuck her tongue out, emitting a hoarse, bawdy laugh.

"It wasn't horrible," Gloria joined the giggling. "But I keep running into him, it's the strangest thing. And he gives me the strangest feeling of deja vu."

"And you're aware there's been an unsolved murder or two in the area in just the past two weeks. This is according to you. The appearance of this character isn't alarming at all? Does he not sound like a character you might write?"

"He didn't just *turn up*. He's been renting a cabin by the lake for the last six months. And, he's not the murdering type, I don't think," Gloria surmised, taking another healthy chug of wine.

Dee emptied her glass and shook it. Gloria pointed to the wine on the counter.

"The box is over there, help yourself," Gloria instructed her friend.

Tuesday nights had become their wine and whine time. When they were high school, they had the same ritual but it involved Miller Lite and *Laverne & Shirley*. It had evolved to boxed wine and reality fashion shows, but it still felt good and familiar to Gloria.

"Say what you will, he's not a killer," Gloria summarized. "And when he dropped me off, Dee, I almost asked him in and you know what…I have a feeling he would have. Then he asked me to meet him for coffee. Tomorrow. And…I know it's not a date, but…I don't know what coffee means anymore. What if *coffee* isn't *coffee*."

Dee was silent for a long moment before giggling, coughing and chuckling. “Well, Gloria Jean, I don’t know what’s come over you, but I like it. And I can’t wait to hear about this date.”

They dissolved into a drunken fit of laughter as the opening montage for Fashion Boat flashed across the small screen.

Chapter 10

She expected to be the one waiting; however, when Gloria ducked into Flossy's at five after five, an act that felt strange and subversive during daylight, Henry was already waiting in the same booth where she'd first seen him. Like that time, he perused a paperback, a glass of bourbon and ice near his hand. He looked up, saw her and smiled brightly, waving her over. She checked the impulse to look behind her. The seven other people inside either day drinking or likewise grabbing coffee did it for her.

"I'm glad you made it," he stood while she took a seat. What the hell with the manners again, Gloria wondered? He signaled Tiny with a casual wave. Tiny appeared with a shy, goofy smile asking Gloria what she'd have to drink.

"You know what - just water, for now." Take that, heartburn.

Henry was wearing a navy button-down shirt, the collar hanging open, sleeves rolled up to his elbows. The shirt, which probably should have been ironed and starched, was wrinkled and worn, the fabric lying seductively across the skin of his forearms. She could see the pewter chain of a necklace beneath his collar and the smooth plane of his collar bone, a bit of dark brown hair trailing down his throat to his chest. Aside from the necklace and a watch, he was free of adornment, except for several small tattoos she spotted on the inside of his left wrist. She found the odd combination bafflingly sexy.

"Thanks for inviting me," adjusting her purse to her side in the worn booth, scanning Henry's face beneath her lashes, Gloria watched him suspiciously. She wanted to say *please tell me why you've invited me*, but held her tongue for the moment. Maybe he'd get right to the point, *I'm writing a blog about the ERA, would you edit it?* Instead.

"I find you incredibly interesting and I'd like to get to know you better." Henry smiled like a Cheshire cat while he made this proclamation and Gloria wondered if he could read her mind, "if you're wondering why I invited you," he finished, quickly adding, "And I'm not psychic if that's what you're thinking now. I could just tell you might have questions about my intent."

"Thank you," Gloria waited an inappropriate amount of time responding, her mind reeling and exploding in tandem. "Thank you for telling me that. I find *you* very interesting as well, though I have to admit, I'm a bit confused by your interest." She gestured to include her entire body.

He nodded sagely, "I think you're cool, Gloria. Just like I said. And you seem like fun. I think we have a lot in common, believe it or not. *You* seem like a very curious woman. Like you like to watch, live at a distance. You'd rather write it than live it. A woman prone to staging her own murder investigations for a little research. Which could mean you're bored right now - by these people or this place. Probably both. Who isn't? I also think a woman like you enjoys a challenge here or there. And I don't want to freak you out, but I've read your books. All three of them. Before you ask, my favorite is *The Stalwarts*, which I've read more times than I can count. *You*…are a beautiful writer - the way you paint the world around your characters. *Therefore,* you must have a beautiful soul because you couldn't see those places so clearly if you didn't. That's what I want, too. One day, I want to be able to tell an ugly story and make it beautiful. Just like you did. *That* is *why* I want to get to know you, Gloria. I think you're fucking awesome and incredibly sexy. And, I think I could learn a thing or two from you." He splayed his fingers in front of his chest like he was revealing a magic trick.

She swallowed rapidly, her mouth dry. Tiny interrupted the trance, slapping down a glass of water, topped with a straw. The enormous bald man backed away, his gaze flitting between the two, before turning and resuming his post behind the bar.

Not. Awkward. At. All. Nor were the other fourteen – no wait, that was Earl Richardson there at the bar – make that thirteen eyes upon them.

"I'm sixty-two," Gloria barked unprompted. *Jesus Christ*. What. was. she. doing? "I'm sorry, I'm nervous, I guess."

"Nervous?" Henry scolded her playfully, arching one brow. "Why in the world would you be nervous around me? Are you worried I've lured you here with impure intentions? Because I likely have, but you won't know until you take the time to get to know me. Deal?"

Gloria shook her head, feeling an uncharacteristic blush steal over her chest and cheeks. Then a rash moment of indignation. Was he screwing with her?

"Awesome, then. Okay. Random facts. I'll play. I'm an atheist," Henry smiled and tilted his head, "what else?"

"Uhmmm," Gloria went with it, "I taught junior college English."

"I like school, and schoolmistresses," he teased. "My turn? *I* am afraid to fly."

"I've never been to Europe," Gloria admitted.

"I was born in England, strangely enough," Henry revealed.

So *that* was the very tiny trace of an accent she'd heard in his fairly straight southern one - an out of place twang here or there.

Gloria broke in, "When did you come here?"

"Oh, I was really young," he seemed far away for just a moment, going on, "So, you live alone now?"

Gloria nodded and sipped her water.

"Always?" he probed, his eyes fixed on her.

She shook her head, "No. Not always. I was married once. I mean, twice. Neither great."

"No kids?"

"Nope." She didn't elaborate. It wasn't a painful topic for her but it seemed destined to invite thoughtless commentary such as *how sad, how lonely, how purposeless your life must seem* - the unspoken (or often spoken) question of *what's wrong with you*?

"Yeah, kids suck," he joked after a beat.

Gloria smiled.

"So, your mom is sick?" Henry inquired. Gloria's face must have revealed her confusion. Henry was quick to supply, "Terry. He goes to see her at the Westbridge, you know. Loves his Nana." *More like he loved the twenties his Nana continued to slip him.*

"No," Gloria admitted. Dottie had never mentioned it, "I didn't."

"I went by with him once. Dottie, your mom, she's a cool cat, ya know. A real pistol."

Gloria smiled, trying to picture the encounter, "What did you talk about?"

"She called me Wade and told me I was a son of a bitch," he shrugged, laughing good-naturedly.

"She didn't?"

"Swear to God," he raised his hand, palm up. "Aggressive lady, that one. And a great kisser."

Gloria laughed and snorted, covering her mouth in embarrassment.

"She's fun," he teased, taking a long draw from his glass.

From there, Henry kept up with a steady supply of open-ended questions that kept Gloria talking about her past and future and everything in between, all while giving away remarkably little about himself. When Gloria next glanced out the window, the sun was slipping behind the pine trees, turning everything green into a dark shadow against the pink and orange horizon. She was surprised by the time.

Dale, walking through the dining room on his way to the back office, did a double take as he spotted Gloria, his eyes widening when he spotted her young companion. Grinning, he stopped and turned toward their table to chat but thought better of it in the end, paused and redirected back to his original destination, shaking his white head dubiously. Most of the evening crowd slipping through the doors took no notice of them. Over the course of three hours, Gloria finished her water, moved onto a tea, finally rounding it out with a single amaretto sour. The sun disappeared as Gloria fretted internally about when she should call it a night. Henry took notice of her fidgeting, glancing down at his watch.

"Getting late, huh?" he announced.

Gloria knew the signal. "Yes, it is. But Henry, it was *really nice* talking to you. And, if you're serious about that writing thing, you should come back to class next week. Write something! Share it with the group. Surprise yourself."

"What do you have going on tonight?" Henry jutted his chin up defensively, acting playfully suspicious.

Gloria stilled, shoving her purse out of her lap where she'd gathered it in preparation for immediate flight. "Nothing." It was true. She'd never be able to get to sleep tonight! Forget it. What would she do with herself in that house alone…think about Henry's sexy forearms?

Henry shrugged, inclining his head to the lake Flossy's Dive-In bar bordered. "You wanna go back to my place, get high and go skinny dipping?"

Suddenly, Gloria knew *exactly* what she wanted to do tonight.

Chapter 11

She rode on the back of his green moped to his cabin, her arms stretched around his waist, the strains of *Cool Rider* echoing through her head, trying hard not to giggle like a girl. Taking her hand on his dilapidated porch, he led her into the dark cabin - a cabin curiously devoid of personal items, just as she'd expected. He threw his keys on the coffee table, clicking a nearby brass floor lamp on with his foot and motioned for her to sit on one of two worn leather couches facing each other across a square room. The couch was further down than she expected. Not the most graceful landing. His amused gaze still following her, he sank down across from her on its twin. She hadn't felt this mélange of excitement mixed with unease and a sense of moral meandering since high school, sneaking out her window to a waiting car. It was invigorating. They should bottle it for retirees.

His dark green eyes stayed riveted to hers as he bent down to retrieve a poorly concealed tray under the couch. From that, he took a wooden pipe, tamped down some grass (was it still okay to call it that now?), held up the pipe and lit the top of it with a lighter. He inhaled a deep puff, exhaling through his nose. Leaning forward, he offered her the pipe.

She hesitated. "It's been a while."

That was an understatement.

"Be careful," he warned. "They've come a long way in the last few decades. This shit will blow your mind."

She took the pipe and the lighter, studying it in the lamp light.

"You just light it and hold your thumb over that hole there," he coached, pantomiming. "Inhale and hold it in for a minute."

She tried but she coughed out a great plume of smoke, hacking and gagging.

"Nice." He laughed.

Her eyes watered. She blinked. What had he said about the strength of modern grass? Gloria tried to retain her senses. Whatever he'd said made sense now. What had he said again? The cabin seemed larger from the inside. Or she seemed smaller outside. Wait, what? What did he say about the pot? Weed? That's what she should call it now. Grass was just grass.

"You rent?" she motioned around the room.

"It's the only way," he took the proffered pipe back and leaned back into the couch, lighting the pipe again and taking a long pull of smoke.

"I don't normally do things like this," Gloria feebly explained. Her feet looked extremely large when she glanced down. When she peeked again, they were a normal size.

"No shit," Henry coughed as he exhaled.

They sat and smiled at one another for a moment in deliciously thick, mutually amused silence.

"You want something to drink?" Henry offered.

Gloria realized how dry her mouth was suddenly, "Water."

Henry stood, handing her the pipe and lighter as he headed to the dark kitchen. She heard the comforting noise of the glass, the ping of ice cubes, the faucet and leaned back against the cracked leather of the sofa, looking around. Several times she peered down at the pipe in her hand but had forgotten how to light it. Her gaze travelled suspiciously around the living space, the only thing of note the original furniture which came with the cabin. There were no family photos or posters on the walls. A couple of dirty shirts littered the backs of chairs and a stack of paperbacks leaned against one side table. But other than that – nothing to tell her more about the mysterious Henry Wynter. She sipped the water gratefully when he placed it on the coffee table before her.

"You ready for that swim?" Henry reminded her gently, his bright eyes alight.

Unable to come up with a suitable excuse to back out, Gloria joined him. They walked in the humid night air across the blacktop road to the piers, down to the water line where the lights didn't shine. She was too baked to back out. Or talk, really.

There was a row of piers in various stages of decay and a parking lot about thirty feet away, but it was empty and dark, the streetlamp long since burned out. Henry had thought to bring two thinning, dingy towels, which he gallantly dropped by the edge of the water. He gleefully, unabashedly stripped in the wavering moonlight and plunged into the dark water with a hoot. Gloria, unsure of how to proceed gracefully, lingered by the shore.

Shivering, she stepped carefully out of her flats, teetering as she slowly stripped her pants off, folding them neatly on top of her shoes. The wind blew across her exposed skin. She removed her bra beneath her top, dropping it to the ground, an old trick passed down from mothers to daughters throughout time.

This entire night felt like happy madness. Not for the first time, she wondered what in the world she was thinking. And then realized she didn't care, she was having fun. For the first time in a long time.

"Gloria Weidman," his teasing voice floated across the water like a game show host, "come on down!"

There was a splash as he dove down beneath the bobbing

green-brown waves of Lake Tyler. A boat house with a bright light about a quarter mile away provided a speck of light and the reflection from the moon on the water gently illuminated his skin, though she could barely make out his lithe form.

Another splash.

"Come on in, Gloria," his voice floated over the water again, his pale form out deeper in the lake. "I won't peek."

She saw the flash of his white buttocks as he dove beneath the water, glad he couldn't see her hungry reaction.

"Please do not!" she shouted as he surfaced, scurrying to get out of her top. She made sure she was deep in the shadows as her boobs flew to their preferred position next to her armpits and sighed in frustration. Next came the sensible panties, thinking… just get to it already. She rushed into the water with a gasp, bending down to more quickly cover her body in the warm, lapping waves. Pushing further into the shallows, she heard his splashes as he swam closer to her, slowly circling her. She ducked under, the water streaming down her face as she popped back up to the air. When she surfaced, he was standing in chest deep water in front of her, his hands floating at his sides, gazing at her with an open face, smiling earnestly, his eyes on hers.

"I may have peeked," he teased. He swam away, sluicing silently past her, a light splash followed.

"Monster!" Gloria splashed water in his direction.

"Like a water nymph in the pale moonlight," he crooned, dog paddling closer to where Gloria floated, the water lapping over her shoulders.

"What would you know about nymphs in the moonlight," she scolded.

He circled her in the water again, the moonlight reflecting from the water to his face. His wet hair was plastered to his head, he looked so young. His skin so flawless. Gloria was momentarily self-conscious.

He smiled, rather sensuously, his eyes sparkling, "You'd be surprised by all the things I know, Gloria," he chuckled, splashing her lightly as he swam away, deeper into the lake and the dark, shouting back over his shoulder, his voice suddenly deep and dangerous, "you really would."

Gloria gasped, shivering as the water around her grew suddenly cold. She saw the devilish look in his eyes and the sharp white teeth as he smiled, his pale skin shining in the moonlight. He looked almost wolfish – wild - just for a moment. Dangerous. Feral. The sensation lifted as quickly as it had fallen. What the hell was happening to her? When did grass get this strong? He circled back, splashing around her, waving her deeper into the water.

"What are you waiting for, daredevil. Let's go," he smiled again and she saw his boyish face, relaxed. She must have imagined it. Perhaps she'd grown paranoid. She *was* still waiting for the other shoe to drop…what had he said earlier, "I just want to get to know you. I find you *intriguing*." It just didn't seem like something that happened to women who weren't about to be murdered or sold into servitude.

Soft, white woman for sale – gently used, retro design, can be trained for light labor or sold for parts. She shook it off, pushing deeper into the water, swimming out to join him. Though her hips were stiff from the moped ride and her knees were groaning, she wanted to enjoy this now. She'd pay later, she always did.

A quiet crunching of gravel signified an approaching car. They turned from their stance in chest deep water, spotting the headlights cruising quietly over the dark road rimming the lake. The car had the unmistakable outline of lights on top of it, coming to stop by the lake line before a large man's form lumbered out of the driver's seat, adjusting his pants and fishing for the flashlight on his belt. Gloria swam to retrieve her clothes but only made it waist deep out of the water before the flashlight snapped on, its beam directly in her face.

"Glory Weidman?" the man's voice asked, a voice tinged with exasperation.

Gloria shielded her eyes, trying to place the voice. The owner snapped the flashlight under his chin, giving himself a grotesque mask of shadows. It took Gloria a moment to place the voice to the face. "Casey Cash?"

The beam of light went back onto Gloria, desperately attempting to both cover and support her breasts, similar to hoisting a bag of oranges for the uninitiated.

"Well, it's Deputy Cash now. But yeah, Glory. What the hell are you doing out here?"

As a child, Casey Cash was the kind of kid that pushed you down, kicked your ice cream out of your hand and farted on you before his campaign of terror abated. The hellion of church socials and birthday parties alike. Casey's oldest sister, Annie, was one of Gloria's best friends in childhood. And, though he stood there in his brown uniform, searching the perimeters for danger, a wealth of wrinkles lining his sun damaged face, he still looked like a harmless, albeit annoying, child to her. She could almost still see the outline of the Kool Aid mustache from his youth staining his face and remembered he'd also lost a brother in Vietnam about the same time she'd lost hers in Germany. It had tempered her interactions with him throughout his youth. Made her more patient with him when others, parents included, were not.

Deputy Cash politely shifted the beam, allowing Gloria to hurriedly don her top. A splash in the water brought his attention to

Henry, waving jovially from his spot treading water.

"Evening, Deputy," he shouted.

"We were just taking a swim," Gloria stated as casually as she could holding her breasts in her right arm. She lifted her left arm, gesturing to the lake behind her. All the while looking Casey dead in the eyes. Deputy Cash seemed a bit scandalized by his findings, his gaze moving everywhere but the mismatched duo.

Gloria could barely keep her composure. She was so high she wanted to sink down into the grass and giggle. Surely Casey would notice. Would they get taken downtown? Is that how it worked? She tried to remember the research she'd done for an article on drug crime in the late eighties. The process of being arrested. Surely, he knew they were on drugs. Were they even still illegal?

"Everything out here copacetic?" He directed this question to Gloria though he said it loudly enough for Henry to hear the exchange.

"Yeah, yeah, of course, we're all good," Gloria nodded as the flashlight went back to her face, water still dripping down her naked thighs. Dammit! She'd forgotten her pants. And judging by the wind, both her buttocks and labia were exposed.

"You've heard about the recent murder, I assume," Deputy Cash didn't seem amused by their joie de vivre.

"I've heard about them all," Gloria went on congenially. "Karl tells Linda everything! You know - family."

It occurred to Deputy Cash he was speaking with the mayor's sister in that moment, in addition to his childhood babysitter. The mayor *in charge of the police department's funding efforts*. He snapped the flashlight off, tipping his head in Gloria's direction.

"Y'all be careful, now. It may not be a good idea to be out

here this time a night. With your clothes off," he glanced towards Henry as he said this, backing to the cruiser parked on the grass bank. "Take care, Ms. Weidman. Give your brother a howdy for me."

As the police cruiser pulled away, the headlights clicking on only after he'd turned onto the blacktop road, Gloria dissolved into the kind of laugh that produced more snorting. Henry joined in her hysterical giggles, crawling up the sloped bed of the lake to the shore, collapsing at her feet. She put her capris on and plopped down beside him in the damp grass and sand, wiping her feet off in an attempt to wedge them back into her shoes.He wrapped his towel around his waist and shook out his wet hair.

"Wanna hang out again sometime?" he asked, glancing sideways at her under his long lashes.

She smiled in the dark, "Yeah. I would."

Chapter 12

A tiny bell tinkled as the creaky, peeling door swung open. Gloria poked her head inside hesitantly when no call of greeting was offered. She shuffled inside with a sweeping peek around the small, cluttered offices of the Gazette - one smaller office to the left and one to the right connected by a common room with three desks of varying styles and ages parked haphazardly in a rough triangle. Outdated, stacked resource books lined the shelves; walls that needed paint. It appeared to be lunchtime, both this and the workspace next door where the actual press was located were empty of living souls. She walked closer to the nearest wall – a wall lined with yellowed articles from, what else, the Gazette on actual paper. Shocking investigations! Honest reporting!

"As I live and breathe, it's *the* Gloria Weidman!" The tone of the deep, familiar voice was almost reverential. He still sounded like he belonged on the radio! Gloria took a shaky breath, turning to face her high school boyfriend, Lenny.

Lenny's camera hung from a leather strap around his neck, along with a leather cord connected to his sunglasses and a leather holster for his cell phone. He looked ready to mount and ride to the nearest corral, to be sold for glue. She noticed his hair was both sparser and longer than the last time she'd run into him – an uncomfortable encounter at Brookshire's around the holidays of '88 when she returned home with her second husband, the fancy editor, in tow. There were several cheery exchanges with Lenny and his first of three wives, Deirdre, Gloria's former twirling partner. False promises for dinner all around, Christmas cards for a few years, and that was it. Now they were old as hell and it kind of took any potential pressure off the situation. At this point in life, she was just happy to see old friends alive and in one piece.

Lenny was a good man, but he wasn't the one who got away. He had been, however, *the first one*. And for that, she'd always have a wry fondness for him. She had happy memories of that time with him. Just not the weeping Lenny who fell to the ground, grabbing her legs and begging her to marry him when she told him she was moving to Dallas for a college scholarship. Not that sad Lenny. *This* Lenny was so cheerful he almost seemed lobotomized. Gloria remembered he was recently divorced again and softened her gaze, trying to avoid *pity face*, recently aware of its pitfalls via one Beverly Kent.

"What in the world?" Lenny looked her up and down, whistling appreciatively. Gloria knew she should be offended but it was probably one of the last times in her life she'd hear such nonsense.

"Lenny!" Gloria leaned in for a quick, chaste hug. His camera and glasses rattled against her breasts.

"I didn't know you worked here?" Gloria admitted with a shrug.

"Ah, you know I dabble here and there," Lenny pointed to the camera. "It's a hobby and Ted, for one, appreciates my work."

Gloria searched her brain for a memory of Lenny with a camera but came up empty. Must have been a talent he developed after she left. Perhaps one of those late-in-life hobbies, like pottery or birdwatching. A beat passed and Gloria realized she was staring. She cleared her throat and Lenny took the cue.

"So, what can I do you for? You here to make Ted cry again?" Lenny laughed at his own joke.

Gloria realized she'd made the Gazette a constant target of her boredom and yet, despite his personal offense, Ted usually published her letters to the editor; letters full of vitriol over what she considered right-wing, conspiracy-laden, misogynistic articles. It was how, over the past year, she'd become *that lady who kept writing in about all that hippy, socialist crap* versus her historical small-town title of *lady who wrote that dirty book*, thought she was hot shit, then failed spectacularly at life. Quite frankly, she *preferred* the former.

"No – quite the opposite, I need Ted's help" Lenny raised his eyebrows in question. Gloria went on, "I need some information about Rusty Fry? The guy that lost his head on Lake Tyler? And the third victim? The woman at the lake."

"Oh yeah?" Lenny perked up.

The bell over the door jingled as the door flew open. Ted Carroll entered with Tammy Johnson, the editor in chief of the newspaper. Tammy was a steely woman in her early thirties, her burnished brown hair reflected the yellow lights of the room, her cheeks rosy. She and Ted paused in their conversation, staring at Gloria with a faint look of fear.

Lenny cleared his throat, motioning to Gloria, "Hey Ted, Tammy – y'all remember Gloria Weidman, right? *Dottie's* daughter?"

"Please give Dottie our best, we sure miss her cookies," Ted threw in with a quick, sweaty pump from his hand.

Gloria tried to subtly wipe the sweat from her palm after this exchange. Dottie never forgot her former clients and busied herself dropping in to check on them over the following years, long after she retired. These surprise drop-ins were greased with homemade cookies. It was only when Dottie grew too confused to find her way around town Gloria had finally taken her car, which now sat waiting, untouched, in the large, detached shed on the backside of her property.

"I'll do that." Gloria promised.

"Gloria was looking for information on that Rusty fella. The one who died on the lake a couple weeks or so ago."

"Friend of yours?" Ted frowned. Tammy moved her svelte figure past him, lingering a bit too long in Gloria's opinion, followed by a quick mental reminder to stop being so goddam opinionated.

"Kind of. Just doing a bit of research, you know," Gloria always hated to discuss her writing when she was in the middle of it; but, she needed information, so out popped the truth. Maybe saying it aloud would force her to finally finish a new work.

Ted cocked his head inquisitively.

"A little story I've been working on," Gloria exclaimed, reluctant to go into greater detail. "Just some little small-town thriller I'm noodling on."

Ted smiled, brightening as if she'd just announced her bid for presidency, "That's great. Real great. Ain't it Tammy? Man! What I wouldn't give to retire and finally write my opus! You know, I've written a few books myself. Mainly science fictions I self-publish. I mean, I'm no Stephen King," he snorted. "But who is!"

Gloria restrained herself from answering, "*Well, obviously Stephen King.*"

Brushing past the trio, Tammy rolled her eyes as she went about her business muttering, "Y'all ever hear of the internet," incorrectly assuming she was out of earshot.

Lenny added "That's really neat, Glory. How can we help you, though? Sit down, sit down." He ushered her to the rickety chair in front of Ted's desk.

Ted slid in behind the ancient wooden behemoth and folded his hands as if in prayer. Gloria fought the impulse to roll her eyes. She needed this twerp to hasten her research.

"I wondered what your angle was going be on Rusty Fry's accident?" Gloria used air quotes. "Now that yet another headless corpse has been found. By my count, that makes three victims."

Ted winked, "Victims, eh? Sounds like we might be reading the same books." He reached for a pad of paper, already copiously covered in notes, from the top drawer of his desk.

"How many headless corpses does it take to raise a red flag in this town?" Gloria began.

"My periscope was up at two," Ted nodded, a look of renewed admiration crossing his bland potato-like features. "Three you say? How's that now?"

"Rusty Fry, obviously. He didn't cut his own head off and transport it away from the scene of the crime. The woman who was found by the Piers three days ago. I'm sure you've heard." She paused for Ted's knowing smirk before going on, "And then there was the suicide near the train tracks by the old market square. No head. Ding. First victim of the lakeside slayer."

"That's got a nice ring to it, Gloria," Ted sat up straighter, licking a pencil lead like an imbecile before jotting some hen scratch on the notepad where a computer should have been. "That what you're going with now? *You* should be a writer." Ted laughed at his own joke. "You mind if I use that for my article?" He went on writing, obviously deciding to move forward with his theft.

Gloria took the compliment. "Help yourself," she answered with an impatient wave of her hand. "So, my point in coming by was to see if maybe we could share information, as it were. We're both seasoned researchers. Surely, we can help one another somehow."

"I don't see why not. You've already helped me!"

"Then I need some information in exchange. I know you wrote Rusty's exhaustive obituary. You must have done some leg work already. What do you know about Rusty's private investigations?"

"He didn't have a license to operate in the state of Texas," he rattled off. "I already checked. But there are the ex-wives to speak to. And I haven't been able to take the time."

"Ex-wives?"

"The damndest thing. All but the current wife worked with him down at his offices. And they all look exactly alike. The four of 'em. Two are half-sisters, so that makes more sense. But, the man's gotta type, amm'I right?"

"And that office is where?"

"It's the old Dairy Queen on the way out to Arp."

"Cross street?"

"You'll know it when you see it." Ted surmised with a squinted eye - as if he didn't quite trust someone who didn't instinctually know the native shape of a classic Dairy Queen. Or the way to Arp. There *was* only one road to and from.

Gloria rose to leave. Both Ted and Lenny clambered from their seats in an effort to escort her to the door.

Lenny offered an awkward pat, "Tell your mom hello, Glory. Was really good catching up, kinda. Have to do it again."

"Sure," Gloria mollified him, pulling her purse to her side as she headed to the door. "And Ted," she turned as her body was halfway out the door, "you'll let me know what you find out about the woman? Anything?"

"Only thing I got from my sources right now is a name. Claudia Hastings. And you'll do the same, of course, if you dig up anything of interest on your paper chase?"

“You can count on it,” Gloria lied smoothly, shooting Lenny a sly wink as she allowed the door to clang shut behind her.

Chapter 13

This class, Henry *was* on time. His hair tucked behind his ears, his jeans worn, boots scuffed. And he was just about the sexiest thing Gloria had ever seen. She couldn't keep her eyes off him during class; his deep green eyes, the sharp white teeth biting his lip in concentration, the hairs dusting his forearms beneath the rolled hem of his sleeves, the one dimple that appeared when he smiled. Her students had to notice her obvious hunger. It was true, she realized. She experienced the most inappropriate emotions when Henry was around.

He joined the circle, nodding convivially to the other students already in a flurry of preparations beginning class. Nerves over their work. Excitement. And when Henry arrived, mystery. Gloria fluttered her hands, greeting the regulars, nodding deferentially to her newest student. Her protégé. Her sexy, sexy protégé.

When he stood as she asked for volunteers to read, she wasn't overly surprised. He'd arrived wearing the doomed look of a death row prisoner, nervous and eager to be done with it as she went through her lesson. He straightened his back, commanding the eyes of the room as he made his way to the leftover pulpit and settled his hands around the pages he clutched. His voice, usually so softspoken and careful, filled with thoughtful words, replaced by what Gloria could only assume was his true voice. A voice she'd never heard until tonight.

He shuffled the white, lined paper in his hands and Gloria saw a discernable shake before he cleared his throat and began to read, his words at first so faint it was hard to hear though as he went, his voice strengthening as his pace grew more lively, finding the rhythm of his own prose.

I was born in a drafty hovel on the outskirts of London. My mother sold eggs at market. And my father, though that memory is murkier, was a stonemason. Not a very good one. I rarely remember him working, as he was a horrible drunk. When I was eleven, he went off to join the Queen's troops without as much as a good-bye and my two older brothers followed the next day. My brothers' names were Edward and Thomas. All three died in the same battle. A skirmish, really, against the Scottish prince. It was too common to lose entire villages of men in a single afternoon during those dark years.

The carnage of the battles left me as man of the house, struggling to help support my mother and a little sister, Elizabeth. England was so very frightful at this time; a crowded lonely place, a place to lose your mind in the filth of the constant rain. Famine, forced enlistments, religious persecution. All things I've tried to forget. Yet, I remember the gloomy weather. The cold, a fragment of my brothers and I roughhousing while my father threatened to beat us all. The smoke curling from the stone fireplace, the rotting thatch of our shanty falling in one quiet night, the lines of soot marbling the rough stone of our walls. Feeling the whoosh of a passing coach and ten, the rough wool of leggings scratching my face as I tried to see around stout limbs and shouting siblings. I remember my mother's callused, cold hands as she pulled me along the riverbank in the snow, down the path to the barns. My cousins, the blurry form of an aunt and an uncle or two.

I remember Nonie, my dearest cousin. Experimenting with one another in my uncle's barn while our Mums walked to market together. Ah, beloved Nonie. I was to marry her. At least, that was the plan I heard whispered around the fire when the adults thought no one was listening. Then there was that icy winter it turned so cold we thought the Earth would never warm and a fever went round. I lost my mother and sister very quickly, then grew ill myself. Yet somehow, I didn't die. Two doors down, Nonie and my aunt were lost – just like that. The girl I would one day marry, black and burned from fever, dead in a shallow ditch with the rest of the world. I thought life was over and I was done. I wanted to be done. I'd already grown tired of it.

Yet I was only sixteen, and nothing ever goes how you want at that age. Orphaned, I joined the Queen's new navy, thinking I'd die in battle like my brothers and father - a noble sacrifice for Queen and country. I knew fuck-all about boats, but luckily, I fell in with one of my brother Edward's old mates, Hugh, and he showed me the ropes. Joining the navy at that time meant you actually participated in the construction of the source of your demise. I wasn't much of a carpenter, truth be told, but I tried my best. I think I may have actually learned a thing or two. By this time, Hugh began to hear tales from returning crews of vast fortunes to be made in the new world, if you could get there, hence the raising of Her Royal Highness' naval force.

And on one of those very ships, those giant new ships of pitch and wood which I'd helped assemble with my naïve hands - the very ship that Hugh's wealthy father had bought him an officer's seat upon – the junior horseman died of a pox and with only a hasty recommendation of my friend, I ended up on the crew. Goddamn, I hated to sail. Yet I was determined to die and it seemed to everyone, not just me who could not swim, that this foolhardy mission was tantamount to suicide. We could well be sailing off of the end of the Earth for what we knew of it then. Yet, for all the terror, it sounded a sight better than working for my old, grey uncle as a stonemason for the rest of my life. Waiting for my other, uglier cousin Tildie to get old enough to marry.

If Nonie hadn't died, I'd have married her, settled down and been dead by thirty like everyone else. A yard full of buried children to show for my efforts. But that wasn't to be. Instead, I went to sea. And to what, quite rightfully, I assumed was my end. And my beginning.

Henry bowed his head; a small, barely noticeable smile illuminating his normally serious expression for just a moment. He pressed his lips together, his eyes still dancing, but his face relaxed back into a carefully constructed canvas of ennui. Ah, Gloria reflected ruefully, what the human heart will do to protect itself from disappointment. She recognized the gambit well.

Now, it was true from time to time, Gloria did stumble upon a gifted student. A student whose talent she tried to nurture. The difference in quality between *this* students' writing and the other pallid tales they'd suffered through previously was obvious to all present. But this! *This* was the first time she'd been physically aroused by the sheer timber of a student's voice. His writing was good. It could be improved upon, everyone's could. But it was good. Really, really good. Rough, though. He'd need help. *Her* help, of course, she decided in that instant.

Several hands shot up as soon as Henry's melodious voice faded, a chorus of questions peppering him, his face reflecting gentle surprise by their interest.

"Who is your narrator?" One demanded, Gloria's resident historian.

Henry shrugged, "Just an English nobody, I guess."

"But what does he do?"

"What year?"

"He's a soldier," Henry affirmed with a smile, "Late

sixteenth century, maybe?"

The student questioning him seemed mollified. And, also kind of into him. Gloria suffered a misplaced pang of jealousy. That young woman was probably in her early twenties. They were much better suited, she thought errantly. Doubt creeping in. But, Henry's voice and his obvious talent stirred her in ways for which she felt slightly guilty. She regretted her choice of underwear as she tried to shake the silky fabric from the cleft of her sweating buttocks, casually wiping her forearms across her skirt to free the fabric from her skin's moist embrace. This maneuver required kicking her thighs apart to fully free the pleats from her folds, gracefully accomplished as she stood to make room for Henry returning from his bashful pose at the front of class, the students clapping.

When the hour was up, he lingered in the back of the classroom studying old artifacts from the previous owner's Baptist regime with knotted concentration while Gloria discussed the literary works of Jared Leto with one particularly opinionated student. The resident historian student paused on his lengthy, limping exit to commend Henry for his choice of first-person subject. After the last of the students dispersed, Henry drifted closer to Gloria, his eyes fixed on her hands as they sorted and stacked the students' manuscripts distractedly. She looked up, trying to affect a look of genuine surprise by his continued presence, but she was sure he was onto her.

"You're very good," she stated succinctly.

He relaxed visibly when she spoke, sliding gracefully into the nearest wooden chair. "You think?" he tilted his head, studying her from beneath his eyelashes earnestly.

"Of course. You must have heard this before. This can't be the first time you've read your work?"

Henry frowned thoughtfully, his eyebrows furrowing. "Never have. But I have been thinking on this story for a while. Just took a nudging to get going, I guess. I owe that to you." His former voice returned, Texas twang and all.

Silence. They both smiled shyly at one another.

Gloria cleared her throat, "I meant what I said. I'd be happy to work with you on it, if you'd like. I *did* teach for years. Should be worth something with a talent like yours." She tilted her head in invitation.

"I'll keep working on it," he promised errantly, fidgeting in a way that signified an exit, "I'll see where it goes."

He made a little temple with his fingers and tapped them together. The awkward silence between them seemed to amuse him as much as it discomforted Gloria.

They stood at the same time, opening their mouths to speak in unison, "I should…"

"Get going," he finished lightly for her. He swept his arms before her, "After you."

She couldn't stop thinking about him driving to her lonely, quiet house where she filled the empty silence with the sounds of nighttime news and the hum of electric lights in every room. The house felt particularly foreign tonight. She longed to wake up once again in her shitty apartment in north Dallas, with its sounds of traffic and wails of ambulances from the hospital on the corner of the freeway. There were times when she had trouble settling back into the muted sounds of her small hometown. The distant roar of a Friday night football game, audible for miles through town. The hum of traffic from the two roads crossing Main Street. The sound of wind, of trees and the hum of the Earth. She could hear all of that here when she stepped out on the porch, her nearest neighbor a good city block away.

Everything about this life suddenly felt odd and misplaced. She felt odd. What was it about this kid? She wasn't thinking straight. She was strangely attracted to him, obviously. But his writing, she was drawn to that, too. Was she secretly jealous of his raw talent? Did she think she could draw some of his creative energy from him like a crazed witch, stealing his youthful zeal? Or did she want to grandmother him, dote on him asexually? Help him find his potential? Or did she, disgustingly enough, want to ravage his taunt abs? All of these, if she was being honest. She felt all of this when she looked at him. And *that* confused the hell out of her.

Chapter 14

Gloria hunched her shoulders, rushing past reception without being intercepted by Beverly. She wasn't in the mood to talk about Dottie's mental decline today. She hadn't heard from Henry since her class the other night. It all felt like a dream now. Like a schoolgirl, she'd spent the previous two days fretting over the fact that *he* hadn't called her. She knew she was being silly, and hopeful. One platonic outing and Henry joining her class didn't amount to much, but it had made her feel awake after years of sleepwalking. And that wasn't *nothing* in her book.

Whmfff! Right into the hard part of an elbow, followed by an inelegant dance around a broomstick and the broom holder. Step, step, cha-cha-cha. The orderly's other hand shot out to steady her.

"So sorry," Gloria shook her head, looking up at the man's broad, tan face. He smiled but the smile didn't reach his grey eyes, the left of which was quite milky, as if cataracted, belying his seemingly early to middle age. He tried to go one way while she countered and turned, stepping the same direction. This happened twice more.

"Care to dance," she groaned internally as she said it.

The janitor made no move to alleviate the awkwardness of the situation. "You okay?" He eyed her suspiciously. "What room are you in?"

She spied the name on his badge, ensuring his employment at the facility. Saint? Ha! What kind of saint had a serpent tattooed across the back of his hand like a prison tattoo, the lines blurry as if applied with rough tools.

Gloria pulled herself straight, huffing, "I'm here for my mother, if you don't mind." Stepping past him, her ego slightly dented, she realized there *were* residents here her age and younger. It was an honest mistake - for which she'd punish him with a rude dismissal.

She didn't see Karl until she ran smack into him, crushing her bag of kolaches as she rounded the final corner to Dottie's door. Boy, she thought, she was on fire today! Karl and Linda were exiting Dottie's apartment, shouting out final "*take care, Mom's*", the smiles dropping from their faces as they resumed bickering in the hallway.

"Well, what do we have here?" Gloria smiled up at her big brother, wondering how they were related. Where she was gold, Karl was dark. Where Gloria was soft-hearted, he was hard; hard-hearted, vain and nasty. Yet *still* her older and *only* surviving sibling.

Linda fluttered her hands, her smile reappearing, "We've been so busy, you wouldn't believe it. Karl *wanted* to *see* his *mama*. Wish we could get by more often, but we know you take the time each day. God Bless you, Gloria." Ugh, she was sincere.

Gloria snorted, "That's great." Her brother's gaze was everywhere but on her as she asked, "How's mom doing today?"

"Out of her goddamn mind," Karl snapped, as if this were somehow her fault.

"She kept calling Karl *Wade*," Linda whispered with a soothing nod in her husband's direction.

"She asked me when I thought Dennis would get home," Karl groused on the verge of tears, uncharacteristically. It softened Gloria for a moment and she thought she might put the bag down and try to hug Karl, but he pulled out his cell phone and began punching it with his chubby fingers, squelching any impulse to comfort her brother. Ah Denny, Gloria thought with a ping of sadness, I hardly knew ya. Had she been ten when he'd shipped out and never returned? It seemed like he belonged to some other family now. Some other family mourned him still. She'd just forgotten the eldest Weidman. For Gloria, he was only a picture on the wall because in their family, they didn't talk about the dead.

"She does that from time to time. It's only going to get worse, unfortunately," Gloria explained.

"It's hard for everyone," Linda nattered on, hands waving indiscriminately in front of Karl and Gloria's faces.

Karl took a break from texting, eyeing Gloria curiously, "So, Glor, I ran into Deputy Cash the other day. He said he caught you skinny-dipping at the lake with some kid? Like, one of your students? Are you teaching again?" Karl frowned, cocking his head to one side, "What were you doing out there?"

Gloria panicked momentarily. What could she say? If it was different, in Karl's book, it was wrong. But what could Karl (or anyone, for that matter) do to her if she told the truth? She was a grown-ass woman, and it was a *community center class*. There *were* no rules.

"I *am* teaching. He just so happens to be one of my students. And I was *swimming*. What *else* would one do at a lake… with an inappropriately younger man. I was ridiculously stoned. And I had a fabulous time. Thank you for asking."

Karl shook his head wearily. Linda barked a laugh, covering her mouth with her hand, her laughter tapering off into coughing. "The lake is dangerous. There's a killer on the loose, you mark my words. Stay away for a while, you hear?" Karl admonished, hitching his head toward the exit down the hall as he pressed his phone to his ear.

Linda opened Dottie's door for Gloria, "Go ahead, Gloria. Good to see ya, hon."

Gloria smiled at Linda, the realization Linda disliked Karl almost as much as she did comforting her in that moment. Linda followed her husband with an apologetic wink in Gloria's direction.

Gloria swept inside, shouting into the entryway, "Mom, it's me."

The front door slammed shut and Gloria could hear Karl and Linda's strident voices nitpicking one another down the empty hallway. Dottie was in her spot in the chair, television blaring, craning her head over her shoulder as Gloria tossed the bag of kolaches onto the countertop with a splat.

"How was your visit with Karl?" Gloria enunciated loudly.

"Your brother is a little shit, Gloria," Dottie swiveled back around in her chair, facing the television again. "It's my fault, I guess. But he was always a shit and he'll be one until the day he dies. He thinks I don't know Dennis is dead. I *paid* for the obituary notice, of course I know he's dead. I have one little slip of the tongue and he's convinced I'm losing my mind. Would you talk to him?"

"I will," Gloria promised. "Mom," Gloria asked a bit more loudly, "Are you hungry?"

"God, yes!" Dottie sighed. "Linda brought some pound cake that tasted like vanilla flavored turds. I'll take anything to get the taste out of my mouth, please."

Gloria hadn't made it by in the past two days, though she rarely missed more than one. Dottie didn't seem to notice.

"Did Karl tell you Nettie died?" Dottie shouted, still facing the screen as Gloria pecked around the kitchen making lunch.

Nettie was Dottie's last surviving cousin, the last of a

group of at least ten. Gloria could remember many a barbeque with Nettie's sweaty brood. Gloria, Karl and sometimes a flash of Dennis in these memories, kids from both sides of the family darting through the throng of adults, grabbing watermelon from their mom's outstretched hands, running and leaping into the lake on a holiday. Sleeping in Nettie's living room, all the kids sprawled on one mattress, a noisy fan and wet sheets draped over them to weather the summer heat before central air conditioning became affordable.

"I'm sorry to hear that," Gloria's shoulders drooped as she mixed the tuna salad. "I know you were always close."

"Yes," Dottie nodded, "we were. My parents raised her after hers died, you know. She was like the sister I never had."

Gloria ignored this old joke. Dottie did have a little sister, Eugenia. Eugenia was still alive, thriving, and living with her ancient husk of a third husband in Fort Worth. Once every fifteen years or so, the two women found time to visit one another and catch up. Maybe a quick phone call every other year. Other than that, Gloria rarely saw her real aunt, but cousin Nettie had been a presence her entire life.

"Poor Nettie," Gloria frowned, "She's been sick for awhile, right?"

"She has," Dottie answered after a beat, her eyes riveted to her talk show.

Gloria finished the salad in silence, interrupted only by Dottie's latent advice, "Don't feel too bad for Nettie. She loved to sleep. Even when we were young. Tony always said he was worried he could lose her to a good nap."

Chapter 15

She stared dubiously at the scribbled address on the strip of ripped typing paper in her hand. Was this it? It was the obvious outer skin of a long-shuttered Dairy Queen, its recognizable aquarium shaped design, the dark stains of signage still legible: y Queen, indeed. A plastic sign leaned prominently in the front window reading Fry Bail Bonds, PI & Taxidermy. A dusty, balding panther guarded the window. One of the glass doors sported a cardboard covering, a jagged hole where the thin glass had been kicked in, the frame dangling from the cracked hinges. The functioning door of the establishment was perched open with a stack of out-ofdate phone books. Some out of state ones as well, Gloria puzzled, shaking the loose gravel from her shoe, popping her head into the shadowy, air-conditioned interior.

"Yoohoo," appropriate warning shot of the South, "Anyone home?"

It had been at least thirty years since Gloria entered a smoke friendly workspace – and *that* was a print shop in the heart of Marlboro country. Yet when she walked through the battered, stickered double doors of Rusty Fry's empire, smoke poured out, enveloping Gloria in nostalgia. This was what college smelled like in the seventies. Every room filled with smoking smokers, smoking their black lungs out. She for one brief semester among them, secure in the sisterhood of sophistication smoking once signified. Then, she contracted a horrid upper respiratory infection and regrettably quit, during which time her then-boyfriend Dan moved into her room to nurse her and never left. An open secret on the floor of her dorm. A semester in the dorm followed by an engagement, marriage and no more college. Ah, the freedom of ignorance! When those pesky warnings on the sides of the boxes were just glimmers in the FDA's eyes. Back when you never really heard about the harmful side effects aside from the odd doctor who put his cigarette down long enough to mention it. The good old days.

"Help you?" A voice enveloped in the smog of the room and, astonishingly, the sole source of the cloud of nicotine filling the space, croaked from behind a floppy newspaper. An actual newspaper lowered to reveal a small slice of an overly tan woman, her long gray hair frozen in time: bangs and dangling earrings competing for space around her heavily lined face, her skin shiny and mottled, the outline of a patrician profile probably quite lovely in her day, still shining through. It was one of the identical sirens from the cemetery. Several empty beer cans were visible littering the floor behind the stool on which she perched over the high wooden desk of the lobby. The lobby was empty, save odd debris. Two partly empty offices were visible over her shoulder.

"Are you-" Gloria was quickly cut off by the woman across from her.

"Yes," she sighed, shaking her head regrettably. "You with the po-lice too or that guy that came by after with the insurance company? Y'all got our statements already."

Ann Delancy would have been smart enough to bring a small notebook and pen. *Gloria Weidman had not.* Dammit! Next time she sleuthed, she reminded herself, she needed a check list and to reread *Death in Leeds: An Ann Delancy Mystery* for tips.

"No," Gloria shook her head, moving closer, peering through the curling smoke, the sizzle of an extinguished cigarette reaching her ears, “I’m not – I’m just – I’m a…a client of Rust-Mr.Fry’s. What happened here?”

The newspaper folded down, carefully placed before the woman looked Gloria over, “Uh, the murder? Or, I’m sorry, *the accident*? And now the break-in? Don’t supposed you noticed the mess.” The woman gestured to an overturned, already long-dead potted banana plant, soil strewn across the cheerful tile of the dining area, a boarded segment of what was once clearly a drive-thru restaurant window, and the distant mess of overstuffed boxes in the storage room beside the restrooms.

“A customer, huh?” the smoke-scented woman grunted, appearing suddenly behind Gloria as she scrutinized one of the disheveled offices. The woman dangled her thin wrist around Gloria’s ribs pointing to the mess, loose papers and scattered manila file folders, each tab labeled with blocky letters in primary colored marker: green, red, orange, yellow and blue. Unfortunately, Gloria’s eyesight wasn’t such she could read the labels to see what secrets they may hold in their paper embrace.

“Didn’t take the money that was here, but I think they’s looking for something specific. Doubt they found what they were looking for. Can’t imagine Rusty having anything of any interest to anyone but a fellow squatch hunter. As you can see, we’re outta business.”

“A what,” Gloria frowned, making mental note of the breakin and the strewn contents of what promised to be Rusty’s private eye client files. What her nosey soul wouldn’t give to get her hands on those babies. It was a small town. No doubt she’d recognize every name surveilled.

“Yep, the po-lice were pretty interested in those files too. But you know, paying consumers got their right to privacy, so we aren’t quite sure what to do with all that. Though I know it’s not for our eyes. Certainly not for theirs. Nope, it's in the lord's hands now. God rest Rusty's soul, you know." Her boney hand rested on Gloria's shoulders, gently pulling her away.

"Kassie, isn't it? You're Rusty's…third wife?"

The woman barked, coughing, shaking her head, rasping, "I'm Susie."

"Oh," Gloria blinked in confusion. The double doors flew open behind her and another, almost identical, version of the woman before her swept into the room with a bolt of blinding sunlight outlining her figure, two bags of fragrant fast-food dangling from her left hand, a very large multi-liter soft drink in the other. As she entered, Gloria could see that her hair was almost white, but still the same out-of-date seventies inspired style as her coworker, the dry strands spilling down her back.

"Kassie, she thinks I'm you," Susie barked, laughing dryly, "Can you believe it?"

"Never in a million years," Kassie answered in a similar brusque monotone, brushing past Gloria to deposit the bags on the desk. Gloria looked back at the first woman, realizing *that* was Rusty's second wife and the one who entered was the third.

"Who's this?" Kassie finally asked, nudging her hair-twin, Susie.

"Customer," Susie explained.

"Weidman. Gloria," Gloria thrust her hand out to Susie who reluctantly gripped it in her own cold one.

"Weidman, eh? I know you," her knowing smile chilled Gloria as she elaborated, "this is the mayor's sister. You remember that dirty book she wrote? You remember that?"

The smile slid from Gloria's lips as her body tightened, "Yes, exactly that one." She pressed her lips together and stuffed her pen into the pocket of her purse. "Well, I can see I've come at a bad time. I'm sorry for your loss. Please carry on with your… cleaning."

Backing out, Gloria made a hasty exit, ignoring the cackling laughter haunting her retreat. She drove away with only a familiar return to an old humiliation and the slightly interesting knowledge Rusty Fry's office had been broken into and nothing of value stolen. What then was the perpetrator looking for in that poorly organized pile of files? She reminded herself to inquire about the break-in with Casey Cash.

Chapter 16

It was almost seven by the time Gloria made it home. Without the once ever-present, too-loud babble from a television in the background - for Dottie Weidman had taken to moving pictures the moment they were available and never looked back - the silence of the small house still rattled Gloria. It felt like she was breaking and entering someone else's property every time she went through the door without Dottie. For all intents and purposes, it was her house now. Or at least, would be one day soon. She lifted her purse with her knee to steady it, scratching around the bottom to find her keys.

"Good evening," his voice came from behind her.

She spun around, hand on her chest, her keys clattering to the porch. "Goodness, you have a way of startling me. Have you been sent to slowly assassinate me?" Gloria teased, her heart racing. Did she have on makeup, she couldn't remember. What nonsense was she wearing? How was her hair? She patted the sides and pushed it behind her ears.

"I guess I do. My apologies." He leaned against his moped, parked under the tree on the other side of the gravel driveway.

She could have sworn he was right behind her when he'd spoken, but he'd been watching from the shade the entire time she'd been fumbling at the front door. Thank God she hadn't wiped her nose on her sleeve, picked her underwear from her butt crack or, heavens forbid, *let one rip* in assumed privacy…all things done before on any given day, thinking herself unobserved.

"I didn't see you there!" Gloria shaded her eyes. She bent with a rueful smile, plucking her keys from the ground as gracefully as possible with a stiff knee, then sauntered closer to Henry, still leaning casually against his scooter. He stood, straightening the jeans he wore with one hand. She noticed a thin manilla folder he clutched in his other hand, holding it aloft in offering.

"I noticed that," he grinned.

She had driven right past him in the shadow of the giant pecan tree. A chameleon with the ability to disappear easily, she thought, realizing she was the same.

"I hope you take hand-delivered assignments?" he asked shyly, holding up the folder, the loose pages within fanning. Henry wore his normal attire; a worn button-down short-sleeve shirt, the chain of his necklace visible against his pale neck, the pointed toe of a scuffed cowboy boot peeking from under the cuffs of his worn jeans. He smiled and his green eyes sparkled, tilting his head to invite her answer.

"Oh," she stammered, greedily snatching the proffered assignment, "you didn't have to drop this by. But, I have to admit, I'm really glad you did. I'm not sure I've ever looked forward to reading a student's work more before." Gloria laughed, clutching the folder tighter in anticipation. She couldn't wait to see what Henry had written about. He was such an enigma in real life.

"Were you visiting your Mother?" he inquired politely.

"I was, yes," Gloria looked back over her shoulder to the front door and back at Henry. "Would you like to come in? I was going to cook dinner. I have some chicken." Smooth, she chided herself. *I have chicken*?

Henry nodded enthusiastically, "I would love to come in. I mean, I came to just drop this off. Then I stayed because I figured you might be back soon. But I'm not going to turn down a homecooked meal, I'm not a mad man."

He followed her through the front door. Gloria dropped her purse on the coffee table as she passed, leading him through the large living and dining rooms, into the woefully out-of-date kitchen. She turned suddenly, bumping into him as he followed close behind, awkward in his presence, the folder crushed momentarily between them.

"Sorry," he mumbled.

She righted herself and placed the folder on the countertop, feeling clumsy and sweaty. At least it was September, maybe he wouldn't notice her glistening discomfort. She motioned for him to sit at the table and took a minute to compose herself under the guise of gathering ingredients, fanning her chest in the cold air of deep freeze as she pulled out a bag of peas. Henry contented himself by gazing around the ancient kitchen with its olive-green appliances and plethora of dusty waxen fruit in bowls she neglected while cleaning.

"This kitchen is awesome," she heard him shout from the other side of the wall, digging a package of chicken breasts from the second fridge in the garage. Why had her mother needed so much food storage? Who had she been feeding with all this?

"That's one word for it," she rejoined, her arms laden with a Styrofoam package of chicken and a bag of frozen peas.

"This might take a bit to cook," Gloria warned.

Henry seemed content to sit at the great wooden table near the window and watch Gloria work. The top of the old oak table was smoothed with age. Henry ran his hands appreciatively across it. "Nice craftsmanship," she heard him murmur to himself.

"I don't have anywhere I need to be," Henry admitted watching her in companionable silence. He rested his chin on his fists, his eyes on her hands as she chopped the chicken into pieces and threw it into a dish with the peas and a can of cream of chicken soup. Glancing at him beneath her lashes while stirring, she realized he looked very young in the waning light of day filtering through the flowery curtains of the kitchen window.

"You eat meat, right? Chicken?" Gloria asked belatedly, pausing her task.

"Yes, of course I eat meat," he confirmed.

"You never know," Gloria shrugged, grabbing a couple of carrots to add to the mix. "I didn't even ask you what your pronouns were when we met. Things change fast. Vegans have invaded the south. I've seen them at the Whole Foods in Tyler."

"What are you making? It looks great?" Henry leaned forward to better see.

"Do you like chicken pot pie?" Gloria kept her eyes on the chopping block.

"Do I? Need you ask? Who doesn't love chicken pot pie?"

"I'm sure someone out there in Borneo or Bangladesh hates it," Gloria rationalized, passing the knife over the carrots for a final chop before sliding them into the casserole pot.

"I think that would have to be because they've never had it," Henry stated wistfully. "It's a pie crust full of meat, vegetables and gravy. How could anyone not enjoy that?" He stood, moving from the table to the other side of the kitchen island, hovering at her side as Gloria mixed the butter, flour and buttermilk together for the crust.

"Voila," Gloria declared breezily, pouring the mixture over the chicken and vegetables into a casserole dish. She clicked the oven on to preheat, explaining, "This *may* be ready to bake sometime tonight." Her mother's old stove was unpredictable at best, slow at its worst. One of these days she'd get around to renovating, she'd promised herself repeatedly while putting it off. "May I offer you boxed wine?" She whipped open the creaking door of the kitchen refrigerator, waving an upraised hand in front of the wine box on the top shelf like a gameshow hostess.

"Of course," Henry smiled, tilting his head toward the nearest cabinet, "allow me."

He opened two creaking cupboard doors before locating the stash of mismatched wine glasses, choosing a long stem champagne flute for Gloria and a smaller whiskey tumbler for himself. He first handed Gloria her own, which she held under the plastic wine spigot with shaking hands. Henry moved past her body with a deliberate graze, serving himself.

She suppressed a smile, sipping her wine as he poured his own before moving to the dinner table and plopping down on the nearest rickety chair. Henry slouched into the seat opposite her with ease. He seemed at home everywhere he went, she noticed. Maybe that was why she was so drawn to him. She always felt like a stranger in her own skin and often thought dreamily, *wouldn't it be nice to know oneself, to like oneself*? She looked up from her dark musing and saw he was staring at her. His dark green eyes were still pools, the color of a pine tree, the ring around his iris particularly vivid. She could almost hear the peace and silence of his mind from the infectious sense of calm he projected. Of strength beneath the stillness.

He smiled, a slow and sensuous smile that unnerved her as much as it intrigued her. She hadn't had a young man smile at her like *that* in a very long while. He looked dangerous again. Feral. And she realized she *liked* it.

She motioned to the manila folder on the table, "Would you read me some?"

Henry shook his head, "You can read it later, when I'm

gone."

Gloria assumed he was insecure, coaching him, "I really like where you're going with your story. Don't count yourself short. Want to tell me anything about it before?"

"I'd rather surprise you," he sat up straighter, leaning forward, his eyes piercing hers with a direct, smoldering gaze.

"I thought you'd say something like that," Gloria laughed, her eyes never leaving his.

He tilted his head, asking, "How long has it been since you've had a lover, Gloria?"

"A long time," Gloria sighed, catching herself and chuckling. She hadn't meant to answer so honestly or so quickly. "What kind of a question is that?"

"Just curious," he shrugged, arching his eyebrows. "I told you I wanted to get to know you better."

"Well, it's rather inappropriate, but why not. I'd ask you the same, but I'm afraid it might depress me. You're very young and quite beautiful, really – leading me to deduce you've either had a lot of lovers, good for you. Or, you've *never* had one. Which might explain your strange preoccupation with a lonely old woman."

"Hmmff. I don't think you're lonely. Or old," he pursed his lips. "And I hate to disappoint you, but I've had *a few*. Nothing impressive, but not *nothing*, if that helps. Furthermore, I wouldn't call it a *strange* preoccupation, Gloria. I'd call it…a *desire. A desire* to know you. That's it. I'm not asking for anything more than what you want. What *you* might desire."

He had such an odd speech pattern, Gloria analyzed… the way he enunciated his words so very carefully, his voice so silky and comforting, flowing around you like a spell. Gloria compulsively smoothed her hair, feeling a blush stealing over her cheeks and chest. Despite her fairly pale skin, she wasn't normally the blushing type, but her body kept betraying her when she wanted to look regal and cool, Helen Mirren-style, not like Hot Flash McGee. There was an uncomfortable silence as Gloria's mind flitted through a variety of deflective topics, unsure if she had the bravery to hear any more of what her mind promised was complete and utter bullshit. Must be bullshit. Because *shit like this* only happened in movies. Usually horror movies.

"Look," Henry sat up straighter, his face earnest, "I know you're leery of me, as you should be of strangers. But the truth is, I'm drawn to you, Gloria. I am inexplicably comfortable in your presence. You set me at ease. That first time I met you, when you picked me and Terry up at the game and dropped us off at the Dairy Queen - the time you didn't notice me - I saw something in you. Sitting in your backseat, I could see your eyes in the mirror as you spoke to Terry. Just about trivial things, but I could see your eyes. You have beautiful eyes. And your voice. I could hear everything about you in the way you spoke to Terry. Other people, they talk to him like he's a loser, but you don't. You see what I see. And when *we* talk, I see a woman with the biggest heart panicking her life is getting smaller and smaller to the point where she feels like she might just disappear. And I wonder why? *How* could *this* magnificent, accomplished, sexy woman forget *who* she is? *Why* is she pretending to be this person here in this town, living *this* life? I think you're amazing and I'd love to know *all of you*. But you know all that, right?"

Gloria stared at him, speechless, clamping her mouth closed.

He raised his eyebrows in a challenge, finishing his speech, "I see the way you look at me when you think no one is looking. I know you like me, too. I don't care what people think. Do you really care what people think?"

Gloria's head was spinning. She felt *something,* he was right. Tingly and dizzy. And flattered. And *alive.* Softer, suddenly? When had she become so brittle? So hard. She'd once loved to dance, to run, to teach and inspire. To write. Done things with that crystalline knowledge there were always more days to come, that her story wasn't even halfway over. Then one day, it was. That surefire confidence fled, and she just stopped…moving…forward. She came home and hid herself away in caretaking. Frozen. But that all ended now with the heat of his touch.

Chapter 17

The oven beeped obnoxiously, startling them. Henry pulled his hand back to his side, standing as Gloria jumped up, relieved to have an excuse to escape the building tension.

"I'm sorry, horrible timing. One sec," her hands shook as she slid the casserole into the oven.

Henry remained standing, his back to her so she couldn't tell if she'd ruined the evening with her sudden flight or if he was thinking of bolder things to say to scramble her brains.

"It's gonna have to cook for at least an hour," she announced, ignoring Henry's bold proclamations. What was wrong with her? Answer him in an intelligible fashion, lady, she ordered herself! Answer him! Lick him. Do something. The irrational part of her mind, the baser part, wanted to rip his clothes off, drag his youthful body to her room and not emerge for several days. But the rational part, the part that *doubted* - the part that knew though she was in fairly good shape for sixtyish, she *was* still sixtyish - was scared. There were so many things to worry about this beautiful boy seeing, judging…retreating from.

Steadying her hands and her heart, she spun around ready to admit she had no idea what to say but turned into his chest as he came to stand behind her, her face muffled into the soft fabric of his shirt. He stepped back with a suppressed grin, peering down at her, his eyes darkening into unfathomable black pools. She could see herself in the reflection of his eyes. He pushed her gently back against the counter and she felt the cold steel of the countertop on her back. He said nothing but deliberately, slowly, moved his right hand to just below her jaw, tilting her chin up slightly. She stared up at him, shocked and paralyzed by his smooth seduction. He moved his face close to hers, his lips less than an inch from her own.

"Is this okay?" he murmured, his eyes never leaving hers. She noticed he smelled like cinnamon and a hint of something more earthy, like lavender. She nodded, unable to make herself talk. She'd never had a man, any man, make a move on her like *this*. And she'd been sexually active in both the seventies *and* the eighties.

He bent to face her, pressing his cool lips to her warm ones, sliding his mouth across hers, pushing his tongue between her lips and circling hers with his own. His hands gripped the sides of her face, his teeth gently pulling at her bottom lip as she realized he tasted like cinnamon, too. Gloria's head swam. Her knees buckled. She could feel him everywhere though his hands were firmly planted where they began. And just as she completely lost her breath, he pulled back, his dark eyes glittering in the dimly lit kitchen, his pale skin flushed and pink.

"Would it be overly bold to ask if I could kiss you again?" He was slightly out of breath.

At the hint of a nod, they moved toward each other, his hands snaking out and gripping the back of her neck firmly, pulling her lips to his, biting her lower lip with his sharp, white teeth before deepening his kiss sensuously, slowly. Dinner was forgotten. Pulling each other down the dark hallway to the bedroom, pausing only to seek each other's lips hungrily, they tore at one another's clothes. She threw open the door to her room, glancing around surreptitiously to ensure there was nothing embarrassing lying around like the jar of mineral ice on her bedside, her reading glasses (who over forty didn't have those?), or *the massager* (thankfully on its charger in her bottom drawer).

Henry pressed his hand on the small of her back, following closely behind her. She spun around as he wrapped her in his arms, bending his head to kiss her neck, then to bite a trail down her shoulder with just enough force to feel good. Was this really happening, she thought fleetingly? She backed up, her knees pressing against the edge of her orthopedic mattress. He bent over her, pushing her back into the mattress, kissing her neck, her collarbone, her earlobes. His body sank into hers with delicious tenderness, her heart beating so heavily she was afraid he could hear it. Her eyes were closed, her arms around the back of his neck. Then, she felt the cold air of the room on her body where his had just been and sat up, confused. He settled back on his knees over her, balancing on his heels, his eyes on her while Gloria leaned up on one elbow, searching his expression in the dark room.

"Something wrong?" she asked breathlessly, her body calming, logic rushing back into her brain. *Of course* there was something wrong! He'd suddenly realized he was about to bed a woman old enough to be his grandmother.

"No," he panted, shaking his head. "I mean, yes." Here we go, Gloria thought.

"Gloria," he said her name softly, his voice full of passion. "I want you to know that I want you very much. I haven't felt this way *in a long time*. But, in one thing, in one way, I feel like I'm being dishonest. There are *things* about my life. *Complicated* things. *Strange things*."

Gloria almost snorted with relief. Ah, to have complicated *early-twenties-things* going on. He sank further back on his heels and Gloria sat up to face him, alarmed by his stern expression, noticing his hand shaking as it fingered the medallion hung around his neck. He held it between his thumb and forefinger, rubbing the back of it absent-mindedly before dropping the medallion back to rest on his pale chest.

"I want to make love to you. Very badly. And if you'll have me, I will. But I should tell you something first. About me. Something you should know."

She felt the chilly fingertips of anxiety slide over her skin, knowing she didn't want this to end. Not yet. Not tonight.

"Are you…sexually confused?" Gloria prodded.

Henry suppressed a smile, shaking his head.

"Do you have VD?" Gloria coached softly.

He laughed, reaching out to caress her cheek, "No."

"Then I don't care," Gloria pulled him closer, her hands reaching for his shirt, tugging at the buttons, pushing the fabric aside to expose his taut, lean torso - a sprinkling of soft, brown hair down the center of his chest, trailing to his stomach. He was thin but tone, the muscles of his forearms bulging as he pressed her back, his body hovering over hers. With the moonlight streaming through the window, his skin glowed pale and his eyes glittered in the dark. His body moved over hers where he crouched like a tiger, sliding his hips into hers, his eyes peering into hers with a look of such deep longing and lust, Gloria felt like she could drown in him.

"Whatever it is, I don't care," Gloria assured him. "Just give me this one night and it won't matter."

He stared intently down at her, the cold medallion dangling from his neck, tickling her chest before his body covered hers. His face relaxed and he kissed her, slowly and sweetly, teasing her mouth with his own before he whispered into her neck, "It's nothing that can't wait."

Chapter 18

When Gloria awoke, Henry was gone. But his manila folder was propped on the table beside the half-eaten chicken pot pie, a flourish of cursive script splashed across the front, a pilfered pen beside it.

Thank you for a wonderful night.

Eternally Yours, Henry

She opened the folder.

Most people are unaware of this fact but there were actually three settlements on and around what would later be known as Roanoke, North Carolina in the late 1500's. Most people have only heard of the final one. The settlement that mysteriously disappeared without a trace to tempt historians into wild conjectures for hundreds of years to come. I won't speak yet as to what happened to those poor settlers, although I do know. But I was on the second exploratory mission to the coasts of wild America. In my day, they simply called it the new country and provisionally named the waters and lands Chesapeake Bay.

That was our destination. A string of islands and coastline bursting with friendly natives, exotic giant animals who practically offered you their pelts, so naïve were they: endless bounty, gold, silver and precious metals, freedom, adventure and the opportunity to start anew. That is what we were told Raleigh's men, Amadas and Barlow, found on their first foray to the area. So much bounty Raleigh rushed to the Queen and had her commission a second voyage, one of her own soldiers and tradesman, professional men who would settle and cultivate a magnificent port town by which

England could begin official trade of its colonial outpost's endless treasures.

These men, myself inexplicably among them. One hundred and twenty men meant to conquer the New World and set up a township where brides would be brought across the sea, families would come and all great English things would be rebuilt in a new place with a more temperate climate and wide empty fields save a few harmless savages. Like Wamenu, the friendly native found on Amadas and Barlow's first visit. A noble native somehow convinced to ride across the ocean on a boat to a world he had previously not known existed, converted, flounced through England in a cage before finally returning to his home with our expedition. He was sullen, yet spoke halting English and could dance an expressionless waltz when commanded by his great friend, Raleigh, as he was presented to the Queen.

Told this story later by a stoic Wamenu, restringing netting one quiet evening aboard ship, I pictured a bear being made to dance by a mean looking man with a stick I'd seen at the Christmas fair as a child. Every fair, in fact, with the same tragic, balding bear. Without the correct language to convey this imagery to my new friend, I'm afraid he logically thought I was laughing at him and so, out of politeness, he laughed with me: a humorless, flat chuckle that made me uncomfortable in his presence. It was not the last time I'd be forced to rethink some of my previously unchallenged beliefs on the superiority of the Englishman as a whole.

Hugh, being among the officers of the ship, wasn't as available to me as I'd expected. An occasional chat during topside exercises and a few mock salutes between us were all I had as far as comradery went – my awkward friendship with Wamenu aside - and I found myself mindlessly observing the others on the voyage.

Whether for some longing to belong, some familiarity to simply witness, boredom, nosiness, I hung back and quietly saw it all. And through my solitary, watchful existence on what turned out to be a very uneventful, even boring, Atlantic crossing through the spring of 1585, I became quite familiar with the people around me: their habits, their dialects, what parts of the ships they fancied more than others, what duties they shirked, who buggered whom and so forth.

Therefore, it came as a great surprise to me when I noticed something interesting was finally happening. People, and more than just one or two, had gone missing. People were disappearing, en route, yet the Captain and the officers never mentioned it. When the cook's boy went missing one starless mild night, I noticed. When the cook took over the boy's additional chores, grumbling ever so faintly in his Welsh slur, I noticed. When the candlemaker, a soldier and a cleric went missing, mere days apart, all in the dark of night while pissing in some corner of the ship, I noticed. I noticed that the others didn't notice and found that quite unsettling that they hadn't.

What if I went overboard, pitched into the water by some rogue wave while defecating into the sea, and no one noticed: no one heard my weak cries, my voice hoarse from disuse except in instances where I half-heartedly mumbled Yes Sir or No Sir to my superiors. What if only Wamenu noticed my worn boots toppling over the side of the quarter deck and just shrugged.

I finally ventured to the officers understood territory on the sunniest portion of the windy deck and cornered Hugh, a tilt of my head indicating my distressed need of counsel. He obliged after finishing his conversation with two overly young officers and approached, a faint look of suspicion in his previously unguarded expression.

"What is happening, Hugh?" I asked him, my voice no doubt carrying across the wind to others.

He ducked his head before answering, lowering his voice, "What do you mean?"

"Have you not noticed?" I gestured futilely to the industrious crew moving about us unconcerned.

"Noticed what?" Hugh looked around us.

"That people," I lowered my voice to match his, "are going missing? Is there sickness aboard? Should I be concerned?"

Hugh shook his head, "Don't be daft, boy. People die on voyages all the time." I'm sure he noticed the doubt on my face, before adding, "And sometimes people just can't tough it out. They...you know." Then he drew his finger across his throat and shrugged as if to indicate those suicides were doing us a favor. "Some people just weren't fit for life in the new world. But we soldiers sure as hell were, ole boy." I remembered Hugh's utter privilege in that moment and pitied him for it. He didn't see what I saw: a grand mystery, a string of murders big and small. And by watching and listening, I could pass my time trying to figure out how to avoid a likely fate. Or not. Depending on my mood. "We can't make a big stink of every little injury or death, surely you understand, it would cause panic and where would that put us. No. It's quite normal. Don't be hysterical."

I returned to my post and continued my unabated watching. And my eyes then fell to someone even smaller, quieter than myself. A young lad - if going by his wide set eyes, stretched frame, oily face and wreathe of curly red and gold hair - was quite likely the youngest now on our voyage since the cook's boy, who'd also looked fourteen or fifteen, went missing.

Like myself, this quiet witness watched the soldiers around him, nervously taking cues on when to eat, where to squat, how to manage himself in the company of other men, all in pursuit of their great destinies, all looking to their own in cramped spaces already filled with secret anxieties and doubts. He seemed so frightened, so unable to speak up, so out of his element, I broke my longstanding vow of disinterest and, over the course of several weeks, took on a rather brotherly, protective stance-albeit at arm's length, and really without language as the lad had heretofore never spoken nor was he to throughout the entire month's voyage.

Myself and another soldier of approximate age, Edmund (one of just thirteen aboard) from Gloucestershire, began to act as guardians for the young lad in tandem. It was as if he saw my small attempts to pass an extra crumb of bread to the boy or point him away from a scuffle or lover's quarrel on the darker sides of the ship and took up the challenge as well. And in that way, with the two of us quietly, suddenly working towards a common goal of ensuring this boy arrived on American soil alive, we were also bonded. Without a word, the three of us became a friendly trio, all based on the goodwill of boredom. For myself, it was the formation of a unit, a pack, to protect against the continued threat aboard. For as the final week of the voyage seemed to stretch into eternity, the disappearances never abated. Four more men went missing as we breached the shoals of the Outer Banks and made our way through a series of confusing channels, eventually beaching ourselves quite far from our original destination and the friendly natives surrounding it, I later learned.

The tale ended abruptly, leaving Gloria to reread it three times to absorb the details of his story. It was a brilliant start. She threw on her sundress, grabbed her keys and, without thinking, drove directly to Henry's cabin, energized with thoughtful critiques and suggestions for his prose.

When he opened the door, bleary eyed and shirtless, she

pushed him back inside, down to the floor and climbed on top of him without a word. Her mouth slanted over his, their tongues meeting and pressing, their teeth grazing the others' lips playfully. She ran her hand down his thigh, pressing her palm across his hard cock, her mouth silencing his moans. He ran his hands through her hair, pulling her hair back to expose the taut tendons of her neck which he bit with his sharp white teeth. Her hand found his zipper, tugging at his pants as she scrambled from her panties, tossing them aside before lowering herself onto him with a silky sigh, slick with sweat, their bodies melting together, panting and wild.

Afterwards, as she creaked and popped and struggled to remove herself from their tangled embrace, righting herself in the nearest chair, her ankles screaming, her forearms bruised, admitting,

"I read your story. You're really talented."

He lay at her feet, smiling up at her with his head resting in the crook of his arm, the other hand slid up her leg to her thigh as she redirected, "We should talk about what you're going to do with this story."

Henry nodded vigorously. Yet, that is *not* what they did.

Chapter 19

"Are you ready?" Gloria announced dramatically to Dee after filling her wine tumbler and taking a seat next to her on the couch. Dee turned her body towards Gloria, her face serious. She took the proffered wine, gesturing with it.

Gloria went on, "Because this is probably the most shocking thing you'll ever hear from me. I swear."

Dee nodded solemnly, bursting into a raucous giggle, sipping her wine.

"Ah mah gawd," she teased, "are you in love with Henry Wynter?" Dee leaned forward slightly, her eyes brimming with anticipation.

"No, better."

Dee's hopeful expression deflated. She frowned.

Gloria looked her in the eyes and gave a small, knowing smile, "I have taken him as my lover."

Dee's jaw fell open, her eyebrows flew up, "Holy shit!" She coughed before taking a great sip of wine, sputtering, "How was it?"

"It was wonderful," Gloria purred. The night of passion with Henry had awakened her somehow. She felt different. She felt different about *many things*.

Dee stared at her skeptically, "Really? He's…so young. You didn't have to…talk him through anything?"

"Quite the opposite," Gloria assured her, basking in Dee's jealousy. "I don't think I've ever been with such a self-assured man in bed before. And he was *all man*. It was wild and…passionate…

and mind blowing and…"

"Ok, Ok, Ok," Dee interrupted, "I get it. The mysterious Henry Wynter is a sexual god. Jesus, Gloria. Are you *dating* now?"

"No, we aren't *dating*. Kids don't date now anyway. They… hang out. Besides, I feel like I'm meant to mentor him, Dee. He came to my writing class and…he's exceptionally talented. I mean, like *get-published* good," Gloria confessed.

"Oh? Exceptionally good, is he?" Dee teased. "But not a man to take out in public?"

"I don't think he's the type. For right now, I'm just going to enjoy it without asking too many questions. At least I'm old enough to know what I'm getting into. What do we call it now? Friends with benefits?"

Dee nodded, sipping her wine, "Amen. When do you see him again?"

"No idea. But even if I never see him again, it was worth every minute of it."

"The scandal of it all," Dee giggled into her wine cup, amplifying her laughter. Gloria joined in her laughter, covering the shadow that fell across her face with a big smile. She couldn't admit to Dee that she tried to record every moment of it. Savor every touch. Every lazy conversation. Every sweet moment stored up in the sponge of her mind and the hollow of her heart. Henry, henry, henry. She wanted to scribble his name with hers in a heart, like a teenager. If she told Dee that - which she knew she should - Dee would snap her out of her trance. She would ground her and it would be over. So, she didn't. She didn't want to hear anything that might burst her bubble. Yet.

Dee, though a great believer in all types of carnal relations and the sort who personally glowed with sexual satisfaction, was much more realistic and matter-of-fact when it came to long-term relationships, hence the five ex-husbands. On the odd yearly phone calls that dotted their adult lives, she was just as likely to update Gloria with "I left Ricky. Bastard was cheatin' on me again. Again." as "Darryl's car broke down for the fourth time this year, so I left him. I just couldn't take it." Life always rolled on and there were always more men to roll with, even in this corner of the world.

Dee left after *Fashion Boat*, forcing several insincere promises from Gloria as she went. First, not to get too attached to her *baby lover*. Second, to use protection – there were all kinds of diseases out there. And third, to call her with all the details if she saw Henry again. And she meant *all the details*.

Gloria sat for a while, flipping through channels, reading online news with her glasses perched on the tip of her nose. Once in bed, her eyes open in the dark, it took a while to fall asleep and when she did, she dreamed Henry was the Lakeside Slayer.

When she awoke with the sun, she was surprised to find Henry snoring lightly beside her. They hadn't discussed his sleeping over, nor had she heard him slip into her bed. He shifted beside her, his hair falling across his face, angelic and unlined as he slept. Gloria smiled to herself, burying any suspicions she had and drifted back into a restless sleep.

Chapter 20

They hadn't left Gloria's house for days. Making love to Henry was fast becoming a semi-competitive sport. Like tennis, but enjoyable. And something she excelled at. These stolen moments of passion had brought her back to the world, out of the precipitous shadow of waiting for things to begin. She had color in her cheeks. She could feel her blood flowing, her skin flushing. She felt everything.

Life had a way of making people smaller somehow, reducing them over and over until their world shrank down to accommodate their new stature. At least that's how it felt to Gloria. That life had made her smaller as she reached for a larger world. But now… she felt different. Bigger suddenly. As if her world expanded and she was as tall as she used to be.

Henry was such a mystery. There was so much she didn't know about him. But there were things she knew already with certainty. He was quiet and shy and unassuming and he, like her, could travel unnoticed through life, without making waves or leaving tracks. Together, they were unremarkable to the world. Though for one another, it was different. They could see each other so clearly. What he couldn't explain, he wrote.

She finally called Dottie and pled illness, but her mother seemed distracted anyway, waving off Gloria's apologies and telling her to come when she could, that she'd live. Which, in the end, worried her more.

"Ha!" Gloria crowed as she unlocked Dottie's door. Henry

stood back, holding several grocery bags. "We made it past Beverly. Success!"

"*Fucking* Beverly," he added supportively.

"Mama," Gloria called, announcing her presence. Her heart raced when Dottie didn't immediately answer from the living room where she was usually parked in front of the largest televisions available to mortals. Henry followed behind, placing the groceries dutifully on the island countertop dividing the small apartment's kitchen from its living area. Feeling guilty she hadn't been by in several days, Gloria stopped by the grocery store to stock up on some of Dottie's favorite snacks. Even the salty ones the doctors frowned upon. She hurried through the tiny apartment panicking when she didn't find Dottie in her recliner or the bathroom.

"Mom!" Gloria shouted, a worried edge to her voice.

"What in the world," Dottie shuffled from her bedroom, carefully closing the door with one hand still on the doorknob behind her. Her cardigan sweater was buttoned incorrectly and Gloria noticed there was no shirt beneath it. She must have been taking a bath, Gloria reasoned. Though Dottie seemed more flustered and confused than usual.

"Are you OK, mom?" Gloria asked again, pulling a sleeve of fresh produce from one of the bags in the kitchen.

Dottie flapped her hand in annoyance, "I'm fine. What's all the ruckus? I was napping."

Of course, Gloria thought, her body flooding with relief. Dottie spied Henry, unloading a plastic bag full of soda cans onto the countertop.

"Who's this?" Dottie demanded, fishing her glasses from her sweater pocket, focusing her eyes with a few rapid blinks as she balanced the owlish lenses across the bridge of her nose. As she brought both hands to her face, she let go of the doorknob she'd held for support. The bedroom door creaked open as Dottie peered around the kitchen, studying Henry with a frown.

Dottie turned to her daughter, wagging a finger, "Gloria, why in the world would you bother bringing him?"

Gloria didn't answer as Dottie's door groaned open to reveal a partially nude, wholly confused elderly man hunched precariously on the corner of Dottie's adjustable mattress. He was desperately trying to pull his left sock further up his calf with little luck. He glanced up to the surprised faces of Gloria and Henry, all freezing mid-action.

"Wade!" Dottie went on, wagging her finger now in Henry's direction, oblivious to the open bedroom door, her voice gaining conviction, "You can't just show up now with one of our children in tow, begging to return. It's over. I'm in love with Bernard. I've moved on." Dottie glanced behind her, dramatically motioning in Bernard's direction.

"Who's in love?" Bernard shouted to no one in particular, struggling to stand.

"I'm sorry," Dottie addressed Henry once more, her face softening with pity. "I want a divorce."

"You're married?" Bernard stood, indignantly struggling to shove his stocking-clad feet into a pair of wooly, brown women's slippers.

Gloria was relieved to discover his ensemble included a fading, worn pair of baggy boxer shorts. Bernard glared at Henry in confusion, glancing between the young man and Dottie in disgust. Dottie raised her eyebrows, her eyes glinting. Henry raised his hands in surrender.

"This is Henry," Gloria enunciated clearly, "Mom? You understand? This is my friend, Henry. Not Dad. Dad is an old man now."

Gloria shot Henry an apologetic wince over her shoulder. He seemed fairly nonplussed, if not slightly entertained by the entire unfolding circus.

Bernard shuffled past Dottie, a blue, terrycloth robe (also Dottie's) slung over his forearm. "I didn't know you were married," he huffed loudly, trundling to the door, his boxers tucked noticeably between his flat, sagging buttocks: all visible through the worn cloth of his underpants.

Dottie completely ignored her lover's ignominious exit, fixing her gaze once again on Henry. This time, she smiled in recognition. "Henry Wynter, of course, you came once with Terry. You buy marijuana from my grandson," she leaned forward to accept Henry's kiss on the cheek. Her gaze shifted suspiciously to Gloria, "Where have you been?"

Gloria ignored the question as she unloaded the groceries, pausing to make lunch. After a short visit, the three of them ate a sandwich while watching one of Dottie's talk shows in harmonious silence. Gloria suppressed her desire to question her mother on the topic of Bernard. She knew she had little room to judge. After lunch, Gloria suggested Dottie get some rest.

Leaving, Gloria almost collided with the same orderly from her dance the other day. Only his nimble feet and Henry's outstretched forearm saved her from a tumble. Now, that would have impressed her young lover. *Nothing like a broken hip for foreplay.*

Henry seemed to pale as she righted herself, "Are you okay?"

"We dance again," the orderly joked, moving on with his chores, his head down sheepishly. Gloria assumed his cataracted eye made it difficult to spot people coming from the right, though she made no comment. Beverly Kent caught them just as Gloria had the exit in sight.

"Gloria!" Beverly trilled, raising her hand as if she was at auction, "Yooohoooo!"

"Shit," Gloria muttered, her shoulders drooping. Henry paused beside her, searching her face, "Just a sec." Gloria turned, her smile almost electric. "Beverly!"

Beverly brightened, then noticed Henry waiting patiently at the end of the hallway by the exit sign, "Is this another grandson? I don't think we've met?"

"Henry," he jovially offered his right hand, "No relation."

A look of surprise crossed her pinched features, quickly suppressed with another benign smile as she stuttered, "We can… talk more later, if you'd like. I'll call you…about…the, *you know*." Beverly nodded, backing up and quickly retreating.

"Yeah! What an asshole!" Henry teased, throwing his arm around Gloria's shoulders as they walked to the car.

Chapter 21

The damn dog was barking again. It was a sunny, quiet day, but the Rottweiler leapt into the air, snapping at the breeze, pulling at a chain tugging a metal stake in the ground beneath a clump of leafless trees. The hum of engines from joyriders on the lake across the blacktop road and the distant buzz of a lawnmower competed with the staccato of his barks.

Dwayne clicked the volume down on his large, boxy television and moved to the window, peering between the creaking aluminum blinds at his girlfriend's dog. Brittney asked him repeatedly to bring Dodge inside during the heat of the day, but Dwayne hated the dog and willfully left the poor creature chained outside while she worked a double shift at the hospital. By the time she came home, the sun would be down, the dog still couldn't talk and Brittney would be none the wiser.

The dog was growling, its great muscles straining and bulging, a rift of hair sticking up from the ridge of his back as he snapped at shadows along the fence. After snarling at emptiness, the dog went back to erratic barks. Dwayne sighed and plopped back down in the leather recliner to finish his game. The barks continued. Dwayne turned the volume up. At some point, one of Dwayne's neighbors shouted from his own backyard, "Shut that goddamn dog up, Dwayne. Or take it inside."

Dwayne reluctantly stood again, adjusting the worn crotch of his sweats, slamming his warm beer down on the side table, storming outside. Dodge barked wildly at the fence line.

"Dodge," Dwayne shouted, "shut the fuck up!" The dog barked faster and louder. "Dodge. Goddammit. Shut the fuck up," Dwayne tried to pull the dog back by the chain as it leapt and thrashed.

"Yeah, thanks Dwayne. Real fucking help," the neighbor's slurred voice taunted from the backyard next door.

Dwayne heard the neighbor slam his trailer door with a hollow clang as he went back inside. Dodge went silent, crouching down, his head bowed in a submissive position. Whining, the dog tucked his tail under his body. Dwayne walked over to Dodge's side, reaching for the chain. *Fuck it*, he thought, I'll put the little asshole in the shed. Maybe give him a fan to keep him cool. Brittney can't say shit about that, *now can she*?

"What the hell?" Dwayne wiped the sweat from his eye with a tattooed forearm, struggling to pry the stake from the ground. The dog bared its teeth. As he separated the chain from the stake, Dwayne heard a soft whump, feeling a whoosh of wind, as if a giant bird had landed beside him and finally glanced up from his crouched, feverish toil.

Dodge's frantic barking effectively muffled the sounds of Dwayne's screams.

Chapter 22

It was silent and dark as Gloria's car idled quietly on the gravel driveway sloping up to Henry's cabin. After peering about the property protectively before stepping out, Henry came around to open Gloria's door. She allowed him to take her hand, leading her up the uneven drive.

"Let's grab some clean clothes and get you back home and dirty!" Gloria teased, gripping his hand tighter.

The moment they stepped onto the porch, Henry pushed Gloria against the weathered door, his hand pinning her wrists, the other hand traveled down her arm, to the small of her back, to her waist, where he pulled her hips into his own. She shivered in delight as he bit the crease of her neck before she turned, her hands pulling his lips to her own her. His fingers brushed lightly down her body as he kissed her roughly, aggressively, his lips moving across hers seductively, nibbling and nipping with his sharp, white teeth.

Henry growled seductively before pulling back, "let's get what we came for and get going." His eyes flitted over the dark perimeter quickly, suspiciously, once more before he caught himself, quickly masking his expression with a smile.

"Shit! My key." Henry patted his pockets, searching.

"You have a spare?"

"You know what…," Henry murmured, kneeling in the darkness, pushing his hands along the deserted flower bed lining the porch, declaring, "Bingo!"

He held the key up victoriously. The black outline of his form lit up with the blue and white flashing of four police cruisers, their lights gyrating in tandem as they whizzed down the dark road behind them - brakes screeching in the distance, the eerie glow of their cars lighting up the neighboring trailer park laying between Henry's small cabin and the lake.

Two more cars flew by without lights, both sporting the boxy, nondescript shape of official city vehicles. The bark and feedback of multiple walkie talkies echoed through the fragrant evening air; wood smoke and lake water brine mixed with the impending autumn.

"What the hell," Henry whispered, his gaze riveted to the scene unfolding down the road.

Gloria looked up at Henry in the light of the moon and shivered, suddenly chilled. "You want to go check it out?" She was, quite naturally, curious (i.e. nosy) as well.

He nodded with a tight smile and Gloria noticed that for the first time since she met him, Henry looked worried. An ambulance sped past. As they walked, Henry took her clammy hand in his cold one. They strolled down the dark blacktop road to the chaotic scene unfolding, passing under the faded Tranquil Pines signage hanging crooked on a tilted frame. Aside from the click of scanners and a low hum of chatter from the crime scene, a quietness engulfed them.

The cruisers, sirens muted, lights flashing, lined the gravel drive in front of the squat, ramshackle doublewide on a tiny brown lot, bordered by two aluminum houses with similarly worn faces; yards full of shrubby green knots poking from clusters of deserted gardening implements, poorly defined property lines bordered by barren pine trees, their brown needles littering the roofs and bald yards like a dusting of snow, a fading, plastic picnic table and an assortment of children's toys being reabsorbed back into the earth. Uniformed police mixed with civilians in the front yard where an exhausted-looking woman nodded with stunned shock as a cop spoke quietly to her under a detached carport. She wore scrubs, her greasy hair pulled into a severe ponytail. As the captain spoke, she buried her eyes in her fists, wiping fiercely at her tears while ignoring her runny nose. Gesturing with her hands, she replied to his questions.

Neighbors wandered near the hastily erected perimeters of the crime scene only to be scolded by the officers, admonished to go home, warned they would be questioned later. One particularly distraught young man was being interviewed by a female officer who nodded, jotting notes as he spoke. "I didn't hear it," Gloria heard him remark, rubbing his red eyes, "fucking dog…barking… Dwayne…. real asshole." "Where's the dog?" the officer asked in response, her eyes travelling to the dark tree lines beyond the property.

A grey Cadillac slid past the spectators, parking crookedly in front of the green single-wide two doors down. Gloria recognized Karl's car with a frown. She dropped Henry's hand, though he was too engrossed in the crime scene to notice. The lone ambulance's engine whirred to life, an EMT taking the driver's seat, lights flashing, otherwise silent. Several officers congregated at the back of the ambulance, talking through the open back doors with the driver who seemed in no hurry to leave, which pointed to a tragedy, not an emergency.

Slamming his car door, Karl shifted the waist of his slacks as he exited the vehicle, heading resolutely toward Deputy Cash who stood central in a circle of men in the victim's front yard. This circle, Gloria realized, was comprised of said deputy, the coroner, the police chief and a stout young woman in jeans, perhaps a detective. *Maybe she could make the detective in her book a woman, too*. Gloria made a mental note.

Karl strode past Gloria before pausing, turning his head to face her, his eyes widening in frustration. "Glory! What *the* hell are you doing *here*, now?" his head swiveled around for the location of her car as he spoke.

Henry appeared at her side, nodding politely in Karl's direction, "Mr. Weidman."

Karl tilted his head, ignoring Henry's outstretched hand, his mouth firming into a line. Kicking his chin toward the house behind him, he fixed his eyes on Gloria, "Get home, now. This is not a safe place to be. I told you that."

Gloria grimaced, "It's fine, Karl. I was just dropping Henry by his house. We had to see what all the hoopla was about."

Karl shook his head, "You should go, Glory." He gave Henry a last, dismissive glance before finishing, "You hear me?"

Gloria smiled, "Oh, Karl, you're too thoughtful. Don't worry, we're going, we're going."

Karl shook his head, turning on his heels before straightening his back and smoothing his shirt, approaching the power circle. The man being interviewed gesticulated, his panicked eyes falling on Henry and Gloria on the perimeter of the yard, excitedly pointing in their direction.

Gloria tugged Henry's shirt, advising in a whisper, "We should go."

"Sir?" The officer called, motioning to Henry, "One moment."

"Henry?" Gloria tried to read Henry's expression. Guilt? Worry? Fear?

"It's alright," he reassured her, squeezing her hand.

The officer approached, her gaze moving from their joined

hands to scan Henry suspiciously.

“Sir, would you mind if I asked you a few questions?”

Chapter 23

Later at the police station, as Gloria sat – looking for all the world like a worried grandmother bailing the recalcitrant grandchild she'd been forced to raise out of jail – waiting for *her lover* to be questioned in the latest mysterious *incident*, she wondered what Henry said that warranted a ride down to the station for further questioning.

She'd tried eavesdropping as the officer, by this time flanked by two other officers and the husky detective in jeans, spoke to Henry, escorting him some distance from Gloria. It seemed convivial enough judging solely by Henry's open-faced passivity during the questioning in question. Moments later, he'd been escorted to the back seat of the nearest cruiser, shouting to Gloria, "Don't worry, they just have a few more questions. I'll call you when I'm done!"

Left with only Deputy Cash in the yard, staring out as the ambulance silently departed the crime scene, the cruiser pulled away with a jarring bloop-bloop. The crying girlfriend continued to honk and wheeze in her grief as Karl gave Gloria a withering look of disappointment and turned his head. No surprise there, he was always one you could rely on in tough times, Gloria thought ruefully. She walked the short distance up the blacktop hill to reach her car. Karl could just go to hell, she decided.

When the phone rang at two am, Gloria answered with fuzzy thoughts, her senses slowed by the weight of uneasy sleep, "Yes?"

Waiting to hear Henry's gentle voice requesting a ride

home, she was surprised to hear Terry's rolling East Texas twang instead. Gloria wasn't sure if she'd heard his voice on the phone since texting was invented. "Aunt Glory, I'm sorry to call so late but Daddy came by on his way home to let me know my friend *Hayes* had some dustup and would need a ride home from the station. But when I got there, Casey wouldn't let me see him and said they need some evidence that Henry *is who he says he is*. I guess he didn't have his pertinents on him when they took him down for questioning. He said you had the key to his place?"

Did she? Wait, he said he'd left his keys in his pants. As Terry went on, Gloria stumbled out of bed and felt around the floor like a blind woman, locating two pairs of jeans and four shirts that didn't belong to her, "Henry asked if I could come get the key and go find his social security card and his license in some shoe box shoved in the back of some closet."

In the second pair of pants, she found a small keychain with four keys attached. Surely one of these would open Henry's front door.

"Don't be ridiculous," Gloria admonished Terry, "you're a good friend, you go back to bed. I'll get his license and take it in. And give that Casey Cash a piece of my mind in the process."

"Aa'ight," Terry sighed. "Call me if ya need anything. You should be able to present his license and they'll let him right out. Tell that boy to stay outta trouble, for gawd's sake."

"I will," Gloria murmured, hanging up.

Gloria experienced the strangest sensation as she drove through the dark streets in the middle of the night, the highway deserted and quiet - a darkness only possible in the folds of the country on a lake perched off the side of the world. Gloria remembered this world so well. It smelled like high school and nights spent around a bonfire at the Point. When the smallness of home was still a snug security and the bigger world surrounding it a beautiful mystery. Nibbles of doubt ate at her as she drove, the radio silenced to fit the mood.

She pulled into Henry's driveway and sat for several moments while the car idled. What was she doing? He was sitting at the station waiting for someone to come and help him. *Why was she dawdling*? Taking a deep breath, she stepped into the still calm of deep night. Hands shaking, she tried pushing the first key in the doorknob. It wouldn't turn. She tried the second, still no click. The third key worked but she had to force herself to enter the still room. Without Henry, this felt wrong. Even though he'd requested his ID, it was Terry, non-curious, non-nosey Terry he expected to rifle through his sparse belongings. Yet by quick, subconscious design, she was here. By herself. With permission (implied, perhaps) to look around.

Unbridled curiosity was a common theme in her life. It was one of the traits she despised the most in herself, but there it was - a constant companion. It was why she'd started writing in the first place. Always wondering while she was driving from the city back home to visit, gazing out the car window wondering what *those people* down *that street* were doing right now. How did they make their living? Did they have a garden? Did they have cats? Did they travel? Did they love their family? Always wondering. Which led to speculation, which led to telling stories to yourself to fill the emptiness. Outright investigation for novels was a newer hobby.

Gloria checked two small closets before she found one that wasn't completely empty. The third closet – a tiny, wood paneled affair located between the bathroom and the bedroom – contained several coats, shirts and four pair of shoes, four neatly stacked cigar boxes and one small mahogany chest that looked as if it at one time sported a lock and more shine. One cigar box contained pictures, at least forty to fifty pictures, though she didn't have time to properly nose through them. The second box contained three very old documents, two still wrapped in rotting silk ribbons, tied nattily closed and a brass key with the number 502 inscribed upon its small face. Another folded paper, the size of a small map, sported an old wax seal, broken and refolded. She pulled one out, carefully smoothing the yellowed parchment with shaking hands. It looked like some type of deed, the black cracking ink faded and illegible. Family antiquities, perhaps? He mentioned he was an orphan. Perhaps this was all that was left of his family records? The third box contained a strange variety of jewelry and snuff boxes, two tarnished gold rings and a few coins - roughly sized with thick metal, darkened with age - and a delicate gold rosary. She held the coins up, one at a time, trying to decipher their origin, but didn't recognize the face on the back of them, though they looked valuable. Maybe this was how Henry made his money? *Maybe* he was a collector. His story would make more sense, as a history buff.

In the fourth box, she found Henry's ID and a small blue social security card. The name on both read Henry Allen Wynter IV. So, he was at least who he said he was. Relief crawled over her skin. She had worried once she started pulling this string the rest of her cloak of ignorance could unravel. The biggest box, a chest, was pushed into the furthest corner of the closet, covered with a couple of worn sheets and quilts. She lifted it out, straining to move it into the light. The box itself was heavy as she placed it on the worn carpet of the hallway, the hall light buzzing overhead before staring at it for several moments. What was she afraid to find? Rusty Fry's head?

The chest hinges creaked as she lifted the lid, peeking down into the apparently empty container. Sliding her hand down into the smooth interior, she slid her fingertips over the rough wood at the bottom until she found two objects: a wooden shingle and another yellowed document, rolled and tied with a leather thong. The shingle, once pulled from the box, resembled a piece of rough bark and fit into the palm of both hands. When she turned it over, she gasped. On the wood, shellacked and sealed, was the astonishingly skilled woodcarving of an ouroboro, a snake eating its own tail. The sheer ferocity of the image entranced her. The carving seemed brittle and old. The rolled document she set aside, her eyes roving over the closet's sparse bounty having found nothing but a few random heirlooms. She slid the leather thong down and unrolled the yellow scroll slowly, worried the aged paper could disintegrate in her hands and smiled at the charcoal sketch she found inside - a one-bedroom shanty, the outline of a shed on a hill with the shadow of a woman tilling in the field, her delicate face barely discernible, a smoky blur on the edge of the drawing. Roman numerals dotted the corner of the sketch. Sitting back on her heels, she sighed and picked up the shoebox with Henry's id cards, aiming to push the rest back into the corner of the closet. The cigar box packed with photos slid off the stack, its photos splattering across the floor of the hallway.

"Dammit!" Gloria barked, checking her watch, dropping to her knees as quickly as gravity would allow to push the photos back into a pile, marveling over the breadth of the collection. Old photos, tintypes, cardboard sepia photos from the turn of the century and a square polaroid that peeked out from the corner of the stack. For some reason, Gloria pulled that photo out and studied the faded picture: a woman, her voluminous hair shining in the sun, winking and posing in front of a black TransAm, her arms flung out with joy. Something tugged at Gloria's mind. The woman's face seemed familiar. Was this Henry's mother? Gloria snatched the polaroid from the cigar box and shoved it into her purse, vowing to return it as soon as she could study it at her leisure.

"Gloria?" Casey Cash's voice boomed. Gloria pulled her hand from the depths of her purse, startled to find Casey's concerned face hovering over her.

"I brought these," she fished out Henry's ID cards and waved them. "So, you can let him go now, you turd." She'd already offered them to the night clerk, who'd dutifully made copies and returned the originals without comment.

Casey frowned, "We were just questioning him, Glory. He'd been *seen* having words with the victim. And, it has been indicated he has an ongoing relationship with the victim's canine?"

Gloria rose to her feet, glaring at Casey, "And that means what exactly, Casey?"

"It's that…well, he…he's been known to feed, water and walk the victim's dog without permission."

"Well, that does it. He must be a killer. Congratulations, case conveniently solved." Gloria full well knew herself to be a class A hypocrite, the stolen picture singing to her from her purse, but she shook her head in derision, "Can I take him home now?"

Casey seemed surprised, "You two shacking up already? You might as well know, he's using you as his alibi. Says he was with you all night until we brought him down. That right?"

Gloria saw the pity in Casey's eyes and bristled, pulling herself up taller, looking him in the eyes confidently, "Yes, that's right. He's been with me. Every night. For at least a week."

Casey opened his mouth but closed it quickly, finishing derisively, "And you'd be willing to sign a document to that effect? Keep in mind, Glory, if we find out he's guilty of this thing, you could be held in contempt."

She heard Henry's voice from the other side of the lobby and nodded curtly in dismissal. Casey disappeared from her side before Henry materialized, waving friendly good-byes to his new friends at the station.

Chapter 24

"What did they want?" Gloria probed, driving Henry the short distance to her house from the station.

"Unfortunately, I was one of the last people to have words with the victim," Henry explained with a tired yawn.

Gloria waited for him to elaborate.

"What?" Henry shrugged, "I told him several times he shouldn't leave his dog out in the yard without water. It's too hot. That was it. Poor guy."

Gloria nodded. But she couldn't stop thinking about the old photo she'd taken from his closet. Or even really explain why she'd felt compelled to take it. *Was it* his mother? And if it were, why wasn't it displayed in his home in a normal fashion? Maybe it wasn't his mother? Maybe an aunt or a great aunt? She'd ask eventually…when she worked up the nerve. But then, she'd have to admit the full scope of her investigative actions. And the fact that those investigations included him as a suspect. He'd realize she was suspicious, too, and he'd disappear. Then she would never know and that was the worst!

The following day and night, Henry was less available, and Gloria said nothing. She felt like she also needed some space with her thoughts as well. He returned, silent and withdrawn, on the evening of the third day and they went on as if nothing had happened. He'd grabbed her hips, pulled her to him and lowered his mouth to hers. She forgot her suspicions for the time. She forgot everything. Everything but Henry.

The following morning, he was gone again, but he'd left

another manila folder displayed on the fireplace mantle, a wilted daisy laid ceremoniously before it. Gloria took the envelope from the mantle, immediately sliding the folder open, the cool white pages slipping out with a hiss and began to hungrily read.

For future reference, early summer is not an ideal time to try and establish crops and food supplies for a fledgling colony - a fact completely lost to greed in the lightning speed of the venture's planning. Several ships worth of wholly unprepared soldiers and tradesmen set forth, myself one of the first to leap from the sides of the ship as we spotted shore, splashing into the cold waters of the Atlantic, pulling our meager supplies to the beaches, our chests puffed with satisfaction and hope.

I wish I could better convey how it looked when we landed and how I felt. But I couldn't write then, so I only have my memory to go by. I didn't learn to write until a great time later at an Indian missionary school in Florida. But by then, this moment was a distant time and I was a completely different person. I know it was beautiful - the huge soaring trees, the moss tangled through the branches, the unfamiliar smells of the land and the emptiness of it. So much flora and fauna and silence. Golden silence mingled with the surf and the birdcalls.

We landed just in time for the summer storms. Grenville and Lane, our noble leaders, turned out to be their own worst enemies. Ignorant in all but rapacious blundering. The kind that gets men killed. First, they allowed our supply ship to sink into the bay, wasting all but a few of our hard brought goods. We salvaged what we could and made immediate work of cutting into the thick vines and saplings of the unfamiliar island, with all but the officers assigned hard labor for the foreseeable future.

I am about as proficient a carpenter as I am a sailor, yet my shipbuilding experience came immediately to the fore. Edmund, the kid and myself were assigned to the lumber line, this being the first time I heard the name Bennett Chappell as Hugh barked our name, rank and orders upon coming ashore. The kid's name was Bennett Chappell. I rolled that over on my tongue a few times, happy to finally have a more dignified appellation for my unofficial charge. He gave nary an acknowledgement nor a flinch when I used this name later that day, only nodding as I explained how to hold the ax head to strike with a great, heavy mallet when splitting a tree.

As our food supplies were feeding the fish in the shallow waters of the inlet, a large contingency of dignified officers, Hugh among their ranks, was dispatched to make contact with our friendly natives and acquire additional grain stores. Five days later, seven of the original twenty in that party returned, bleeding and traumatized. Hugh was among them, the returned, empty handed - all with harrowing tales of sorcery and survival. It was to chill an already cooling enthusiasm for our mission.

Bloodied and dazed, Hugh appeared back in camp, walking silently with the remaining few through our shushed ranks, directly to the officer's tent. It was only later that night at the urging of Edmund that I snuck to Hugh's side and demanded he tell me what had happened. Without ever looking me directly in the eye, instead focusing on the flames of the fire, he recounted in a dry recitation that the first of them disappeared while on patrol during night one. One, then two, then four the third night, and finally – six taken, all silently drug into the unlit shadows of the night on the fourth and final day. Nary a scream, never a sound.

The first missing soldier was found on the third day, blocking the path of the group, his insides spilling about his corpse; a corpse grotesquely strung between two trees with his own ropy tendons. The second and third were never found and the six officers taken on the fourth night were later seen as rattling heads, the gore of their severed necks trailing down the spears of the savages who held them, shaken at an already shaking, rapidly shrinking group of terrified boy soldiers, wailing and wetting themselves - finally, mysteriously, left alone again as the rain abated on the final afternoon.

The Indians, savages painted in soot, never fully materialized. They terrorized by heckling the men from trees and throwing stones and pinecones at their retreat, only arriving en masse to reveal their terrible visages during a deafening thunderstorm, springing from nowhere to melt back into the trees after a series of high-pitched yelping, wild gesticulations meant to frighten, a bit of face-to-face taunting and the aforementioned severed-head-shaking.

All said, with the recent depletion of our officer stock and the mysterious losses endured on the voyage over, we were down to just ninety-seven men. English crops had been immediately planted, far too late in the season if judging by the sweeping theatrics of Wamenu, consulting with the farm team before he disappeared into the night-presumably to return to his own, wiser people camping nearby. Our hardy English seeds failed miserably in the moist Carolina heat, leaving us to forage for food in an unfamiliar forest. The results were, as one could imagine, less than stellar.

On some occasions, a native (my guess, our old ally Wamenu) would leave us a skin of fresh deer meat or a pile of weevily corn, and we would gratefully drag it behind the wooden pikes with which we'd walled ourselves into the compound and wave in thanks, pulling the sad offering behind us in the dirt like refugees.

Grenville, rightfully assessing the situation, almost immediately took our remaining ship and several lucky crewmembers and returned to England to fetch supplies for our flailing settlement. We never saw him again. Or at least, I didn't. He left Governor Ralph Lane in charge, a decision immediately regretted as he was even more of a charlatan than Grenville and began a very strange campaign of terror against the local tribes: a sullen, unhelpful lot who by this point silently lingered feet away from us as we traipsed about their lands, pulling the trees from the Earth around us to build lopsided long houses and tilling futilely into their salty coastlands. Lane's foolishness culminated with the killing of a local chieftain, not intimidating the local tribes, but enraging them instead. Our friendly native allies melted into the countryside and never returned.

Gloria sat for a moment when she was done, marveling at the details of Henry's story. It was brilliant, though unsettling. She got up, unable to shake her sense of general unease and busied herself making coffee and cinnamon toast, spotting the blinking light of the message button on the house phone with a frown. Gloria tapped the button on her messages. To her surprise, she had several voice mails.

"Gloria," Dee's strident, gravelly voice filled the room, "give me a call. It's Tuesday. I haven't heard from you. I take it our whine and wine night may be canceled? Let me know you're alright. I guess we'll catch up next week." They hadn't.

Message two.

"Glory Jean," Dee commanded, "give me a call. I'm getting worried. You take a lover and you disappear. Unfair…and not like you. Call me. I'd like details, you whore." Gloria winced.

Beep.

"*Gloria Jean*," Dee again, her voice exasperated. Gloria asked her repeatedly over the years why she never texted like the rest of the world, but Dee would only shrug, saying her cold fingertips made the activity damn near impossible."I expect to see you this Tuesday for the usual. If I don't, I'm calling the police."

Beep.

"Gloria? Ted Carroll here with the Gazette. So, uh hey, I've come into some sensitive information regarding the uh, local incidents. But I have to admit, I'm a little dubious of my sources, so take what you may from it. Maybe you could swing by the office here soon. We can discuss. Or call me."

Chapter 25

Now *here* was a *Dairy Queen*! Gloria stared over the plastic swirl of her straw at the sign in front of her, whole and functional. Sucking fruitlessly at the last of her Oreo Blizzard, a building headache between her eyes, her gaze travelled again to the files peaking from under the peeling leather seat of her car. She tossed the phone into the seat and placed the depleted Blizzard in her cup holder with a reluctant pull, leaning across the emergency brake to run her fingertips over the fan of files on the floorboard of her car. Five of them! One so thick a jumble of notes and receipts tumbled from the bulging pocket of the file folder. Two were labeled Wynter, Henry. One titled Schaeffer, one titled Saint Hanover and the last with no label to identify its possible contents, which *felt* like stiff photos, crinkly receipts and thick-papered records. She made a mental note to look through these later. When she had privacy, wine and more courage than she had today. When she recovered from the shock of seeing Henry's name on two of the files. She wanted to look inside so badly. But what an invasion of privacy. She didn't think she had it in her. Her liberal conscience wouldn't allow it.

Ted had been uncharacteristically out of the office when Gloria dropped by, but Tammy efficiently handed over a stack of manila file folders marked with a yellow post-it labeled *GW*. As she exited the Gazette, she could have sworn she heard a rustling behind Ted's closed office door and giggled thinking he might be hiding from her to evade further questions. Slamming her car door closed, she pushed the files under her passenger seat and sped away, her stomach dropping into a freefall.

Now, feeding her shaky feelings with a melting shake, she couldn't stop thinking about the block letters in various prime colors drawn clumsily onto the manila label tab of the files. Blue, red, orange, green - connecting them very quickly to the pile of similar files she'd seen more recently at Rusty Fry's defunct PI offices. She knew what they were the minute she'd seen them. Why in the world would Rusty Fry follow *Henry*? *Who* had hired him? How in the hell had Ted effing Carroll ended up with these files? How did Ted fit into this? Had he stolen them from Rusty's agency? Why, Ted Carroll, you dirty dog, Gloria mused. What would that man *not do* for a story?

She didn't recognize the other name, nor the name of the Saint, so she set those aside. Going through these files would be a massive breach of ethics. She knew she *should* return them to the Fry Agency at once. Or better yet, report this to the police, take the files to Casey and tell him exactly where she got them. *And maybe she would.* One day. *When* she was done with them. But she still couldn't bring herself to look inside. Things were too good with Henry to ruin with this now.

She didn't dare bring them into the house either. There was no rhyme or reason to Henry's quiet comings and goings and she'd rather he didn't realize she was still actively investigating the murders around him. Actively investigating *him*. He needn't know she didn't trust him enough to tell him about the files or believe him fully when he spoke so casually of his innocence.

She was halfway home before she even realized she was driving, pulling her attention back to the road just as the car in front of her braked short at the light. Gloria's tires screeched as her car slid to a stop. A hand from the driver in front popped out the driver's side window with a timid wave of apology before puttering back up to speed. One of the color block-labeled files slid out as Gloria braked, its contents strewn across the passenger side floormat. On top, a square photo of an older woman taunted Gloria: her face loose and cheerful, a recent shot from the Longview Lion's Club, the background a painted backdrop of fall foliage and a pumpkin. Someone honked as Gloria sat a moment too long at the light, her gaze riveted to the exposed snapshot. There was something about the woman's smile that resonated.

Gloria recalled the photo of the Lakeside Slayer's murder victim from the obituary Ted ran in the Gazette. She remembered her name was Claudia Hastings. The woman was sixty-eight. In a flash, Gloria realized she was *also* the beautiful young woman smiling in the photo she'd taken from Henry's closet, the same woman from the photo in her purse! Forty years older, but the smile remained the same. Spots danced before Gloria's eyes and she pulled quickly to the side of the road, trying to catch her breath.

Gloria swept the photo back under the passenger seat of her car with the rest of the files. She didn't have room for more doubt in her relationship with Henry, if what she had with Henry could even be classified *as* a relationship, because the mysterious Henry Wynter remained just that – mysterious. But she knew enough now to realize she should be more careful going forward. And, if she had any faith in Henry whatsoever, she needed to confront him about her suspicions before she opened those files and found the answers she was searching for herself.

Chapter 26

I had, in the months between our landing and the wet fall wherein I and the men around me lay in exhausted heaps in a half-finished fort, the sagging skin of our bodies and our sharp features stretched into grimaces, come to regret my involvement in the whole affair. Several men, apparently of weaker mental character, disappeared into the shadows of the imposing forest beyond our camp as starvation and madness set in. We subsisted on what we could gather and boiled sassafras tea. Sassafras, it seemed, was in limitless supply.

I was still quietly watching everyone and everything, my conviction that a killer was among us only waning slightly in light of the actual murders (of the soldiers, of the natives) taking place. However, now that the cook - once my main suspect due to his access to both cutting implements and methods of disposal - had ironically died of food poisoning, my investigation slowed.

Through it all, Edmund and I continued our watchful preservation of Bennett Chappell who, after nine silent months, finally spoke. Once, when an axe head imbedded itself into his thigh, I heard him yelp, miraculously unmarked except for a small red line of blood which quickly scabbed over, saved by his thick woolen chaps. I knew then he wasn't mute. The second time, I heard him clearly say as the remaining four officers faced us one wind bitten morning and asked for volunteers, "I'll do it," in a peculiar, vaguely Northern European accent, his voice reedy and nasal as one would expect from such a young lad.

Though I'd grown too thin and my hair too long, I was in better condition than some of the larger, more muscular men after our trying winter: most having lost hair, teeth, nails and more than a few extremities from the axes, starvation and cold. I'd also successfully avoided ever leaving the enclosure once we'd erected our piked fencing, thereby protecting myself from some of the more unwelcoming aspects of our new home, such as the animals and the Indians. Bennett, however, was completely unchanged. Perhaps because of the great care and extra rations Edmund and I had provided or by lucky genetics, Bennett's cheeks were still oily and plump, his body showing none of the wear and tear myself and the others experienced. Despite his continued muteness, Bennett Chappell seemed to be enjoying his days in America, miserable though they were.

"I'll go as well." I was almost as surprised by my own impulsive volunteerism, but my initial instinct was still to protect this boy. Hugh nodded, giving me a secondary, thankful inclination of his head. I guess volunteers for sure death were hard to come by anymore.

Five of us headed off to our assumed demise, tramping through the cold and wet to present ourselves to a nearby tribe of former friendlies. It was a pathetic camp, a small collection of ten adults and seven children – rabbit carcasses drawn on sticks smoking over a smoldering fire, the women topless and stringy, the wet winter having affected our neighbors' supplies as well. An ancient crone sat atop a small pile of – what else - sassafras, sorting and picking, seemingly disinterested in her guests.

We held our hands out in front of us, palms up, as instructed by Wamenu and I mumbled a few words of nonsense we'd memorized. The children hung back as several wiry adults approached us. This is when the sassafras crone reared her head, exposing us to her toothless smile and a sightless white eye. She hissed, her one functional eye widening in fear and she let out a torrent of gibberish, her hands pointing our direction then back to the sky and ground. The adults froze and the children disappeared without a whisper. Our detractor abandoned her pile of sassafras and with her toothless lips twisting into louder and louder proclamations, finally spat in our direction and hurried from the camp without a single glance behind her.

Our attention focused on the frightening hysterics of the old crone, we'd failed to notice the Indians had produced a small pile of what we would later learn was hemp, a haunch of one of our own missing horses and a bladder of fermented honey then disappeared themselves, back into the trees leaving the remnants of their fire and all of their worldly possessions behind. We took what we could carry, returning to the cheers of our comrades and the expectation that we could get as lucky again.

And we did, again and again, enough to keep us limping through a desperate end to winter. It was the strangest thing – anytime we approached a small tribe, they shook in fear and handed us whatever we demanded, right down to the skins off their backs. This, when they didn't just recede into the woods and leave us to our fancy. It took us several shakeups in personnel before realizing the key to it all was Bennett Chappell. We assumed it was the boy's red hair that made the Indians lose their minds. If he wasn't with the patrol, negotiations invariably failed. When he stepped forward, the world was ours as far as the heathens were concerned. They wanted none of him.

When we received word through a Scottish trapper that Admiral Drake and his ships were prowling through the Caribbean and up and down the Florida coast harrying our enemies - in this case the Spaniards - we cheered and pictured a scenario where the explorer would glide up to the Carolina beach, draw us to his bosom and carry us back home. By this time, it was widely accepted that Grenville had left us to our destinies and would never return, so we'd sent our desperate messages with trappers and traders, hunkering down to hope.

The jubilation when we received word back from Drake help would come was as palpable as it could be among a group of defeated, half-starved madmen. Hasty plans were drawn to rendezvous with Drake's ships by the coast, a plan involving one last minute scout for travel supplies. Bennet was immediately drafted for the honor and I volunteered as well. As it was, one of the only other available of any stamina was my old friend Edmund, spared of the rickets and ruinous mangling so many of our men at arms endured.

The three of us - for one last run. I'd grown braver through our forays and, secretly, I'd spied Wamenu on our perimeters from time to time. Due to the fact that he hadn't killed me and quietly gone his way from whatever spy mission he was on, I assumed we were special friends and didn't report it. Even so, I was deathly afraid to leave the fort. The odds of something going wrong on this one last commission felt immeasurably raised. A sense of foreboding settled upon us as we left the compound with nary a wave from our incapacitated comrades. It was rainy and foggy and humid and grey. Bennet, however, was somewhat jovial- a smile on his face, a bounce in his step. Edmund and I shuffled along in the boy's radiant shadow.

The forest was full of eyes. I could feel them on us, every step. I heard their trills and yips and birdcalls, saw the smoke signals. There wasn't a creature in that dark country that wasn't keenly aware of our presence and yet, we saw no one. Not an animal, not a person, not a thing. For three days we walked, desperate, but the countryside was stripped and dead. Every campsite deserted. Every storage pit depleted. Just the scraps of someone's grand plan.

Night was worse. We huddled around a smoldering fire, the green wood smoking just enough to ward away the spring mosquitos, defeated. Bennet silent as always, Edmund praying to some god somewhere across the sea. I was angry. To have wanted to die, to have come all this way, to never see the resolution of my mystery, only to find there was no mystery - people just die, horribly and often - and now that I wanted to live, desperately, I would probably die. In this shitty little hovel of a country an entire world away from where I should be dead to begin with – a classic existential crisis. It all seemed so ridiculous.

Edmund went to take a piss on the fourth night, as we made our way back to the fort in defeat, empty handed and hungry. I'd fallen asleep and didn't realize he was missing until I spied his empty spot 'round the guttered fire the next morning. Bennett shrugged, seemingly unaffected by the loss. Edmund was my best friend, I muttered, hastily wiping a wasted tear from my eye. The goddamn Indians were at it again. Here it goes I thought, any moment expecting to have my spine severed or my heart pierced by marauding savages, I've come to my end. But that never happened. I was alive when we finally reached the fort two long days later.

The scent of death was in the air. Blossoming within me was a horrible, roiling sensation of pervading doom, cemented as we approached the perimeter of the fort and stumbled upon a new sight. Three mutilated black-skinned persons swinging from a rope round their necks in a lonesome tree on a hill. Their shriveled corpses exposed by their nudity, frail bodies curved in death. Two were sliced across the midsection, viscera spilling out, rocking in the breeze. The hemp ropes squeaking intermittently. Silence. Wind.

Creeeeeaaaaak. Bird call. Silence, wind, creeeeaaaaaaak, bird call. We had no way of knowing from where these unfortunate folk hailed. Perhaps there were black natives in this land too.

I would find out much later that to accommodate our crew on the return voyage home, Drake ordered the release of almost one hundred slaves he'd acquired in raids up and down the Caribbean and South American coasts. These slaves now gathered near the beach, displaced, frightened, angry and hungry: seeking vengeance for their murdered brethren killed almost surely by the soldiers in the fort. Our only defense in the coming weeks would be their ignorance regarding how many soldiers truly remained behind the walls.

Tacked upon a listing door with a rusty nail, a door affixed to an unfinished wall holding up half of a timbered enclosure, gaping and sagging under its poor construction, was the letter. A fancy flourish of penmanship (I could not yet read) informing the three brave volunteers who remained behind we were to hold our posts, continue our construction of the fort and await reinforcements. Drake's men had arrived early and, due to the storm clouds on the horizon, immediately evacuated the settlement to his ships, racing away from the coast to outrun the advancing hurricane. When I handed the torn pronouncement to Bennett and he read it aloud in his tinny voice, he laughed and laughed. After a while, so did I. What else could you do? They had sentenced us to a horrible death. No one was returning to this hellhole to reinforce this failure of a fort. We were forgotten entirely.

The dreaded hurricane began with just a plop of rain on the beaten dirt, the wind picking up, ruffling our hair as we stood like nincompoops at the threshold of our half-done fort. I thought that death would come swiftly and silently. It did not.

"Are you kidding me with this," Gloria sighed in rapture,

throwing one naked leg over Henry's lap, reading the pages of his manuscript as fast as her eyes would allow. "When did you write this part? You just gave me the other part a few days ago?"

"What can I say," Henry drawled, running his hand from her thigh to her foot, his gaze travelling appreciatively down her leg as he skillfully ignored her question, "I've been inspired, Gloria. It's flowing out of me now that I began. What did you think I'd been doing on those nights at home alone?"

She hated herself for allowing the small trickles of doubt she already felt. The time they were spending together was the best she'd had in years. Maybe ever. But, there was mounting evidence leading Gloria down a spiral of self-doubt. Trust her instincts or look at the facts? She *wanted* to believe Henry was innocent. She was falling in love with him. And though he'd been cleared in the most recent accident, his ID and his alibi enough to convince the police he wasn't involved, there were at least two other unsolved murders now as well. And the picture of one of the victims once hidden in Henry's closet, now secreted in her purse. Was she being a fool?

Chapter 27

The hoedown was in full swing. She could feel the speakers barking their country tunes from the dark parking lot behind the old downtown mercantile. She'd clicked the engine off but there was a strange electricity between Gloria and Henry that seemed to smoke in the air between them.

"I can't believe I let you talk me into this," Henry groused good-naturedly.

"There are several events you just don't miss, townie or not. That includes the annual fall Hootenanny in the Brookshire's parking lot, the Yesteryear festival, and the homecoming game somewhere in between," Gloria corrected him with a laugh.

Henry reached for the passenger door, but Gloria placed her hand on his arm to stop him.

"I have something I'd like to admit to you. And something I'd like to ask you," Gloria probed with false cheer.

"Oh yeah," Henry angled his body to face her more directly, "what's that?"

"I took something," Gloria looked him the eye. His expression flickered from calm to surprise and back to calm as she spoke, "from your cabin. When I was there…to get your ID the other night."

He raised his eyebrows, inviting her to continue. Gloria's hands shook as she reached into her purse, pulling the polaroid from her pocketbook, holding it aloft. She handed him the photo, her eyes downcast with shame.

"I don't know why I took it," she mumbled, Henry's eyes scanned the photo. His lips turning downward to a frown, his expression inscrutable. "I mean," Gloria hastened to explain, "I know why…I looked at the photos. But, why I took this one? I'm nosy. You know that about me. And I know it's the woman who died. Her name is Claudia Hastings. From Longview, where she's lived most of her adult life. Raised in Mississippi. Married three times. I don't know who she is to you or why you have her photo but I know I was curious enough to take it. I didn't put it together at first but I've been doing some research on my own. Are you investigating this for another reason? Something other than what you said? Is this why you're here?"

She didn't want to hysterically blurt out her first thought… *that he had a type* and she was not unique. Claudia was even older. But that didn't explain the photo from the early eighties, the mysterious reflection in the shiny hood of the black TransAm the only clue as to the original owner, the blurry outline of a man, any man in his prime. Maybe Henry's father? The woman had been smiling for a lover in the photo. Gloria knew that for a fact. But now Gloria knew she was the same woman who'd been murdered by the lake and she wanted more information,

"Were you involved with her?"

"Don't be ridiculous, Gloria," Henry held his hands out in mock surrender. His jovial response heartened her. "I've lived here for almost a year. That's not my lover. She was…a family friend. Like an aunt. So, there! I *do* have an interest in who killed her but it's all a horrible coincidence I even have that photo. I hope you know if that becomes common knowledge, I could get picked up again."

"Oh!" Gloria sighed in momentary relief as they stepped out of the car. A family friend! He'd said it so readily, of course it was the truth. Maybe she was letting her fears run away with her common sense. It still didn't explain why he'd omitted that fact. "But you knew her? Why didn't you say? Surely you recognized the photo in the newspaper."

"I was going to," Henry assured her, pulling her into his arms, crushing the photo between them as he kissed the top of her head, murmuring, "I was going to tell you everything. Don't worry It's nothing. Really. Just give me time."

Gloria shook off a wave of misgivings from the innocuous statement. She glanced over Henry's shoulder and saw the sun dipping into the trees behind the park. Henry followed her gaze.

"You know what," he stepped back, beaming down at her, "let's not let this spoil the evening. Let's have a good time. I can tell you more later, I promise. Just trust me."

Gloria forced a smile, nodding as he kissed her gently on the lips, his fingers cupping her chin.

"Promise you trust me?" Henry asked, his eyes childishly hopeful.

Gloria hesitated, noting the worry darkening his features before shaking her head, "Of course I trust you."

Henry frowned, his eyes crinkling suspiciously as he regarded her, instructing ominously, "Remember that!"

Chapter 28

Gloria tried to relax and enjoy the festivities, but she was still unsettled from her brief talk with Henry in the car. The volume was deafening. She scrunched her shoulders and bobbed her head to the country music. Three fiddlers ringed the singer; their strings singing even louder than the vocalist. "Excuse me?"

Gloria looked down to her side, expecting to see a child. Instead, a lithe young woman with vibrant, almost plum-colored hair stood before her. The girl couldn't have been more than sixteen or seventeen. Gloria peered around for Henry, hoping he'd return with their food and save her from having to admit her fading memory, knowing he'd instantly introduce himself to the girl in front of her. The young woman's shaped eyebrows arched in delight as she smiled up at Gloria, a picture of youthful innocence in pink.

"Ms. Weidman?" the girl ventured hesitantly, as if surprised to see Gloria at the annual celebration. Gloria searched her mind to match the face, scanning through a litany of friends' children and years of students.

"Yes?" Gloria hesitated.

The girl's carefree smile transformed into a smirk, her smoky grey eyes narrowing to hard diamonds. "We have a mutual friend." The smile faded completely as the young woman tilted her head up, her eyes burning into Gloria's before the cheery, hollow grin reappeared with a break in the music, the crowd pushing into them, parting around them.

"Are they in my class at the community center?" Gloria went on, paranoia tickling her senses.

The young woman, her cheeks bright, the rich color of her hair spilling across the pale skin of an unblemished forehead stepped up on her toes, suddenly leaning forward, the scent of strawberries filling Gloria's nose, stirring a wild compulsion to grab the flaxen tresses floating around her and sniff them again.

A hidden, deeper voice than the lisping tone used just the moment before hissed into her ear, the decidedly seductive timbre of the redhead's melodic alto sending a violent chill down Gloria's neck and arms, "Tell Henry Liesl misses him."

Confused, Gloria searched the crowd around them for Henry. When she looked back down, the seductress was gone. The crowd around her was exactly as it had been before. The music abruptly started again as the audience erupted into applause.

"Care to dance," Henry reappeared by her side, two sloppy brisket sandwiches on white bread balanced on a plastic tray, the paper wrapping soaked in barbeque, a sloshing beer gripped in the other hand.

"Why don't we have this sandwich," she suggested, her eyes scanning the dance floor to find the girl. "Some young friend of yours stopped by to say hello," Gloria shouted over the music as they picked their way further from the dance floor. "She made me kind of uncomfortable if I'm being honest," Gloria admitted, perching inelegantly on the back of a hay bale, the tray of barbeque settled between them, adding, "she gave me a message for you."

Henry's eyes narrowed suspiciously, "What message?"

"She said…ah, let me see if I can get this right. She said to tell Henry…Lisa misses him? Whatever the hell that means. About seventeen, maybe? Had crooked front teeth. Ah, and the hair!" Gloria nodded, how could she have forgotten, "That shade of red, almost purple. Auburn, I guess you'd call it. Baby voice?" Henry paled, "Did she say *Lisa* or *Liesl*, Gloria?"

"Oh, you know," Gloria wiped her chin, only glancing over at Henry as she spoke, her own intentionally light manner dissipating under his worried glare, "it could have been either. It was *Liesl*, maybe? How odd. Is that German? What is it, Henry?"

Henry stood, his eyes raking the crowds around them, fists clenched at his side. He leaned up on his toes, searching the dance floor, the tables and wooden benches ringing the crowded space.

"Henry?" Gloria stood, touching Henry's shoulder. He pressed his lips into a thin line, his jaw set, his eyes haunted.

"Stay here," he commanded. "Stay right here. I'll be back."

"Where are you going?"

He was gone before she finished asking, returning a few minutes later and sliding onto the horse blanket beside her with a rueful shrug and an apologetic wince.

"Mind if we leave a little early?" He requested with an exaggerated yawn, squinting up at the sky. It was close to nine by the dying light. Gloria frowned, surveying the merriment surrounding them; portly, greying husbands two-stepping clumsily with their round, beaming wives, little girls in boots and prairie skirts dancing together, teenagers gossiping on the edges of the crowds: young singles clumped together in patches, draped over hay bales.

"Sure," she agreed, the hair on the back of her neck prickling with unease at his reaction to this girl.

Henry's eyes were wild and panicked as he rose, pulling Gloria to her feet with a disingenuous grin. Grabbing her hand firmly, he pulled her through the crowds, away from the dancers, the hanging Chinese lanterns and the haybales, down the dark, muted sidewalks of the old downtown. They had almost reached the parked cars lining the town square when Gloria stopped, pulling hard against Henry's hand, shaking hers free.

"Are you OK?" Gloria pressed. "What is wrong with you?" Henry opened his mouth, closed it and dropped his head, pushing his thumbs and forefingers into his temples.

"We need to get out of here," he muttered, shifting his gaze to the sky overhead searchingly.

"Why?" Gloria demanded, looking up at the dark sky as well. "*What* are you looking for? *What's* happened? *Who* was that *girl*?"

"I'll tell you everything later," Henry promised, "Now, let's go."

"Wait?" Gloria felt dizzy and weak, her eyes refusing to focus on Henry's wavering features, demanding, "Why are you acting like a psychopath? Stop right now. I won't go a step further with you until you tell me *what…anything…*is going on?"

"Liesl," he muttered, his voice soft and sad, "the girl."

"Okay?" Gloria took a deep breath, her eyes refocusing on Henry, "And?"

"She's my wife."

Chapter 29

The door slammed shut behind them. Henry's cabin was silent and cool, a fan humming cheerily overhead. Crickets from the woods behind his house shrieked in unison, their song throbbing in the tense air. They'd both been quiet and stiff on the short drive over, Henry's eyes scanning the roads and the dark spaces beyond the surrounding trees of his property as they went inside. He seemed scared. And that scared Gloria.

"I'd love to know what you're thinking?" Henry threw his hands up, dropping his body onto the worn leather of the couch.

"Would you?" Gloria stood near the door, hesitant to go any further inside. Henry didn't answer as she went on, her voice trembling, "I think you're scaring me. I think that, for sure. First, you have a photo and a prior relationship with a dead woman and a prior history with a dead man. You have a very mysterious past. And by that, I mean, you don't. There's nothing. Nothing online and nothing around town I can find. No one knows *you* but *me*, *Terry* and my delusional mom. So now, I'm thinking…hey *dummy*, this guy isn't into you, he's into little, old ladies and their retirement checks. Or… lucky you…he's a serial killer and he's using you as an alibi. That's all I know, Henry. Because that's all you've given me. I realize more and more I don't know a single, *real* thing about you."

Henry stared at the floor before lifting his gaze to meet hers, his mouth twisting into a frown, "I was afraid that's what you were thinking."

"Which part?"

"All of it. I would. You have every right. But I hoped I'd have more time to tell you…everything. So you'd understand. So you wouldn't be scared of me. I hoped I'd get to write the end of my story. Then, it would all be clear to you. I don't know where to start," Henry shrugged and sat up straighter, covering his face with his hands. Taking a deep, raspy breath, he dropped his hands and raised his eyes to meet hers.

"Why don't you start with your Aunt Claudia. Then ease on into your teenaged wife, Lisa?"

Henry winced, squinting as he admitted, "I did know Claudia. A long time ago. I told you that part. I don't know why she was here. I haven't seen her since a visit…over a year ago. Not until I heard about the murder. I promise, this isn't what it looks like. I think she came here to warn me."

"Warn you about what?" Gloria went on, her voice quivering in panic. All her fears - being lied to, being made a fool of, sleeping with a murderer - coming true. "Your teenaged wife?"

"I'm just as shocked as you to see her," Henry explained plaintively, "I thought she was dead."

"Awesome," Gloria deadpanned. "Great. What?"

Henry hung his head for a long moment. When he raised it, his eyes were cold and his voice transformed from his normal southern drawl back into the crisper, curious accent he'd used when he read from his manuscript. "Tell me. What did you see when you went through those boxes, Gloria? When you found the photo of Claudia?" He gestured behind her, to the hallway closet where she'd found his boxes of keepsakes.

"I don't know," Gloria stammered, thrown by the turn the conversation had taken from her planned tongue-lashing and righteous exit. What *had* she seen? "Photos. Some old photos and antique documents. I don't know? What was I supposed to see? Trophies from your victims?"

Henry looked crestfallen and shook his head, "No. I expected you to see *me*. *Me*, Gloria. Everything I have. *Everything* I am. My whole life…is in those boxes. My whole. *Long. Life.*" He let the words hover between them, continuing without looking at her, "I've seen you look around here for clues to who I *am* and I know you've asked me about my past. There's *a reason* I don't talk about it…why I don't talk about my family." He turned to face her, his shadow engulfing her, "Do you remember the first afternoon when we met and you asked me about myself?" He peered at her, searching her face for her reaction as a shiver of fear slid down her spine.

"Sure," she answered in a quiet voice. Of course, he'd joked he was…

"*I* was born in a hovel on the outskirts of London. *My mother* sold eggs at the market. Her *name* was *Angelina*. And my father…"

Gloria shook her head violently from side to side. *This wasn't happening, she told herself.* Of course it was, she thought. He was clinically insane, she rationalized quickly. Of course, he was. *This* explained *everything*! She put her hands over her ears to stop the noise, repeating to herself, "No, no, no, no, no, no, no, no."

Henry continued, his voice raising over her frenetic protestations, his tone more severe, "*My father* was a stonemason. That is *my* story, Gloria. *I* came to this country in 1585. *I am* four hundred and forty-eight years old. I didn't lie. I'm sorry I didn't tell you before, but I wanted you to get to know me first. Before you judged me. Or thought me insane. *Please* believe me. I've been trying to tell you through my story. The one I've been writing *for you. My story*, Gloria. *Mine*."

Gloria's vision blurred. She shook her head to clear the ringing in her ears as Henry watched apprehensively. She went completely blank. How *did* one address such an absurd confession - from a very good writer. A wonderful storyteller who was apparently *way too into* his latest work. Inappropriate laughter bubbled up through her throat and she doubled over, laughing so hard tears streamed from her eyes. Fanning her hands in front of her reddening face, she tried to still her compulsive giggles but only laughed harder.

"Of course," she managed to choke between guffaws before collapsing into another fit of laughter.

Henry clamped his white lips together, standing and pacing away from Gloria to stand in front of the fireplace with his back to her, opining, "I can tell this isn't going as well as I'd hoped."

He sighed, turning to face her, a wounded expression clouding his normally open countenance. Gloria's giggles tapered slowly to hiccups.

Henry shook his head, taking a deep breath before going on, "Gloria, please! Listen to me, I can prove it. I need you to believe me. I have wanted for so long to tell someone about my life. And now that we've met, this is everything I've ever wanted. I want us to be together, Gloria. And we can be! Believe it or not, there's a way we can be together forever." With that, he sidled up to the window, peering out behind the curtain to scan the sky before remarking, "You just have to stay with me. Now, until it's time. Otherwise, I don't know if it will work."

Gloria reeled from his insane proclamations. *What* was she *still* doing here? She had to get out. This was ridiculous. Dangerous even, now. How had she not seen it? He was obviously delusional and who knew how far the delusion went, how deep?

This level of mental illness *and* a wife. *No thanks*. She shifted her purse, marching resolutely to the front door.

"I'm sorry, Henry," she explained, "I can't do this. You're a beautiful writer, you really are. But, it is a story. That's all. Your first person character, *the one you researched, he* was born in a hovel outside of London. *You were*…I don't know where you were really born because I realize now I don't know anything about you. But I know you need help. I really hope you get help, Henry. I don't know what you could possibly get from this…charade…but I can't play along."

She suddenly felt very foolish and very scared. Every little odd look she'd received in his company from the people in town came back to haunt her. They all knew how dumb she looked and now she finally realized it, too. The embarrassing thought hardened her resolve. Henry stepped in her way, but she pushed past him. Now she was truly frightened. How had she overlooked all the signs?

"Gloria, stop, please," he begged, his voice cracking in despair.

Get out, she told herself. Get out now. This never ends well. In a flash, he was in front of her, blocking her exit with his body. She pushed him aside, struggling to get to the door.

"I'm leaving, Henry." Tears gathered in her eyes. She needed to get out before he saw she was afraid. "We can talk more tomorrow. Really."

He looked down at his hands, stricken, moving away from her as she grasped the doorknob.

"Gloria," he shouted from behind her.

She turned and saw him standing with a large, curved knife - a knife she'd spied earlier propped on his fireplace mantle. Her heart dropped, realizing she was too late. What a fool she'd been.

This was how she'd die! *How humiliating.*

He stepped toward her as Gloria screamed, backing into the door, reaching behind her for the elusive doorknob, then dropping her purse onto the tiled entryway with a clatter instead. She stilled, regarding Henry warily as he approached, the knife held down at his side.

"Wait, please," Henry implored.

Something in his voice made her pause. She dropped her hands to her side, standing straight as she accepted her fate with dignity. Henry lifted the knife, his left arm extended out and plunged the sharp blade at least an inch into the soft pale flesh of his wrist, slicing decisively up the length of his forearm.

Gloria screamed in horror, covering her eyes, her screams tapering off as the room went quiet save for Henry's steady breath and her own ragged panting. She peeled her fingers from her eyes, bracing for a grisly scene. Henry stood, a passive shadow of sadness in his eyes, the corners of his mouth curled in a frown, the knife still gripped in his other hand. But there was no blood. *Where* was the blood? There was just a pink scar where he'd cut himself and even that was rapidly transforming back to unblemished flesh before Gloria's eyes.

"Do you need to see any more parlor tricks to believe me?" He spat derisively. "Do you want me to rip off my shirt in the sun like some sparkly pedophile. Or levitate. Turn into a bat? Because I can't do any of those things. I don't even have any fangs. Just *really sharp* incisors."

"Now you're a vampire? What is all this, Henry? Are you trying to make me feel crazy?" Gloria whispered, close to panicked tears. Usually, she just got an *it's not you, it's me. This* was completely out of her wheelhouse.

"This is no trick. Do you need to see more?" he pressed, an

edge to his voice.

"No," Gloria sighed. She knew what she'd seen. But she'd also lived long enough to know the mind played tricks on you when stressed, when gaslighted or distracted. A sleight of hand, that's all. And who didn't love a good magic trick?

"I didn't kill those people, if that's what you're thinking," Henry offered softly, placing the curved knife back on the mantle top and striding back to the couch where he plopped down with a petulant frown. "But I *may* know who did. Sit down," he ordered firmly, studying her face. "I'll tell you everything about Liesl and my life until now. I'm sorry I didn't before. I thought she was gone, long ago. And I thought I had more time."

Gloria shook her head, clutching her purse to her body protectively, "This is too much. I have to go."

Henry was by her side in an instant, reaching for her. She pulled away.

"Gloria, there's not much time left before this all unravels. And I have so much I want to tell you. So much I need to share with you. There's so much *more* to *all* of this. You could be in great danger. I have no idea why Liesl is here, now, but it can't be good. You have to stay with me. I can protect you. I can make you stronger and you will never get hurt again."

Gloria backed her way to the door, gripping the doorknob, promising Henry, "Tomorrow, okay?"

She had to get away, process everything she'd just been told and everything she'd just seen. *She had to tell Dee*! Dee would know what to do.

Henry nodded in resignation, tilting his head up to meet her eyes, "I love you, Gloria. You know that, right?"

Gloria laughed harshly, tears welling in her eyes, "Yeah? Well, that's just great."

Before he could respond, she was gone, the crunch of sand and gravel beneath her feet as she scurried to her car, throwing open the creaking door, tires squealing as she pulled away and drove like a woman fleeing a crime.

Chapter 30

Dee arrived ten minutes after receiving Gloria's EMERG-C text, accidentally replying JK instead of OK. Dee hated to text - said her old lady ghost fingers made it damn near impossible. But she answered as soon as she heated her fingertips by rubbing them on her jeans. The conversation, which as always began with boxed pinot, didn't go *quite* as Gloria hoped.

"So, he's a vampire? Who happens to be *married*? That *is* what you're saying? Right?" Dee placed her glass full of wine heavily on the side table, clutching a throw pillow to her chest. She looked stricken, as if Gloria told her she had cancer. "But he had… *nothing* to do with the two…no wait – three…murders that have taken place in the last month?"

"I'm saying he's *maybe*…immortal. Though he never used that word. Thank God," Gloria expounded pointlessly.

"Do you hear yourself?" Dee demanded, the color draining slowly from her plump, shiny face. She reached out blindly for her wine glass, tipping the contents down her throat in one large gulp. Gloria had always been the most rational friend Dee had. It's *why* their friendship worked so well. Making this turn of events even more horrifying to her.

Gloria's mouth fell open. Dee was normally her biggest supporter.

"Gloria?" Dee barked when she didn't respond.

Gloria snapped out of her trance, "Yes! I know what it sounds like. But it might be true, Dee. You have to believe me. You didn't *see* what *I* saw him do. I have to have someone to talk to about this!"

"*No, I don't* and *no,* we do not. I will not entertain such bullshit, Gloria. And neither should you. He's a charlatan and you're acting like a feeble brained nitwit in love with a Nigerian Prince you met online. You need to call the police. You *need* to tell them what you know."

Gloria shook her head back and forth, "Dee, he showed me how he spontaneously heals and, whatever movie magic he's using, it's convincing. Is there any way he is actually almost five hundred years old and I am *not* the world's slowest cougar?" Gloria realized she was slightly drunk.

"Jesus! Gloria, this kid is hustling you. Either *that* or you're dating a serial killer. Congratulations! Take your pick." Dee lectured.

"He isn't the Lakeside Slayer," Gloria heard herself deny fruitlessly, the energy behind her conviction waning.

"And just how did Mr. Wynter come by his immortality, Gloria?"

Gloria realized she didn't know. "I'm not sure, he hasn't finished his story."

Dee pressed her palm to her forehead, "Jesus, G. I'm really starting to worry about you. This story this kid is conning you with…it's starting to sound an awful lot like one of those thrillers you've been reading. Or honestly, it could be any one of *your* stories. Are you sure this is all coming from *him*?"

"It could be real, Dee," she pleaded weakly. "I need your support. I know he's done some suspicious things…I'd…a…be a one to admit that. But…ip…he's been with me during the last two murders. He was…with…me? Could he move that fast?"

"If he was a vampire he could." Dee snapped, rolling her eyes, "You *need* the name of my doctor, Gloria. Really!

You would have my support if you were having a purely sexual relationship with a hot piece of barely legal ass, which is more than most people would give you. But if you demand support of your relationship with a *vampire*? Well then, I'm afraid *he's* clinically insane and you're *suddenly, ridiculously* gullible. You need to move away from this psychopath now. You hear me? Right now. Stop it down. And if you know something…anything…that might *implicate* him in these murders, Gloria, you have to go to the police. Now."

"Dee, it's not like that. I want to believe him. I mean, its clear he believes it. And I can't help it. I care for him," Gloria trailed off as she spoke, noticing Dee retreat from the conversation. She should have expected as much. Would she believe Dee if the shoe were on the other foot? Had she believed Dee when Dee was dating that *divorced* guy from the neighboring town? No, she'd pushed until Dee admitted he was married and then shamed her until she broke it off. So, no, she wouldn't believe herself either. Dee was just trying to be a good friend.

"Gloria Jean," Dee shook her head compassionately, placing her hands on Gloria's shoulders, forcing Gloria to look her in the eyes, "you are being tremendously stupid. Don't wait until this boy hurts you. Or worse, kills you. Get out of this now!"

"I don't know if I want to," Gloria admitted, her eyes locking willfully with Dee's.

Dee remained silent for a moment, squeezing Gloria's shoulders lightly, dropping her hands to her side. She reached for her glass, heading to the kitchen for a refill, shouting over her shoulder, "You know I'm right."

"You're right," Gloria conceded, not seeing Dee's shoulders fall in relief while refilling her glass from the box. After a few silent minutes, each woman drinking and eyeing the other wearily over the kitchen table, Dee left.

Gloria sat for a moment, trying to remember every little thing Henry said earlier tonight. She checked the locks and her phone again. Surely this was an elaborate ruse. Surely there wasn't a *vampire* living in a small town in east Texas? *That* was the stuff of novels. Her brief levity cooled when she pictured Henry's tragic face…his eyes imploring her to believe him. *Why* did she want to believe him so badly? Was she already losing her mind?

Chapter 31

It rankled Gloria's sensibilities to break a promise, but the next day she was too paralyzed by doubt to face Henry. Creeping doubt. When the phone rang, she ignored it. She ignored his texts. When he pounded on her door the second day, she hid in the shadow of the hallway waiting for him to leave. When his frantic messages abated the fourth day and her doorbell uncharacteristically sang out, Gloria tiptoed to the door, annoyed it was Henry again.

Instead, she threw open the door to a sour-faced Karl, sweating in his cheap suit, a scowl pushing his prominent brows more closely together.

Gloria sighed. "Hello, Karl. Everything alright?"

She tried to recall - had her brother ever just dropped by before? She saw Karl's gaze travel past her, searching the house, then the driveway and beyond.

"Can I help you find something?" She deadpanned, moving aside to allow him to fully see inside.

Karl paused his surveillance, a slight smile of embarrassment lacing his puffy features. He swallowed audibly, leaning in, "I just thought you should know…they…they are going to issue an arrest warrant. For Henry. As soon as the DA signs off. And that could happen any moment. They want to question him again. Seems the, uh, victim at the lake had Henry's address on her when she died. I…think he may prey on older ladies, sis. I don't mean to be rough, but I wanted…I thought you should know."

Gloria nodded, her face blank, her heart quietly breaking just a small measure more, "He's not here."

Karl shrugged, "Okay. Look, I know y'all are *special friends* and I didn't want you to be…caught unawares. You should be careful, you know. I'd hate for you to get mixed up in this mess."

"It's over," Gloria supplied lamely, shrugging like a sixteen-year-old. "So…but, *you know*."

Karl pressed his lips together, a look of impatience covering the small moment of concern they'd shared, "Good. okay. I gotta git back to the station." He meant the gas station, of course. Not the police station. He turned and stopped, swiveling back around, squinting into the late afternoon sun, "You take care of yourself, sis. I mean it." Swiveling around, he hustled back to his car where he lifted his form laboriously into the front seat, uncomfortably adjusting his suit. Gloria watched as he drove away, her heart melting just a shade for her normally useless older brother.

She thought about calling to warn Henry. She wanted to but froze with indecision. Should she just go to him now and admit that even though she didn't trust him, she would help him turn himself in? She decided she had to at least warn him. She still loved him. She owed him that, at least.

Rushing inside, Gloria grabbed her purse, moving down the hallway to fetch her shoes and a stash of emergency cash in her bottom dresser drawer. What was she thinking? Would she lie for him? How far would she go to help? She hurried to her car.

"Gloria." Her name in her ear. She could feel his breath hot against her neck. Henry!

Her heart leapt. She spun around, but there was nothing there. Just an old swing creaking under a distant tree, the wind and the bird calls. She experienced a moment of vertigo, wobbling on her feet, the lightheadedness passing as quickly as it had come. Sliding behind the wheel, she aggressively punched the engine to life. She had to see him, even if she no longer believed in him. He was just sick. He needed her help.

Chapter 32

The police were already there when Gloria's car screeched to a stop on the gravel drive. Henry's front door hung open ominously, two police cars quiet and waiting, their engines still clicking and dripping next to hers. Four officers prowled around the shady interior of his cabin, but Henry was apparently nowhere to be found.

"Did you know he was going to flee?" Casey Cash wheeled around from his study of the curved knife on the mantel, his expression incredulous.

"How would I have known that? I haven't seen him in almost a week. He didn't even call." Gloria admitted.

"Do you know when he left?" Casey demanded.

"If I didn't know he was leaving, how would I know when he left?" Gloria posited.

Casey pursed his lips, his brain whirring audibly. He pressed on, "You know what I mean, Glory. Where would he go? Family?"

"I was told none. And I don't know. He mentioned a wife before he left. A *wife* who mysteriously appeared at the Hoedown, as it were. Right before all of this," she supplied, her eyes darting around the room for clues to Henry's whereabouts. Surely, he was only hiding. Surely, he hadn't *really* left town without a word after professing his undying love?

"Is that so?" Casey stroked his greying, omnipresent five o'clock shadow, "Her name?"

"No idea," Gloria lied smoothly. "Maybe…Lisa something

or other. Lisa…Wynter…if I had to hazard a guess."

A stocky, baby-faced fellow officer whispered something furtively in Casey's ear before posting himself a foot away.

Casey stood straighter, adjusting his holster, "You shouldn't be here, Glory. I'm gonna have to ask you to leave. We got a warrant, so you can rest assured this is all legit. But *you* can't be here."

Without acknowledging Casey, Gloria moved toward the knife, her hand outreached for the dangerous curved blade to test its fidelity. Casey grabbed her left forearm, gently arresting her approach and attempted theft.

"No can do," Casey shook his head regretfully, his eyes scanning the damning weapon, expounding needlessly, "Evidence."

"But I wanted to see if…"

"No. Can. Do." Casey stated again, motioning vehemently to the open front door, a line of sweat appearing on his brow.

Gloria fumed as she made for the door, casting a baleful glance over her left shoulder at what promised to be a real clue. Why hadn't Henry mentioned he might leave? And where in the world would the mysterious Henry Wynter go?

Chapter 33

Gloria was still fuming when she arrived home. So, Henry left, had he? Without any warning! Well, she'd left first, goddammit! And forget about trust! Pffft! She slammed the front door, marching through the living room to toss the files she'd pulled from under her passenger seat across the oak surface of the kitchen table with a gratifying splat. The five manila folders slid out like a fan. Swinging her purse into one of the kitchen chairs, she yanked the polaroid of Claudia Hastings from the outer pocket, slapping it atop the pile. Why hadn't she done herself a favor and looked through these the day she'd picked them up?

Her plan *now* was to turn these puppies over to Casey Cash, though she couldn't do *that* in good conscience if she didn't know *what* she was passing along. It could all be ridiculous hooey, she rationalized. Who hired private eyes anyway? Wasn't there some type of law that prevented stolen information like this from being used in court? And *how in the hell had Ted Carroll gotten his hands on these* and why did he want *her* to see them so badly? Because of the files on Henry, no doubt. But had *he* broken into the PI agency himself to get these for a Gazette story? It seemed a bit extreme. Even for Ted. She poured a large juice glass of boxed wine.

Her shaking hands hovered over the files for a moment, before pulling out the first file - the file labeled Schaefer, Lisa in red marker. There were several sticky notes affixed to various papers and receipts and these seemed to be in a different print from the file label. Ted's notes, perhaps?

It was a fairly easy chain of events to follow with the included paper trail. The first note in the file was a handwritten half-sheet of paper reading Lisa Shaver 898-555-5555 inside a coffee ring. There was another full sheet of paper with the following notes, handwritten in the same tiny half cursive script as the phone number, the top of the paper stripped from a spiral still sporting the shredded ruin of its liberation: The first line read Hanover Saint with a paragraph underneath that had been redacted with a black marker. Ah, Gloria realized, sliding the fourth file out from under the top two and comparing the name. Hanover Saint was *a person. That* made more sense. She had thought Hanover an odd name for a saint. Folded at the bottom of the Shaver file, there were copies of three oldfashioned traveler's checks for $250.00, each for *services rendered* on May 26th the previous year.

Moving into that file, *Saint Hanover* in green, she deduced for whatever reason (as Rusty Fry certainly hadn't notated it in his spiral bound paper notes), the PI continued watching Hanover at no charge once his surveillance job for Lisa Shaver was complete. There were no notes, but there *was* a small, neat stack of copied documents and several photos, dated accordingly. Per a change of address postal request, Hanover Saint arrived in the area from Boston over a year ago, first staying in the larger city of Tyler, then making his way to Whitehouse where he leased an apartment, shown via a copy of his rental agreement with Great Oak Leasing, Consolidated. Paper clipped to the inside of this manila envelope was a crude surveillance log empty of notes, again, as Rusty Fry seemed to do his best work with the camera. There was a series of rather prettily composed black and white glossy 8x10's, presumably of the hulking outline of this Hanover fellow going about his life. In the last few photos, the same oft photographed man was now armed with a long-lensed camera: a camera trained on yet another, smaller indistinct figure in the distance. Which led to an absurd, candid photo collection of one person surveilling another who didn't know they themselves were being surveilled. One of these was a blurry color photo of the shadow of Hanover Saint taking a photo of a man with Henry's coloring and build entering Westbridge, her Mother's retirement facility, at dusk. According to the date on the post-it with a big red question mark beneath, the picture had been taken over a year ago. Before Henry met Terry. Right after her mom moved in! Before she knew Henry even existed. Her stomach fell. Gloria took a healthy swig of wine, shaking her head cynically.

Rusty Fry had, at this point, lost interest in Hanover Saint. Yet, as recorded on the surveillance log paper-clipped into his file, continued following Henry for the better part of three months; the time covered by the two files labeled Winter, Henry 1 and Winter, Henry 2 in blue, blocky letters.

In these folders, pictures of *him!* Henry! In Longview, sitting in a small diner - across from him, Claudia Hastings, smiling like a doting grandmother. A receipt of cash paid to Henry for an antique pocket watch at a collector's pawnshop in Dallas the previous July. A picture of Henry walking the murdered neighbor's now-missing dog. Gloria's heart dropped a beat with every piece of damning information. In Henry's file, the last entry on Rusty Fry's exhaustive surveillance log was August 19th. Two days before his gruesome murder. It read SUN, dawn??? Meet H. Three days before that, another log entry reading THEIR WATCHING. They are watching? Both entries were highlighted. The color drained from Gloria's face.

The information contained in bottom file, labeled Miscellaneous (abbreviated MISL, likely through want of correct spelling) in yellow block letters, was sparse. There was the small cutout of a local story involving an unnamed victim found by the train tracks on the outskirts of town: male, Caucasian, approximate age twenty to twenty-five. Gloria recognized the story from the Gazette. She'd long maintained this supposed train *accident* was likely the Lakeside Slayer's first victim. But *who* was *he*? The copy of an autopsy report for John Doe was folded, stuck to the back of the news clipping. Gloria wasn't a doctor, but she could read a diagram well enough to see the victim was missing his head, though that little nugget had been left conveniently out of Ted's story.

She realized she needed to get back by the Gazette as soon as she could. She and Ted needed to talk *before* she turned his files over to the police. *This* was all the proof they would need to see Rusty Fry was meeting 'H', obviously Henry, the day he was killed!

How could she have been so wrong about Henry? She still didn't know what to think. She'd convinced herself what she saw that day with Henry was a parlor trick, an illusion. But now? She had to face facts. She didn't know Henry, at all. And the real Henry might be far more dangerous than she'd ever imagined.

She laid her head on the table, exhausted, her thoughts swirling. She felt warm. Was she running a fever? She had just closed her eyes when her phone pinged. Stretching, she rubbed her neck. Good grief, it was almost two in the morning.

Usually, it was Gloria who sent the text. For the first time, it was she who received the call-to-action EMERGEN-C text from Dee and immediately drove to her, no questions asked, her heart pounding out of her chest with fear.

Chapter 34

Relieved to find the door unlocked when she couldn't find Dee's spare key under the doormat, Gloria rushed inside without knocking, the aluminum clink of the storm door heralding her arrival. Dee, characteristically nude except for a large towel wrapped around her midsection and uncharacteristically shaken, met her in the front sitting room, inexplicably angry.

Pointing frantically toward her open bedroom door, Dee stuttered, "I…got out of the shower. And there was this man. Here. In my room."

Gloria craned her neck to inspect the room behind Dee, the curtain blowing out the one small, rectangular window open over the bed. Gloria swept past Dee, sliding the window closed, taking a moment to look beyond Dee's small, chain linked yard and its twin across the alley. This is how Ann Delancy, PI would enter the scene of a crime. Though Gloria saw nothing except two roaming strays patrolling stoically through the night.

"We need to call the police."

"No," Dee insisted, stopping Gloria as she reached into her purse for her phone. "He said no police."

"What do you mean?"

"I mean the intruder said no police, Gloria. He said he wasn't going to hurt *me,* but he had a message for *you.*"

"Was it Henry?"

"No, it wasn't Henry. But this was *about* him, Gloria. I don't know *who* this man was, it was dark. I was drunk…I just saw his outline in the moonlight. I don't know. I don't know! He had silvery eyes…he was really tall. I've never seen him before." Dee took a deep breath, shivering from the memory, "I came out of the bathroom and he was looking through my dresser. I thought he was burglar or a pervert, so I grabbed my pistol - the tiny one I like - but he knocked it out of my hand. He moved so fast I couldn't get away. I thought I was going to be attacked but instead, he handed me this towel and told me put it on. Then, he asked me how well I knew *you*. He told me Henry was dangerous and *you were in danger*. He said Henry was leaving a trail."

"A trail for who?"

"I don't know, Gloria. Spit on the messenger much?" Dee retorted, her voice rising as she lost her dearly tested patience. "He said you were running out of time and you were in danger."

"What do you mean running out of time? Henry's gone. Was it a hit man?"

"No, Gloria," Dee plopped down on the bed, her towel riding indecently up her thigh before she went on, grabbing both of Gloria's hands in hers. "He said…it was your *soul* that was in danger. Not your body, Gloria. *Your soul*."

"Are the Methodists reaching out to lapsed members?" Gloria joked to lighten the tension in the room.

"Gloria, this isn't funny. I was scared shitless. I still am. Henry's got you all mixed up in this…whatever the hell *this* is. I'm not sure what to think. Murders? Immortals? I come out of the shower and some man is waiting to tell me that my best friend's soul is in danger then crawls back out the window without a fare thee well or…even a catcall. Do you know what that does to my self-esteem, Gloria? I just trimmed. Do you know what this shit is doing to my anxiety?" Dee huffed, struggling into her kimono robe. "Of course not, because it's always the Gloria show. Since we were teenagers, it's always been all about Gloria Weidman. So, no surprise here. Once again, the *center* of attention. Even from my attempted rapist."

Gloria didn't know how to respond. Everything Dee said was true. She had been focused on herself, for years. Sort of a '*who else would be*' situation was how she'd seen it; but of course, that was all narcissists. Self-centered people rarely noticed they were so singularly centered on themselves because they assumed everyone else was focused on them as well.

"Look, I said I'd pass the message and I did. And I don't want to be involved anymore," Dee pouted.

Gloria took the hint, gathering her purse to her body, "Are you sure you wouldn't rather…I stay? If you're scared, I could keep watch."

"Troy'll be here in a bit. He's working second shift, so I'll be fine," Dee jutted her jaw out defiantly, lifting the tiny pistol from her bedside table and pressing it into Gloria's hands as she left.

"Are you sure? I can stay? This is all my fault," Gloria tried again, worried by Dee's obstinate coldness.

"No, Gloria. I've done my part and told you every goddamn thing he said. Now, I love you. Go home. Windows are locked. I have my other gun, locked and loaded. I'll check on you tomorrow. Keep that weapon close."

Gloria reluctantly hid the pistol inside a long-expired paper map in her glove compartment, leaving it in the car. Yet when she stepped inside upon returning home, Gloria realized someone or something had been in the house and regretted the impulse. The energy in the rooms had shifted somehow, the sounds coming from the wrong angles. She first paused entering the front door, shrugging off her unease heading to the kitchen where she felt a light breeze rustling the napkins and newspaper circulars littering the tabletop. Then, she heard the whistle of the night wind through the open window over the sink, a broken bowl and plate dotting the linoleum of the kitchen floor. The back door was still cracked open, creaking. The files were gone. The property was otherwise silent in the predawn vacuum of noise. A wolf howled in the distance, startling Gloria as she tiptoed around the ceramic dish shards to the sideboard, pulling a large breadknife from the drawer with a hiss of metal on wood. She didn't know why she bothered arming herself. She could feel, almost like a bat with radar, there wasn't another living soul in the quiet space of her home. And she knew in a flash exactly *who* had been here and *why*.

Her brain had played with that puzzle the entire, short drive home. Why bother scaring her friend with a toothless message? Why not just scare *her* directly? Her file thief had to have been the same man who'd accosted Dee. *That* was just a distraction. A way to get her out of her house. She just had to figure out exactly who that man was because clearly this wasn't *just* about Henry anymore. It was also about *her*.

Chapter 35

With no new pages of Henry's story to review, Gloria took to rereading sections of the existing manuscript, searching for clues in his words, any piece to this puzzle, the full shape she couldn't quite see yet. The finished assignments from her students were due in a matter of days and she was upset for a multitude of reasons she'd never get to read the end of Henry's story.

The late autumn wind was moving in. Every other day the temperature would drop and she'd draw her sweater closer around her arms and look to a horizon darkening with the season. The next day, per Texas protocol, the temperatures would soar, and she'd throw off the sweater, looking toward a brighter and warmer colored sky. Today, Gloria left the storm door open, the crisp air whistling through the screen.

"Gloria?"

Tap. Tap.

Gloria jumped from her seat on the couch, spinning around and displacing the pages on her lap.

"Lenny?" she squinted.

Lenny stood taller, a bemused smile reaching his lips, a hand shielding his eyes from the sun as he peered inside, sighing, "This place seems so much smaller now that I'm old."

He had been such a catch in high school, Gloria reflected. Her gold, shining baseball hero. With the sun behind him, for a just a moment, he looked like he was here to walk Gloria to school, the years and life falling from his physique in a trick of shadows and light beams. He stepped out of the sun. Yep, old again.

“Come in,” Gloria motioned him inside, glancing out over his shoulder.

She’d felt, just the past few days, that someone was watching her, but attributed it to her mounting paranoia after the break-in. Aside from the stolen files and her failure to report said theft to the police, all had been rather boringly normal since. Henry was just…gone. Shutting the front door behind him with a thud, she noted Lenny clutched a large white envelope.

“Wow,” he murmured, following Gloria as she picked her way back through the cluttered house to the dining room, “this is so far out. It looks the same. A little dirtier.”

Gloria motioned for Lenny to sit at the table, “Why are you here, Lenny?”

He plopped down, taking a seat in a worn, shiny wood chair at the end of the table. The same one he’d favored in their youth. He ceremoniously produced the envelope, a stiff photo pressing its edges through the thin paper of it, remarking, “Ted found this the other day when we were sifting through our yearly Yesteryear retrospective edition.” Lenny slid the envelope across the table before tapping it with his forefinger, “thought you’d get a kick out of it. And I wanted to check on you, Glor. Been worried about you with all the gossip, you know.”

“What is it?” Gloria asked, pulling the white envelope to her chest. She opened it, producing a rectangular black and white photo. In it, a sign hung over the old intersection of town reading Yesteryear ’61.

“An old Yesteryear photo?” Gloria analyzed the old picture with an apologetic frown, searching the sea of black and white faces for resonance before handing the photo back to Lenny, embarrassed to admit she thought it was just a blur of old fashions and slightly yellowed nostalgia, not even particularly well taken.

Lenny frowned, his eyes scouring the photo, tapping his finger impatiently on a spot near the edge of it, "No. Look there, there's Dottie. See? And…there *you* are. Couldn't be more than maybe two, three. See? Anyway, you can keep it. Your mom was such a bombshell, right?"

Gloria glanced at the photo dismissively, "Notice she's left her three-year-old standing by herself on the edge of a busy parade route while looking so fancy."

Lenny whistled appreciatively, his eyes still on the photo, "You come by it honestly, G."

Gloria laughed, flattered, before glancing uncomfortably around the room thinking how absurd that it almost felt wrong to be sitting here flirting with another man.

"Would you like a drink?" Gloria stood, the chair groaning as it slid behind her knees.

Lenny opened his mouth to answer, then closed it, cocking his head and pressing his lips together before responding with confidence, "You know, I would like a drink. Very much. Thank you for asking."

Gloria tried to casually extract more information about Ted's investigation as she mixed their drinks, raising her voice from the kitchen to inquire, "So, when's Ted's article about the Lakeside Slayer coming out?"

"Soon. He's really gone overboard with this one. I'm starting to worry, honestly. Coming and going at all hours. And last week, he kept going on and on about some secret informant with mystery connections to some whack-job searching for werewolves, or was it Bigfoot? I think that was a dead end, but he was looking into some wacky theories there for a bit. Truth be told, Ted hasn't been himself. I think he might be having an affair. I thought maybe he was on a fitness kick at first…he seemed really energized and healthy. But it was an aggressive energy, for Ted. So then I thought, well maybe there's steroids involved. These young men and their shortcuts, you know," Lenny shouted, lowering his voice when Gloria reappeared.

"Mmmhnmmmm."

"I just don't know. Ted's always been a bit…grandiose." Lenny caught himself and smiled, trying to lighten the sudden maudlin atmosphere. "But enough about all this nonsense, Gloria. How are you, really? You still seeing that kid? Was that true?"

Two hours, three rum and cokes and several old stories later, Gloria was feeling pretty good about things. The gravity of the unfolding situation seemed less heavy. She was reminded of who she used to be when she dated Lenny, who she *wanted* to be back then. A journalist or an activist - anything other than what she'd become. It sounded like Lenny felt the same. They were both a little lost it seemed.

"The Gazette is gonna end up shutting down. Just can't compete with the internet these days. Too big. I guess I'll retire then, but I can't imagine what I'll do with my time," Lenny shrugged, slurring a bit.

Gloria felt so sorry for him in that moment, so sorry for herself, the mood shifted and they both grew morose. Lenny stood, wobbling as he glanced out the window, his eyes darting up at the starless sky, an apologetic grin on his lips, "Guess I should get going. Gotta feed the dogs."

Gloria stood to escort him out. Before she could speak to thank him for the visit, Lenny closed the gap between them, taking Gloria's face between his moist palms. He pressed his dry lips into hers rather forcefully, moving his lips against her own. Gloria *tried* to respond to his kiss. She searched her body longingly for any kind of response, any burning of her loins, but came up empty-handed. As she studied the kissing as if she were outside herself, from afar, she felt the unfamiliar sensation of nausea and was just able to step back, pivoting her body toward the planter behind her before vomiting into the dying fern - voluble sound effects of retching and heaving accompanying the spectacle to really to complete the scene.

Lenny jumped back, his hands in the air, apologizing, "I'm so sorry, I thought you…I?" He stopped his rationalizations and rushed to her side, his arm gripping her elbow to balance her as she righted herself from her sudden, clumsy lunge toward the potted plant.

The room was spinning as she wiped her mouth, waving Lenny's apologies away, "Oh Lenny, it's not you. It's…everything else. And a little too much to drink. I think I need to lie down."

"Sure, sure," Lenny agreed, waiting only a pat moment of decency before announcing she should put herself to bed while he saw himself out.

Gloria brushed her teeth, the room still dancing around her, waves of nausea and chills moving over her aching skin. She put herself to bed that night and dreamed of Henry. She woke at dawn drenched in sweat, another fever building inside her and kicked off the blankets she'd piled over herself in the night, drifting back into a dark and dreamless sleep.

Chapter 36

It was the worst flu Gloria had ever experienced.

"I was sick for a week. I still haven't recovered," Gloria confided to Dottie, voice hoarse. Her lungs ached with every breath.

"I missed you and I was quite worried. You have to take care of yourself," her mother advised. "You're too much like your father in that regard. Karl, too."

Gloria had been self-sufficient from birth as Dottie was never that natural of a nurturer, though she tried. She'd had other heartbreaks to attend to through Gloria's developmental years. The Weidman women had always possessed an innate hardness within them that ran through the entire female line - from their Pict ancestors down.

"Where is your young man now?" Dottie sat up straighter, pulling the cuffs of her sweater down to cover her spindly wrists.

"I told you, Mama. He left," Gloria repeated impatiently. "We are not seeing each other anymore."

Dottie nodded knowingly and winked, "Henry's wonderful. Isn't he? He thinks I don't remember him from when I was younger, but I do. How could you ever forget those eyes?"

Gloria only heard the last part of Dottie's statement, her focus on her aching head. Shaking it in confusion, Gloria demanded, "What do you mean, Mom? You just met Henry?"

"You should get your flu shot, Gloria," Dottie spoke slowly, turning her attention back to the talk show on television. "It's dangerous at your age not to."

"What did you say about Henry? Mom?" Gloria tried to recapture her attention.

"You said you'd broken up. What *should* I say?" Dottie harrumphed with a shrug, swiveling her body more fully forward, away from Gloria's questions, changing topics, "Are you going to the Yesteryear festival with Dee again this year?"

Gloria assumed that was the plan, though things had been a bit strained since the night of Dee's attack. Dee had been the first person to drop by with soup when Gloria fell ill last week, but their bedside patter was superficial and light with no talk of Henry, the mystery intruder or romance of any kind.

Upon leaving, Gloria retraced the conversation with her mother over several times to determine if it was she who had become confused, or Dottie. In the weeks since Henry's disappearance, she'd taken to looking for him everywhere, even in other people. In anything said if it could conjure his image, could help her make sense of the facts she'd learned about him since he left. Any evidence that could make his lies the truth.

Chapter 37

Whistles from the majorettes filled the air over the screaming and cheering of spectators and the gentle swells of conversation, music and horseplay from the crowds lining the streets. In front of the majorettes, a team of tractors slowly driven by husky, thick necked, floppy-haired high schoolers sporting sleeveless tees and acne; the tractors pulling trailers populated with letterman-jacket clad 4H members and their animals - ignorant, cheerful animals to be processed at the end of the year for finals - cute piglets and calves standing nervously on the moving platforms beside their human overlords. Squawking chickens lined the beds of red flyer wagons, attached via rope to the trailers. Since the parade moved so slowly, the town wasn't overly concerned with the usual, regimented safety regulations of, say, a Macy's parade on Thanksgiving as the creatively themed Yesteryear Festival celebrated its yester years, every year.

A poorly designed float supporting the thrones of the Yesteryear King and Queen, scions from the town's oldest and most important families, cruised down the main thoroughfare of town. The parade was followed by a weekend-long arts and craft festival and fair, drawing the curious, hipster crowds from nearby cities. The craft fair was punctuated with carriage rides through historic downtown, the old storefronts lining the railroad reopening to serve ice cream and barbeque, roped booths hawking jams and *doilies,* fresh produce and handmade soaps. It culminated with a carnival in the one public park – a hastily erected deathtrap filled with cotton candy, zipper rides, a creaking Ferris wheel and a darkened, indoor hard rock centrifugal ride to nauseate and deafen the rider in one shot.

Gloria peered down the road at the horses. Pretty, long-haired girls kicked at their sides, hooves dancing back and forth across the street with a hollow clopping. Little girls in frilly old timey dresses in small, gaudily decorated carriages being pulled by teams of goats. Dogs in saddles riding goats. Large men on tiny motorcycles. Just a dude on a four-wheeler and a lady in a go-cart. The entire shebang, as Dottie would say, though she'd opted not to attend for the fifth year in a row, even with Gloria offering to pick her up for the event. Gloria was pretty sure this was the last stand of her mother's legendary vanity.

That, and the fact the Gazette's latest edition dropped the afternoon prior with Ted Carroll's long-awaited expose titled *The Lakeside Slayer* in a bold, splashy font. Beneath this, several unanswered questions in a smaller, less attention-worthy font reading: *Is the Slayer a local drifter? Did the Lakeside Slayer's lover unwittingly aid and abet him? Meet the victims.*

Since it was published, Gloria had fielded no less than fourteen phone calls from old classmates, casual acquaintances and distant neighbors to simply 'check in on her', code for calling to mine her like a mineral deposit for gossip to go with the sensationalistic write-up. And, though Ted hadn't mentioned her by name, it was clear who the *older, local author* might be.

Gloria had the sensation of being observed, admitting, "I feel like people are looking at me."

Dee shrugged, patting Gloria's shoulder, "No one is looking at us. It's a travesty, I tell ya."

Dee butted her shoulder into Gloria's playfully, wiggling her eyebrows. Their voices were drowned out by the baritone wall of sound from the middle school band marching past in staggered lines.

"You wanna walk over to the park and check out the carnival?" Dee shouted over the din. Waves of distant joyful screams filled the air in intermittent bursts with the swooshing Scrambler and the hum of an engine fueling the endless loops of the Starship ride. The food booths were doing brisk business with their lines of sweating customers twisting throughout the foot paths.

The carnival had, as it had every year, appeared in the early hours of the morning, a great line of old trucks hauling the skeletons of the rides and booths. In an eerie silence, the roadies emerged in the morning mist, ninja-style, and quickly, silently, snap together the joints and pieces of the entire fair ground, unfolding it together like reverse origami. By mid-morning, the carnival stirred to life and the Yesteryear attendees made their way into the empty spaces of the grounds like zombies. By noon, it was as if the carnival had always been there on the soccer grounds of the city park, the swelling of noise rising over the bark of the PA from the parade, the town compact enough one could view snatches of the Yesteryear parade from the top of the Ferris wheel.

Gloria felt the snap of eyes on them as they passed through the familiar crowds. Perhaps she had careened into pure paranoia? Was she feverish again? She still felt like she was experiencing the lingering side effects from her bout with the flu.

A tall, balding man with olive skin nodded convivially and pointedly at Gloria as he passed, his dark grey eye lingering only momentarily on Dee, the other eye…clouded. Gloria nodded in response, her brain actively trying to place the memorable face. A face which made her instantly uncomfortable. It took her just a second after the man swept past them to realize he was one of the orderlies at Dottie's facility - her dance partner - his tight smile never wavering, never quite reaching his eye. The man whose uniform read *Saint*. She gasped - that was *Hanover Saint*! Hobby stalker and scarer of women. She opened her mouth to warn Dee. Too late!

"Oooooh!" Dee trilled, spotting a booth selling locally sourced candles, shouting over her shoulder as she bolted away, "I'll be right back."

Why was that man *here*? Gloria panicked. Was he watching her? Or was he looking for Henry. Had he come to warn her? Thank God Dee hadn't noticed her midnight attacker casually strolling the fairgrounds. Gloria turned to follow him, determined to ask why he was here, but he'd disappeared. There was only one major fairway at the entrance, but the tall stranger was nowhere in sight. Perhaps she was imagining things. Imagining people. Someone bumped into from behind.

"Gloria," her name was whispered in her ear. She shivered as she felt breath on the back of her neck and whirled around but there was only a small child holding tightly to his mother's hand as she negotiated with a honey vendor. The dark head tilted up, the child's attention on the bright flag reading Ellington's Honey fluttering from a nearby pole, a wooden sword drooping from the other chubby hand. He smiled innocently up at her, stabbing the stick aimlessly in the air.

"Gloria," her name was whispered into her other ear. Seductively. The voice sent ripples of pleasure down her spine. Spinning around, she found no one, not even the little sword bearer who'd been led away by his mother's hand. Gloria panicked, searching the crowds pressing in around her for Dee's unnaturally brown hair.

"Dee," she shouted, much to the consternation of the people

surrounding her. They began looking around for *this Dee* with her, panicked by the panic of an elder in their midst. *Who does this Nana belong to?* Spotting Dee in a jam booth several rows over, Gloria wove unsteadily through the crowds, her eyes alert and searching.

She scurried past the dark alleyway of the old town square, currently serving as a photogenic selfie backdrop near the last row of the market stalls, rushing to catch up to Dee and get away from the concerned patrons around her.

A cold hand clamped over her mouth before she could shout for help, an arm wrapping around her waist to pull her back into the dark, grassy corridor running between the old brick courthouse and the antique mercantile.

"Don't scream," Henry commanded, his mouth against her ear, her body molding into his. His arms wrapped around her shoulders to hold her against the length of his body. She could feel her heart beating frantically against the calm of his deep breaths. The electricity in the air crackled between them.

Chapter 38

Gloria stopped struggling as Henry released his steely embrace, allowing her to pull herself righteously from his arms and whirl about with the fury of a woman confused. When she opened her mouth to give him the thorough dressing down she'd been dreaming of since he'd scrambled her brains with his vampire nonsense and fled town, she was stopped by Henry's lips crashing brutally into hers, his tongue darting out, the force of his body pressing her own into the damp, peeling wood of the building behind her, his hands running down the hot skin of her arms.

She felt her own body respond, her hands running up his back, pulling his hair to bring him closer, closer to her as their mouths ravaged the other, tongues dancing, hands pulling and pushing. Her skirt rose, his fingers trailing up the soft flesh of her thighs, slipping into her. She gasped, fumbling clumsily with his zipper before Henry pushed her hands aside impatiently and thrust himself into her, silently, suddenly, fiercely. Gloria came as quickly as he entered her, a guilty moan escaping her lips. Henry followed suit, gripping her hips with his hands as he stilled and buried his head on her shoulder, breathing heavily.

Gloria cooled, pulling herself from Henry's frantic embrace, straightening her skirt while furtively glancing about to ensure they remained unseen in the dark shadows.

"You can't be here," she warned as Henry adjusted his clothes.

"What did you tell them?" he demanded.

Momentarily taken aback by the accusation, Gloria sputtered, "Nothing. What could I? I *may* have mentioned a version of your wife's name, if that helps. Henry, you have to tell me. Are you involved in these murders? Did you do this somehow?"

He tried to take her hand but she pulled it back, straightening her top and crossing her arms in front of herself as if she could protect her heart. Henry shook his head woefully, his eyes travelling over Gloria's face, desperately trying to read her, "You know I didn't. I was with you."

"But the first…"

"It wasn't me Gloria. I'm not sure what Liesl did, or who might be with her. Do you understand?" He pressed.

"Henry, please. You're scaring me. You really are. If you know who did this you have to go to the police. You have to explain."

"Explain what?" Henry exploded, his voice raising, "That my dead wife just might be in town to…what…have dinner? Catch up after two hundred years? Maybe kill a few people? How do I explain *this*?" He held his arms aloft as if to indicate the world around him.

"But I can help you, Henry," Gloria went on, sensing a breach in his defenses. "I can. If you'd just turn yourself in and tell them what you know. We can explain. We can explain that you're sick and we're getting you help."

"Sick?"

Grief washed across his face as Gloria went on, "You're just confused, Henry. I think you're just confused. You're mixing up *your* story with real life. But we can get you *help*. And when you're better, I can help you finish it. We'll get this all cleared up and get you help and it will be fine, Henry." She realized she was speaking to him as if he were a child. Which, she also realized, he kind of was. He was just a very young man with a potentially life-threatening mental illness wrapped up in a very serious situation. And he was probably as dangerous as he tasted.

His eyes narrowed. He grabbed her upper arms and pushed her back against the damp rotting planks of the wall behind her, his voice low and feral, “I’m not sick Gloria. I told you exactly who I was and I didn’t lie. For the first time in a very long time, I didn’t lie. You can do all the research you want. I know you have. All of those roads lead back to the *truth*. Don’t you see? I told you the truth.”

Distant screams from the rides carried over the breeze, freezing them both in place for a moment, their breath heavy. Henry relaxed his grip, dropping his hands to his side guiltily.

“I will never hurt you, Gloria,” he whispered plaintively. “I love you. I don’t want your help,” he spat, continuing more softly, “but I do want you.”

“I’m not yours to have, Henry,” Gloria reminded him gently. “And I love you too. I really do, God help me. But, it’s not - we can’t - you need help. And we need to think about getting you a lawyer and some medical intervention-“

“Stop,” Henry commanded, his head drooping, “I’m leaving here, Gloria. You can come or not, but I’d love it if you would even consider joining me when this is all done. You may not feel the same way after all this is done. You may not feel like yourself.”

“Join you?” Gloria almost laughed, “Henry, this isn’t a joke.”

“Didn’t you read my story? We *can* be together, Gloria. Forever, if you’d like,” Henry rushed his words, his eyes traveling furtively to crowds beyond their hidden alcove, up at the sliver of exposed sky overhead, squinting hopefully before his gaze moved back to her, "I'll explain it all later, but it's time. It's finally time."

The crowds screamed again. But this time, they were louder and shriller.

"I can't," Gloria shouted over the din, a look of complete heartbreak on Henry's face as she admitted, "Henry…you can't be here. I'm going to have to let the police know you've been in contact with me."

Henry's eyes narrowed before he leaned forward, kissing Gloria tenderly, beseeching her, "Why won't you believe me, Gloria? I've told you nothing but the truth."

"It doesn't sound like the truth, Henry. It just sounds like you're a great storyteller."

"Then finish reading my story, Gloria. And it will tell you everything you want to know."

Tears spilled from her eyes, she sniffed, "I'd love to, but I don't know where the story *is*."

The screaming from the midway grew louder. Gloria wiped her eyes, opening her mouth to plead with Henry to turn himself in, but he was gone. Gone in an instant as the waves of noise in the distance grew in intensity.

Gloria ran toward the merchant tents in search of Dee. Rounding the corner, back into the sunlight, she was met with Dee's disapproving wag of a finger.

"Where were you?" Dee scolded.

"It…was Henry," Gloria squeaked, still confused from his sudden appearance and even more sudden disappearance. "He said he was sorry. And that he wasn't responsible for the murders."

Dee frowned, her eyes scanning the crowds around them uncomfortably, "We have to report that. I hope you know why."

A cacophony of actual screams, easily distinguishable from the joyful cries and cheers she'd heard earlier with Henry, rose from the carnival. The shouts transformed quickly into a panicked babble of barking voices and loud exhumations, layered with wails of terror. Looming over the center of the fairgrounds, the Ferris wheel was frozen, its carriages still squeaking and rocking. Tinny music from the park's PA carried over the entire town on the crisp October breeze with a haunting tinkle.

Dee, several plastic bags dangling from a wrist, grabbed Gloria's hand in hers without a word, as if they were girls once again, and marched them down the main thoroughfare of the fairgrounds toward the melee with her head held high.

Gloria noted horrified onlookers staring up at the Ferris wheel. Several passengers aboard had their heads buried in their hands, crying. One young girl continued screaming from her captive seat. The carriage at the very top of the wheel was empty, still rocking with an eerie creak.

Chapter 39

A crowd gathered at the foot of the ride, pushing and jostling to get closer to the center of the disturbance while others scurried away. There was another peal of shouts and pleas as Deputy Cash muscled his way through the throng, pushing spectators back from the body on the matted grass; its neck turned, blood seeping beneath a gory head wound, the left leg folded back in a ninety-degree angle. Gloria backed away, her gaze riveted on the body. The outstretched hand, the corners of the fading tattoo, an ouroboro - a serpent eating itself.

Dee sucked in her breath, her voice shaking with fear as she leaned closer to Gloria, whispering, "*That* is the man who was in my house that night."

Gloria didn't answer, unable to admit she already knew and said nothing. To protect Henry. Her knees almost buckled as her eyes searched the crowd for him. *Where* was Henry? She had to warn him. Karl pushed past Gloria without a nod of recognition, joining Deputy Cash at the scene.

"I knew it," a familiar female twang sighed in her other ear. Gloria turned to see Linda, her many golden rings aflutter as she shook her head, pursing her pruned mouth. "It's a serial killer. Karl was right again."

Gloria realized then she would eventually be forced to admit she'd seen Henry mere moments before the sensational murder. If he wasn't already suspect number one, he certainly would be then. Dee looked pointedly at Gloria when Deputy Cash asked if anyone had seen anything amiss and Gloria remained silent before pushing her forward. And, when Casey Cash asked her exactly *when* she'd seen Henry and in which direction he fled, Gloria lied, admitting only that she may have spotted him earlier, loitering near the parking lot seconds before the accident occurred, even going so far as to look around the fairgrounds as if searching for him.

Dee waited patiently while Casey Cash ineptly questioned Gloria, much to the amusement of the few spectators lingering to watch the short exchange between the notorious Gloria Weidman and the deputy regarding her murderous lover. Once done, she shuffled back to Dee's side, defeated.

Before Gloria could open her mouth, Dee swept her up in a fierce embrace, releasing her only after squeezing her uncomfortably tight for an inappropriate amount of time, demanding, "Are you okay? Did Henry hurt you? Did Casey hurt your feelings?"

Gloria took a deep breath, looked Dee in the eye and started to cry.

"Oh, don't cry, are you OK?" Dee hugged her again, "Tell me Henry didn't hurt you?"

"No!" Gloria sniffed. "*He* didn't hurt me. I mean, *my heart* hurts, Dee. Because he's gone. But Henry would never hurt me."

Would he, though, she wondered silently? She wasn't so sure now.

"Well, whatever actually happened, you're still the talk of the town. And everyone *is* staring at you now, so," Dee informed her, leading her toward the parking lot, "you can scratch that off your list of to-dos."

"He really left. That's all. He…he thinks he knows who's killing. And suddenly he has a wife. But he thought she'd been dead for over two hundred years. Obviously, I can't tell the police that. They'd have me committed."

"Ah, yes, the mysterious Henry Wynter's mysterious vampire wife. Yeah, I see your dilemma."

"What are they saying?" Gloria gestured back toward the thinning crowds of the festival.

"They…specifically Ted Carroll and his great big expose… are saying your young lover is this Lake Slayer and when the police came calling, he cleared out his house and ran. Now, he's back and has killed again, at random, after attempting to murder you in broad daylight, right behind the corny dog stand. I didn't correct anyone. Oh, and now Karl's telling everyone *you* broke up with *him* when you got suspicious he was the killer and that's why he lost his shit and murdered again." Dee took a deep breath.

"I did break things off…before," Gloria confirmed as they reached Dee's multi-colored through rust-and-ruin-vehicle, her brows furrowed. "He's sick, Dee. Don't you think he just needs help? He's no killer."

Dee plopped herself into the driver's seat, leaning across to unlock the passenger door manually. As she stretched, she lectured loudly, "You still believe what he told you? There was a *dead body*. Right there. *Henry* is a fugitive. And might I remind you he tried to kill *you* that day after the Hoedown. *Kill you*! To your face," Dee laid it out, disapproval lacing her features.

"No," Gloria sighed as the fairgrounds shrank in the rearview mirror, "I don't know what I believe. He's not a killer, Dee. I know he's not the lakeside slayer, but I don't know exactly *what* I believe anymore. About him." She didn't bother to explain further so Dee wouldn't think she had any doubts about Henry. She flipped Dee's rearview mirror down to touch up her lipstick and quickly wiped away the smear of blood that appeared on the finger she passed it over her bruised lips. Leaning closer to the mirror, she spied two distinct puncture marks on her bottom lip, a souvenir from her and Henry's illicit passions. Pressing her lips together, she savored the last sting of pain.

"Well, here we are," Dee announced as they reached Gloria's house, inviting herself in to putter about in Gloria's inherited kitchen as Gloria sat motionless on the couch, staring into the dark corners of the room.

The tea kettle whistled through the quiet house as Dee's shadow moved through the kitchen, bustling about with the *ting ting* of China and spoons. She returned and thrust a steaming mug of tea into Gloria's hands. Staring down into the amber liquid, her head spinning momentarily, Gloria blew the steam from the mug and took a tentative sip.

"Hey," Dee startled her from her reverie, "it's okay. We all make mistakes. This, too, shall pass. Everyone will get over themselves. And they," she gestured to the space around her, "will grow tired of boring old you and move on to a real story."

"I just don't know how I got here."

"Well, like a lot of great women before you, I believe you fucked your way here. But no one's holding you in this place. And you have the power to move beyond it," Dee reminded her cheerily.

Gloria grimaced, raising her eyebrows, acknowledging ruefully, "That's true."

Dee glanced at her watch, "I gotta git. Told Troy I'd watch JR and Lovie tonight while he works a shift." Dee placed her cup on the kitchen bar, heading to the front door. Gloria followed her, swinging the door open as Dee adjusted her sunglasses into place.

"Thank you, Dee," Gloria hugged her tightly.

Dee peered down at her oldest friend in the world with

a tired sigh, “You be careful. Dating’s not the same beast it was when we were young. Love is absolutely dangerous by comparison these days. I’m sure you’ve noticed.”

She was right, Gloria realized. Love *was* dangerous, in so many ways. It had the disappointing habit of creating chaos where none existed before. And chaos…*chaos* hastened *horrible* things.

Chapter 40

Ignoring fresh tears, tears that threatened to appear with very little provocation since the fiasco the day before, Gloria took a ragged breath, sinking into the couch. The house looked like a pigsty in the prying rays of the late afternoon sun. This entire affair made her act so unlike herself. Perhaps it was allergies or maybe she was still sick, but she felt decidedly under the weather again the minute she realized Henry was gone for good. This felt like… heartbreak.

She inhaled and exhaled slowly, meditatively. *Why* hadn't he called her? Her own desperate texts to him had gone unanswered. The skid of tires on gravel and the quiet whoop whoop of a siren startled her. Next there was the gentle tap tap of knuckles on her door which she swung open, a frown creasing her visage.

"Gloria. Just doing my job here," Casey explained sheepishly. There was a second officer standing a respectful distance away.

Without a word in response, Gloria turned, retreating into the dark house, leaving the door ajar for the officers to enter and ignoring them as they gingerly picked their way through the living area and gave a cursory glance into each room. Gloria returned to the couch, clicking the television on with the remote while wondering for the hundredth time…how did she, Gloria Weidman, the most methodical, predictable woman in America, *get here*? Duped by a pretty-faced grifter. The laughingstock of the town. Did she imagine the whole affair? Was she that far gone?

As she escorted the search team to the porch, Casey pulled Gloria aside, holding the grainy copy of a traffic camera picture out for her perusal. Gloria took it, the paper snapping in her hand, her brow furrowing as she gazed down at the fuzzy image - a black and white shot of two occupants in a vehicle she didn't recognize.

She shrugged, "What am I seeing?"

"Henry," Casey poked his forefinger into the paper to indicate the passenger before sliding it to point to the driver, "Is this that Lisa girl? The wife?"

Gloria squinted, her stomach dropping, "It could be. When?"

"About an hour after the Yesteryear murder. This is getting on I20 going north from 69…leaving town heading towards maybe Dallas or Fort Worth? Looks like maybe she's helping him flee. Best you got out when you did, Glory. I shudder to think what he had planned for *you*. Why he…well. Just best." A quick, hidden look of pity crossed Casey's normally stoic features. His eyes moved back to the door as he went on, "We couldn't find a marriage license, so I don't think this little gal is his legal wife. At least not here in Texas. Hell, I can't find her anywhere at all, for what it's worth." Casey nattered on as Gloria walked him out, "His house was empty, as you know. And folks said he'd been spending nights *here* before, you understand. So, when he tried to approach you before the murder yesterday, we figured he might try to get to you again. That's why we're here. For your safety. We aren't here to say if he's guilty or not."

Gloria slammed the door shut in his face, leaving the embarrassed deputy speaking softly to a closed door, the officer stationed behind him trying not to laugh openly at the insult. She hadn't thought of *that*. That Henry had used her to some nefarious end all while on some criminal streak in cahoots with his wife.

Surely not. Why would he bother with her? She wasn't anyone to anyone, anymore. She certainly didn't have anything to steal.

She hadn't imagined everything, though? Had she? She'd once been so sure of herself in life. But now, now she doubted everything. You'd think a person got smarter as they got older. But no, they just became wise enough to realize the breadth of their ignorance.

She could still feel the tender skin of her hips where Henry's hands gripped her so tightly as they'd made fierce love in the alley just the afternoon before. She touched her tongue to the bruised flesh of her lower lip, pressing her lips together as if to taste his kiss just one last time. At least she hadn't completely imagined all of *that*.

And as for what he told her about his life, or may have written for her, she had no idea what to think. She needed to get her hands on Henry's completed story. Henry seemed to think it was in her possession. But where was it? Had it been left at Henry's house?

She reminded herself to check with Casey.

She kept retracing her last encounter with Henry. Could she trust her instincts? Between the wine and the doubt, she hovered between believing everything he said and laughing at her own stupidity. Surely, Casey would tell her one day the knife they'd confiscated from Henry's cabin was just a trick knife, a prop. Maybe Henry had even lied about the story he'd written for her.

She had an endless reservoir of tears for Henry now, it seemed. Once the tears started, she couldn't stop them. For him, for the loss of him. But mainly because she felt so stupid about the entire affair. Which is, truthfully - aside from grief and anger - one of the only real reasons women ever cry.

Chapter 41

As Gloria headed out to drop dinner off for Dottie, she glanced out the window, spotting Casey Cash at his evening post, parked in an unmarked police car two feet from her drive. Sighing, she quickly cut another couple slices of her leftover meatloaf and pulled the loaf of bread back down from its perch atop the microwave to make a second sandwich.

Casey startled as she rapped on his passenger window. His car idled with a quiet hum, the air conditioning rushing out as he leaned over and manually rolled the window down with some effort, leaving him sweating even in the path of cool air.

"What can I do you for Glory?" He smiled apologetically.

Gloria held the meatloaf sandwich aloft, bending to lean into the window, "It is more what I can do for you, Casey."

He accepted the foil wrapped sandwich with surprised delight, "Wow! Thanks."

Gloria took a moment to critically survey the interior of the vehicle, "Jesus, Casey, you've got to get bored in here. I know you have a job to do, but I do question the wisdom of this old-school stakeout. You're wasting your time. He's gone. It's been over a week since he left with his wife. We broke up weeks ago. It's all over."

Casey shrugged, moaning inappropriately as he bit into his sandwich, giving Gloria a thumbs up as he chewed.

"Any leads?" Gloria queried innocently. Casey shook his head, still chewing as Gloria went on, sharpening her acting skills,

"Any thoughts on when your team might be done with the things they took from Henry's house? Like maybe a manuscript? Or what looked like a stack of typed pages. Or there was that knife… the one on the mantle. I mean, I know it's just an old prop, but I'd really love to see it," she lied smoothly. "Morbid curiosity. For research. For my book."

Casey scrunched his craggy features in confusion, shrugging good-naturedly, "I don't recall finding anything of any interest of yours, Glory. Now I ain't saying I think he's guilty like everybody in town, but you have to admit…it doesn't look good. Don't get caught up in this. You say he's not around? Well, good. Keep away from him. He's dangerous."

If only you knew, Gloria thought. Nodding, she pulled her head out of the car, "Understood, Officer Cash. I'll see you tomorrow night about this time. You like roast beef? Never mind, everybody likes roast beef."

Chapter 42

Terry generally got along with all stoners. Truth be told, at his age, dealing weed was how he made almost all of his friends. First, they were customers. Then, they were friends. They liked him and he liked them. They told good stories. Funny stories. And they came in all shapes and sizes, all ages. Generally, he didn't sell to the young ones aside from his lone weekly drop to the local high school, a large order to be marked up and distributed by a six-foot-four, twenty-one-year-old senior: an aspiring rapper who went by the moniker Tyler from Tyler. Aside from that, he kept to himself and, on the whole, discouraged drop-ins to preserve his anonymity in a nosy town.

Terry noticed the dribble of oil seeping into one of the few clean spots left on the living room carpet. Mom would kill him. He'd pretty much ruined all the furniture and flooring he'd inherited upon his much-vaulted move to this family-owned rental house, which he was instructed to fix up in his spare time to later sell for a profit. However, you see, if it 'twere never quite fixed up, then it could not be sold and he would not have to enter into the tedious prospect of moving. Or, working harder to pay for said move. He shifted the pan, clanging his head with a dink on the motor. He pulled back instinctively, almost slicing his leg on one of the industrial mower's left blades, which he'd tilted vertically to preserve the beige carpet. He probably shoulda done this in the yard but he didn't want to take a chance with the Community Center's property. It was one of his duties to maintain the equipment both inside and outside the facility. And to that end, once a quarter, he drove the mower - a supersized Kubota donated some years ago by a wealthy town elder - the 1.4 miles to his house, over two-lane country roads, past the schools to the outskirts of town as motorists patiently idled behind him.

Once home, he changed the oil using his own supply and swapped out the spark plugs. Not clean work but he enjoyed it. Unfortunately, it was dark by the time he reached the house and his porch light wasn't quite bright enough, nor would the one lamp he owned reach far enough, its orange extension cable having been sliced through on his last foray into nighttime mechanics.

"You OK?"

Terry swore, trying to rise without banging his head to spy the owner of the sultry, girlish voice at his open doorway, the screen door obscuring her features where she stood.

"Yep, yep," He assured her, wiping his hands on his jeans. He didn't recall selling to her before. He frowned. Young, he noticed first. Striking, though. Beautiful, really. Her features a bit pinched, reminding him of a fox, her hair spilling over her shoulders and down her pale arms. With those eyes, she could have been anywhere from fifteen to forty. He was a poor judge of people's ages.

"You lost?" Terry squinted, his gaze traveling over her shoulder for someone else. There was no car. Had she walked here?

"Can I come in?" She smiled, her teeth white and sharp.

He gestured to the mess around him, "Kind of dirty in here. What can I do for you?"

"I'm a friend of Henry's," she put her hands on her hips and tapped her fingers impatiently. "Can I come in?

"He not with you, is he?" He asked suspiciously, having

heard a small bit about Henry's recent legal entanglements.

Her eyes swept the room behind him, "I was hoping maybe *you'd* seen him."

Terry relaxed, stepping back to allow her to swish past. Her hair smelled like strawberries.

"I don't suppose you've seen our friend *recently*? Have you, Terry?"

Two minutes later, Terry – shackled without preamble to the Kubota, his phone conveniently placed out of reach – realized his folly. Crash. More glass breaking.

"Where is it?" she shouted from the adjacent room. Terry heard another small crash, another tinkle of breaking glass. He didn't have much to begin with. What else had she found to break? The severity of his décor seemed to enrage her further.

"I done told you, honey," Terry volunteered, unsolicited. "I keep my product in a box under my bed. You can smell your way there. It's the room on the left. Could you not-"

Another crash, a curse and then the fox appeared beside him, a disgusted look on her face, "The manuscript, you moron? I'm looking for *the story* Henry said he *left* with *you*. The stack of papers?"

Terry was genuinely confused, and not for the first time that day. He thought for a moment - a brief flash of a memory of an assignment Henry had asked him to pass to his aunt at the requested…ah, time! How had he forgotten? Henry probably failed the class, he realized guiltily. Perhaps he'd misread Henry's sense of urgency the day he'd dropped the folder stuffed with typed pages into Terry's hands, casually mentioning he might leave town for a bit before asking Terry turn in the assigned story on his behalf. Terry assumed his taciturn friend and his aunt had parted ways romantically, none of his business, and promptly forgot about it.

"Now I don't recall anything other than a paper to be turned in for him at his writing class." He glanced around nervously as he spoke, his normally unrufflable equilibrium quite shaken by the amount of chaos this small lady had wrought in a fairly short amount of time. It hadn't seemed that important. But after what that girl had done to his house looking for it, he realized the assignment must be worth more of Henry's grade than he thought. There was a reason he hadn't bothered with college.

"Jesus," the strawberry fox rolled her eyes, sauntering to the screen door. She sighed, her back still to Terry, before turning and bending down to peer into his eyes. "Thank you, Terry Weed-Man. You're a champ."

Before he could utter an appropriately witty repartee, the girl vanished before his very eyes. Taking a step off the porch, there was a poof of wind where she'd stood, the swoosh of a blur to the tree line and she was gone.

Terry remembered belatedly that though his intention had been to turn in the finished assignment for Henry by the specified due date, he'd left the stack of pages in his car, still parked in the old shed behind the Community Center where the Kubota normally sat. He eyed the mess around him and the phone just beyond his reach with a sigh before stretching his left leg out from a low yoga squat he'd seen Sissy perform one Saturday morning. Placing the rubber toe of his work boot gently across the lip of the phone case, he carefully dragged the device across his dirty, napped carpet, cawing victoriously as his fingertips connected with the device. He paused before texting for help. Man, Aunt Glory was going to have his hide for this.

Chapter 43

Finally. The end of Henry's story, at last! Gloria's hands smoothed the curved, stained pages of the manuscript. Terry was a turd but thank goodness for his bad memory. And his safety. He'd been overly apologetic when he'd dropped the end of Henry's manuscript off earlier, bruised and chagrined, hopeful it would still count toward Henry's grade, accepting his aunt's grateful hug as forgiveness. He didn't mention the embarassing reason he finally remembered it.

After being abandoned on the wild shores of America by our crew, Bennet and I hunkered down, fortified what we could and waited. After the storm died out, the noise began. At first, it was a gentle drumming from the tree lines. It sounded like a celebration and went on for several days, followed by some piercing screams obviously meant to unsettle the fort's remaining occupants and a couple of flaming arrows that went pfft into the sodden dirt and did no real harm to the wooden structures. The threat was implied. Then some keening and ululations for long stretches of time from transient groups of natives, usually women, who stood in a row just in sight of the front gate and trilled endlessly, it seemed, often ending these songs by spitting at the fort.

Occasionally, a brave group of liberated slaves would arrive in between the Indians' performance to demand food and supplies in their native tongues, only to slink away when ignored. Neither group ever organized enough to storm our pathetic defenses. Wamenu snuck into the compound during the second week of our slow siege and bid me to come away with him.

Bennett had developed an odd habit of disappearing for several hours before dawn each day. I always pretended to be asleep when he returned, assuming he was searching for food he didn't have to share. It was only natural he fend for himself. I sure wasn't any help having given up entirely to napping in light of our current predicament. It was on one of these mornings I awoke to find Wamenu cross legged beside me, making a small circle around my ragpile bed with a handful of precious salt. He smiled when he noticed my eyes on him and motioned to his salt circle.

"Come with me," he said in perfect English, better than I'd ever heard him speak in the company of others. "You must come now, before the red star crosses the sky and you are lost."

I actually looked up when he said this, staring heartily through the rotting rafters of the unfinished ceiling, searching. I saw nothing through the bald rushes.

Without rising, my body too weak at this point to bother with manners, I shook my head. "I can't leave the boy," I explained. "You have to wait for Bennett to get back."

Wamenu turned to me, panic in his eyes, imploring gently, "The boy is dead, you must come or die as well. There is evil here. It is no good for you."

I bolted up, pushing myself against the sticky resin from the seeping logs of the raw pine wall, "Bennett is dead? How? When?"

Wamenu shook his head, standing and proffering his hand, "Come."

I stared at his hand, horrified, convinced he was tricking me to lure me to my death as well. He dropped his hand, giving me one last pitiful nod and backed away, slipping into the fog of the morning just as Bennett reappeared. I pretended to sleep as the boy dropped down to his pallet opposite mine and closed his eyes, an unfamiliar scent filling my nostrils I couldn't readily identify wafting over me as Bennet adjusted his form. It was the smell of flesh and sweat, blood and smoke and something else, something like rotting fruit. All smells I should recognize well enough by now. I was relieved by Bennet's reappearance, enough so I didn't question where he'd been or why Wamenu lied about his death. What purpose could separating us possibly serve? We were the easiest marks that ever lived.

I was dying. I could feel it. My body was weak. We hadn't eaten in days, with days between the days before that. I'd developed a wracking cough and it shook my entire body of bones each time it gripped me. I must have been delirious because I thought Bennett was in the same shape as he lay across from me on his own pallet of scraps we'd collected from camp. It was only when he held my head up and forced mouthfuls of water from a dirty wooden cup into me that I noticed how positively healthy he still appeared. Weeks of starvation, illness, sorrow and fear and he was virtually unchanged from the day I'd met him almost a year before. Unchanged.

For the first time, I grew leery of this boy. The one I'd protected and nurtured for so long without a word of thanks or acknowledgement. I'd never had the time to really ponder our odd arrangement, to think whether or not he'd even needed my help. He hadn't, had he? He never sought me out or gave me a second glance. I was the one who'd pressed my energies on him. I was the one who'd watched over him like a brother.

This water, this succor, was the first sign of humanity I think I'd ever seen from this silent child. It touched me even though I was becoming suspicious of him. How had he survived so well and wholly to even now show not one sign of hardship? My voice failing me, I grasped his hand as he sponged my forehead with a rag.

"I know nothing about you, Bennett," I implored, "tell me about your life before I die."

A rather dramatic declaration but I made it all the same.

Bennett shrugged and continued, muttering, "You're not going to die, my friend. Not now. Likely not ever." I ignored the strange comment, delirious as I was. He went on in his crisp, odd accent, "But I will tell you a funny story."

He sat back on his haunches, crouched, his eyes still locked on mine and went on, "Did I ever tell you my mother sold me, to a man who wanted to feed me to a tiger? Can you believe it?"

I couldn't, because he'd never said and, though I was too weak to acknowledge it verbally, this was the most he'd ever spoken, at least to me.

"Well, she did, that bitch. But it wasn't a tiger he fed me to, Henry," he said my name. I had never heard him use it, "it was just a man."

He settled back on his pallet, my eyes following him as he stoked the fire a bit and sat down, pushing his back against the spindly wall behind him. "I remember it was summer and I loved the season because my people, we'd walk and walk and walk, hunting all through the spring, then in the warmest months, we'd find these fruit trees, all in a field and there would be such a celebration. And ceremonies and the feasting and people fucking by the fire in center of camp. It was a wild, wild time. I was just a child, so no fucking for me. But my mother, unlucky woman, agreed to sell me to a man she'd just met. He offered her a tidy sum, I imagine, and I had several brothers and sisters so it was no real loss to her, maybe she'd fucked him by the fire, I'm not sure. So off I went, a rope around my neck, like those poor bastards out there."

He motioned jovially towards the hanged slaves still swinging from the tree at the perimeter of camp. "You see, on the long walk back to his camp, my captor told me there was no tiger, but there was a wise man he wanted me to meet and he would leave it to the man to decide my fate. If the man thought I was virtuous and clean, he would likely keep me as his own. If not, I could very well be eaten by a tiger when I was cast out, which in my case meant certain death since I was only twelve and a small twelve at that.

Now finally, we came to a cave – a dark cave - and he led me inside. I was convinced he was indeed leading me to my death in a tiger's lair, but as promised, we came to a small firelit chamber and there was a man. Just a man of some great age, propped on a rock with only a few crude pieces of furnishings around him. He had smooth white skin and marvelous white hair and his teeth were sharp and white. He paid my captor, who retreated and left me to my fate. I knew I was enslaved and, quite frankly, for the times, it wasn't that odd of destiny.

My new master smiled. I was petrified by his sharp teeth, and then I realized the joke about being fed to the tiger, because this man resembled a tiger with his teeth and his strength and the way he paced his chambers like a great golden lion I had seen in a caravan the summer before.

He told me the story of the beginning, when a man and a woman were placed on Earth inside of a giant seed. This invisible hand planted the seed in the bare soil and buried it very deep. There, a tree of fruit grew from the seed and when it was ready to harvest, the man and the woman crawled out of the soil from the tangle of roots from the tree and then picked and ate the fruit. The fruit made them sick, so they spit it into the soil, where the seeds grew new people to populate the Earth."

With that, Bennet struck his bare foot out through the flames of the fire and, with the side of his foot, scattered the salt ring Wamenu had drawn beside me. Despite my chills, I pushed myself up to sit, staring through the flames trying to focus on Bennet's face as he went on with his story. "This man, he said he was the son of one of these seed people, one of many sons and daughters. But he himself never had a wife and he couldn't find a woman who lived as long as he so that he could have a family who never died. He said I would be his son and he would raise me and educate me and give me eternal life. And he did. I stayed in the cave with the Tiger for over three years, learning everything I could. Mathematics and alchemy, medicine and philosophy. Then one day, just as he'd promised, the red star returned to move across the eastern sky after two hundred years of waiting and gave him a sign. He knew it was time to give me the same gift that I'm going to give you, Henry. You know, you're very lucky. I know you wanted to die – back in England and the voyage over. But you want to live now, don't you, Henry? You should because when I'm done with you, you're going to live forever, just like me. But I won't keep you like the Tiger kept me. I'm going to let you free. I had to kill him to get away, to be free, but I did - and it was hard. Hundreds of years of being his fine son, but I finally got away. And now, you'll be my brother, not my son, and I'll give you your freedom."

My eyes were wide with fear. I shook my head to clear it, sure I was hallucinating it all. When I looked up, Bennett smiled and it was then I knew he was telling the truth. And my mystery - my silly mystery was quite solved. It was Bennett, every time.

His eyes sparkled as recognition washed my face to ash. It was Bennett who had killed the men on the boat coming over, it was Bennett who killed the soldiers on the first raid, it was Bennett who killed Edmund, who strung up those slaves. It was always Bennett. And, when he laughed, I saw those sharp teeth, those needle-pointed incisors that were so fine I'd never noticed. Invisible almost. The Tiger's fine son.

"Not now, silly," he guffawed, waving away the horror on my face, "but soon, very soon. It has to be the very right moment. I chose you, Henry. I did. I know it seems like I got stuck with you, but I made sure we'd be together when the time was right. The Tiger told me I'd know when the time was right. And I do. I could feel it. I've felt it for years. Just like the last time. And the time before and the time before that. That red star is coming! I can't see it but I can feel it. And when it does, I'll do it just right. It won't hurt. Just get some rest."

He smiled and I immediately felt sleepy, despite his dire warning and my mortal fear. Somehow, I fell asleep. And I dreamed of tigers.

Chapter 44

This time when Ted Carroll left a message, his voice quivered with fear. Instead of his usual grating, overly-confident warble, this Ted whispered forcefully, his voice traveling to and from the earpiece as if he couldn't keep still long enough to leave a cohesive message. Beep.

"Schmmmmms…mutual friend."

Gloria leaned forward as she listened, as if this would somehow help her better decipher the message on her ancient machine, "But I was looking through… (static, silence) … archives… year. Found…something…Lenny said he'd brought… (silence, garbled noises) look at it—I can come…come to you or you drop by. But there's so much more to this (muffled noise) think (more static) worried. (Garbled noises). New source, but it's…but there's a catch... (interference)." Then a dial tone as the message cut off midsentence. He hadn't called back.

The desperate message was from three in the morning, four days prior. Gloria had so few actual messages over the past year since assuming Dottie's mortgage, she no longer bothered to check the machine and hadn't noticed the blinking light. When she swept into the open front door of The Gazette the following day, still rattled by her inability to reach Ted by phone, it took her a second to process what she was seeing.

There was Lenny - standing over a pile of scattered photos strewn across the floor, two overturned desks and a broken window allowing a cool breeze to whistle through the room, stirring the papers carpeting the creaking wood floor. Both Casey Cash (who seemed to materialize and dematerialize based on Gloria's location) and two other officers were speaking in calm, low voices to Tammy, tears streaming down her face, her arms crossed protectively in front of her body.

The door to the press room was tilted from its hinges, the lock obviously shattered by some force. Gloria peaked inside noting what appeared to be a bloody handprint on the wall with a matching, rainbow-shaped streak inferring the owner of the bloody hand fell to the ground after bracing themselves against the wall. Gloria stifled a gasp, leaning forward to see if Ted's body lay on the floor beneath, but Casey moved his generous form to block her view.

"Gloria," Casey tipped his head in her direction, scowling. "This is a crime scene. I'm afraid you can't go in."

Craning her neck to gawk around him, Gloria was relieved to spot no signs of a corpse, "What happened?"

Casey shrugged, casting a quick glance across the trashed offices of the Gazette as Tammy informed the officer questioning her, "I mean, the Gazette runs inflammatory articles all the time and the most we seem to get is hate mail." Gloria heard Tammy sniffle, telling the young officer in a hushed tone, "He said he felt like he was being followed? But I'm not sure why anyone would bother following Ted."

Casey shifted his focus from Tammy to Gloria, demanding, "Why are you here again?"

"Ted called me." Gloria shrugged, adding noncommittally, "Said he found something for my book. Probably nothing."

No doubt the police were already aware there had been a crime, Gloria rationalized internally. No need to muddy it up with additional details regarding Ted's garbled message or the stolen files and inviting more scrutiny to herself.

Casey rolled his eyes, "Why am I not surprised you're mixed up in this too? *When* did he call and what about?"

"It was a message about some research he was doing – for a story. Maybe four days ago? Why? Mixed up in what?" Gloria protested.

"Ted's gone. He's missing. His wife hasn't seen him since he left for work yesterday morning. Gloria, I think we've got another homicide on our hands. And they are all orbiting around you! Is there *anything* you want to tell me?"

"You think *I* did this?"

"I *know* you didn't, Glory. I was parked in front of your house when it happened. See? Good thing, too. Is *he* back? He's back, isn't he? *Henry*?"

Gloria looked around the demolished offices as Lenny swept the photos and papers up from the floor where they'd fallen out of their organized and labeled files. Surely someone should stop him from moving evidence from the scene of a crime.

She shook her head, the hairs rising on her neck, "If he is, I haven't seen him, Casey. And *why* would a twenty-two-year-old kid give a shit about *The Gazette*?"

Lenny stood, wiping dust from his knees, helpfully adding, "Because Ted did that expose on the Lakeside Slayer and he was onto something?"

Gloria pressed her lips together, shaking her head back and forth, declaring passionately, "Henry would never hurt anyone."

"Well, someone did. Now Ted's probably dead as well," Casey surmised, narrowing his eyes as he surveyed the wreckage of the offices. He strode away, consulting with the other officer as Gloria snuck quietly out the open front door.

She reached her car, breaking into a cold sweat. It took a

moment for her hands to stop shaking before she could drive the short distance home.

Chapter 45

Gloria pushed Henry's manuscript aside in frustration, unable to focus, her burning eyes as the black ink danced across the pages in nauseous waves. Her fever returned and, as she hadn't fully regained her strength from the previous malaise, Gloria began to worry something more insidious was happening inside her. With frightening visions of cancers and heart failure dancing in her head, she put off making an appointment with a General Practitioner for several days during which she grew weaker and weaker, her fever spiking and receding in disorienting waves. Time seemed to slow as she slept and fretted and tossed and turned with the heat or the cold. She found she was quite paralyzed with weakness. Her body simply, rapidly, shut down.

At some point, she heard a tremendous crash and the looming form of Casey Cash hovered over her, Karl flanking his side, both sweaty and wild-eyed. Casey leaned over her speaking, but she couldn't hear him. She tried to tell him to go away, swatting feebly at him, her hand glancing off the rough cambric of his uniform. Karl stared down at her, his lips twisting silently. Gloria could feel the sweat pour from her skin. She kicked her feet to dislodge the blankets tangled around her.

Gloria saw her brother swoop down, arms outstretched, and could feel herself being lifted; the whoosh of air cooling her slick skin. Her head fell back as she slid into a quiet, dark place, the hum of her blood singing to her as her pulse beat louder and louder until she could hear nothing else and see nothing else. She drifted away - the strange sensation of being handled by others, of being touched by others. Hearing voices and mechanical beeps, but hearing them from far away, as if they were no concern to her snuggled down into her cozy cave. Then, silence. Golden silence.

Pneumonia. Beep. Anemia. Beep. Rampant, inexplicable, idiopathic anemia. More tests to follow. Reasonable concerns about lymphoma or leukemia. A tinny alarm and the sound of a pump. All the words juggled past her ears while she lay in a daze, followed by an all-around relief when she finally opened her eyes.

"Ah, thank god," Dee crowed, her hoarse voice calling out for the nurse. "She's awake!"

Gloria struggled to sip the water from the cup Dee held under her chin. "How long?" she croaked.

"An entire day, Gloria Jean. An entire fucking day!" Gloria noticed Dee's lips quivered as she went on, "There will be more tests, of course. But you're going to be okay, I just know it."

Dee pat Gloria's hands and Gloria looked down, startled to find an IV taped to her forearm and monitors on her finger and ribs. A frazzled middle-aged doctor appeared, clucking over Gloria and poking her with the blunt end of a pen, running the same chewed pen top over the soles of her feet to test her reflexes.

"Wonderful," he proclaimed. "Your fever's broken and your body still seems to work."

The aforementioned list of potential culprits was reviewed next with promises of more tests the following day, culminating with another, full once-over by a summoned nurse before she was ordered to rest, alone. After a litany of tests, blood scans and consultations, the doctors landed on hyperthyroidism - potentially Hashimoto's disease – sending Gloria home with a referral to an endocrinologist in Tyler, plus a hefty hospital bill with instructions to get some rest.

She was wheeled from her room to an awaiting police cruiser on the third day, surprised to find Casey Cash in the driver's seat. He rushed from his position, helping her from the wheelchair to the passenger seat, his jacket offered in lieu of a blanket for the ride home. Gloria was weak enough and still sick enough to accept the gesture with gratitude.

"What did I do to deserve curbside service?" Gloria asked, her voice raw and weak.

Casey grinned, "Figured I took you to the hospital, least I could do was pick you up. I was heading back to your place anyway, if that's where you're going."

Gloria leaned back in the seat, suddenly exhausted, closing her eyes, "Of course, that's where I'm going."

She slept until the bump bump bump of Casey's car alerted her they'd pulled onto her potholed, gravel drive. Gloria turned to face Casey. "I don't know how to thank you,"

He shrugged, blushing pink as he held her purse out to her, "Yeah, well, I don't know that it matters. It's what you do."

"Not always," Gloria surmised, waving back to Casey as she made her way inside.

The house was warm and airless, still in a general sense of disarray. Gloria made her way to her bedroom, lowering herself to the corner of her bed stiffly, eyeing Henry's manuscript strewn across her sheets and bedroom floor in the upheaval of her rescue. She touched a page, pulling her hand back to her chest warily before shaking her head ruefully while gathering the full manuscript back into a tidy stack again.

Chapter 46

I kept thinking I should run. Then, the eternal beating of the tom tom drums and the shouts from the slaves and Indians alike would convince me there was nowhere to run. Now that he'd spoken and told me my fate, Bennett kept up a lively patter of conversation. He was downright chatty, though I'd lost my own voice at the end. I realized I was quite paralyzed, but whether that was sickness of the body or of the mind, I'll never know.

I lingered in this twilight state for what felt like months but was really only a matter of weeks. One crisp, pink morning, Bennet returned from his daily patrol, his white teeth dipped in blood, a wild look in his eyes as he announced, "Today's the day, my friend. Let's get you up and dressed for the full moon tonight!"

It took me a bit to notice there was only silence. The keening, the drumming, the throbbing of insects was all gone. The sun was shining when Bennett hoisted me into his arms as if I was nothing and carried me to the stream a mile away. There, he tenderly placed me into the shallow edge of the water and bathed me quite like one would a child. As he held me in the cold water, me shivering despite the fever burning through my blood, sluicing water over my body with a cupped hand, I stuttered, "What happened to the Indians?"

"The savages were politely asked to leave. And, they've obliged."

Bennett leaned over my right shoulder to look me in the eye, "We needed the quiet, you and I. For our ceremony."

"But the slaves?" I checked the tree line around us, my

eyes wild with heat. "Have been reminded of their place and won't bother us again." I caught his smile from the blurry corner of my vision.

"Ceremony?" I slurred belatedly. It was as if his voice was coming to me through one of those long ear-funnels I'd seen the gentry use in London.

"I mean, it's not really necessary." He shrugged, lifting me effortlessly from the water and gently laying me on the grass, my skin exposed to the weak rays of the spring sun. Shaking his wet hair, his dripping clothes sticking to his hairless, juvenile body, he settled beside me, leaning over me to hear me speak.

"Not?" I repeated hoarsely, hope flaring for just a moment between my delirium. Perhaps? Perhaps.

"You're already transforming, can't you feel it? It only took proximity. I only had share myself. Get close to you. Breathe the same air. Drink the same water from the same cup."

I struggled to raise my head. I was so very weak. I could only make out one word.

"Transforming?" I repeated.

"Yes!" Bennett swiveled about to face the water, a look of absolute ecstasy on his face. "You are transforming, Henry. I thought you knew." He looked up at the sky, shielding his eyes with the back of his soft hand, fervently searching the clouds. When he spotted what he was looking for, he relaxed.

"There she is!"

I tried to stare up at the sky, but the sunlight blinded me, splitting my head into pieces with its light. I closed my eyes. When I opened them, Bennett was poised over me - a smile on his lips, his sharp teeth glistening and white. He positioned his face directly over mine, obscuring my view. Lifting his head to peer down at me, he used those sharp teeth to puncture his bottom lip, the blood welling up in quick bubbles. I could see my reflection in the red and black swirls dripping from the needle points of his incisors. Mesmerized, I only whimpered when he lowered his lips to mine, a kiss so sensuous and salty, his tongue raking my eyeteeth through my protests, my weak push against his chest futile.

With that – with the brush of his bloodied lips against my own - he pulled back, his eyes affixed to mine. He licked his bottom lip, a self-satisfied grin turning the corners of his mouth as he turned back to the water, away from me.

"There!" he declared nonchalantly, "Now, you're well and truly infected. Not that I had any doubt before. Look at you." He stared down at me, a moue of pity on his lips. "You'll thank me one day, Henry. You never have to be this pathetic again." He shook his head, "You never have to be weak like this again." He got up, his shadow falling across my naked body. "The ceremony is just a formality – to show you who you are now. So you know what you can do. We'd better get you dressed. I can't wait to show you what I found while I was looking for supplies."

He picked me up as if I were a brace of wood and carried me back to the fort. A magnificent collection of finery was laid out on the one plank table we'd cobbled together. He propped me on the bench before it to admire the pieces after first wrapping me in our only quilt.

Bennett motioned to the jewelry, bird bone chest plate, crockery, silken ties and stockings, several gold nuggets, a beaver hat speckled with dried blood, a silver rosary (the kind only priests wore), several woolen chemises and two stained pantaloons made of twill. A repository of the dead, I realized. All the treasures Bennet had collected on the voyage over - and since. Hands shaking, my racing brain suddenly awake from my terrific daze, I fingered the Indian chest plate, lifting my eyes to meet Bennet's.

He shrugged, gesturing to the goods in front of me. "Take your pick. You should look your best for the ceremony. I think I'll wear this."

He grabbed the rosary, chuckling, and placed it around his neck. He turned to the rickety chest in the corner of the room we'd used for storage and pulled out a clean cambric shirt, which he tossed to me. I was still so physically weak I could barely pull the shirt over my head. Bennet helped tie the sleeves on and pulled me up, sliding a pair of brown pantaloons over my calves and up to my waist. Hands on my shoulders, Bennet pulled me to stand.

"You look good," he assessed with a nod. "The sun will be setting soon. I'll make some tea."

He left me on the bench and went off to shuffle about in another room, humming and clinking a pewter spoon against a wooden bowl and cup to prepare the aforementioned tea. I willed myself to stand and tiptoed slowly, painfully, toward the open door...if I could just make it to the trees, past the swinging slaves and into the shade of the forest where I could lay down and hide... Ignoring my failing legs and my burning brain, I painstakingly placed one foot in front of the other until the world became black and slid away. I heard a soft thud as I hit the ground, my body seemingly falling through it and floating down to nothingness. I thought that meant I'd made it and I congratulated myself as everything moved away from the now.

Pink-pink-pink. Clang. A moan. Was that me? I was moaning? Cold water hit my face and there was Bennett grinning down at me, the wooden cup still in his hand, a porcelain mug full of tea in the other. The sun had set and there was only a small, hot fire and one sputtering candle for light.

"Won't do you any good," Bennet proclaimed cheerily, setting his tea down carefully and pulling me to my feet like you'd

lift a water bucket. Dripping, contrite, resolved to my fate once more, I joined Bennet on the bench when he patted the seat beside him and assured me, "Oh, Henry. I'm not going to hurt you. You are...special. Didn't anyone ever tell you that? You're a watcher, not a doer. I like that. The world needs more people to watch it burn."

He reached into the fire pit in front of us, pulling out a burning ember with his bare hand – a look of amusement on his face as he opened his palm in front of me. "I like to set things on fire."

The coal winked with blue and white flames that pulsed in and around it before he tossed it into the pile of bed scraps we'd built up in the corner of the small room for him. The kindling of the cotton scraps popped and smoked before almost immediately bursting into yellow flames. My instinct to danger was always to flee; but, as I ordered my legs to rise up and move, Bennett placed a strong hand on my thigh.

"No," he ordered, pulling me back down beside him, "this is part of the ceremony. Don't you see? This is how I show you who you are now. First, there was water. Now, there's fire. You should be happy I'm doing it this way. What the Tiger did to me was so much worse."

As the flames licked closer and closer to our feet and traveled behind the flaming bedclothes, up the rough pine logs of the wall, I felt the heat building inside me and out. The fever cracked my head with throbbing paroxysms of pain. The fire behind my eyes mirrored the fire at my feet, now devouring the walls, scorching the hair of my arms as it breathed into life like a roaring dragon.

Still, Bennett held me in place. The rotting thatch of the roof gave way in a whoosh of sparks, falling onto my clothes, which promptly caught fire. Strangely, I heard Bennett's voice over the cacophony of the flames. He looked up, a wild look of exhilaration in his eyes as he chanted three lines over and over.

It was a language I'd never heard before and have never heard since. Maybe it was made up? Again and again, he repeated the three lines, stringing the words together until they became one word, louder and louder, rising over the rushing inferno of the fire around us. My skin blistered under the waves of heat and flames and I watched the fabric burn from my legs, yet I strangely felt no pain. This must be what death is like, I thought. At last, one mystery solved. This is death, I thought, as the fire consumed me and I heard Bennett's voice, louder and louder.

As I had the sensation of my hair catching afire, the burned fibers of it lifting up with the maelstrom of wind funneling through the open doorway and up through the collapsed timbers of the roof, I saw the glint of a wicked looking blade - a curved blade like that of a scimitar - the orange flames and my shocked expression mirrored in it's silver tip. Bennett brought the knife down and I saw it protruding from my chest and, as the blood seeped into my lungs, he stood - his own clothes afire, his own hair burning.

"I'll see you, my brother," he shouted over the din as if taking leave of me in some pub. Without another glance back, he walked through the burning fort and into the night. I fell back, the darkness mounting in my corner vision, aware my clothes had burned and my blackened skin was about to burst like a roasting pig. I stared down at the blade in my chest, choking on my own blood, one last chuckle rising in my throat at the calamity of my end. I realized as I faded away, Bennett was right – it hadn't hurt. He'd at least been right about that.

The next morning, I awoke. I woke to hear the birds chirping, the remains of the fort smoking still. Yet I was alive and whole. Snowflakes fell around me, brushing lightly on my cheeks and I thought for just a moment, I was home in England, a boy still. But then, I tasted the sulfur on my lips as the warm breeze blew over my exposed skin and I opened my eyes to realize the snowflakes were just ashes. They were ashes…because the world had burned around me. I was still there. And it was…beautiful.

The End.

When she turned the final page, Gloria realized her little mystery was quite solved. It was Henry, every time.

Henry had set this whole thing in motion to get to her.

Everyone who had died, died because of her. And now, she would die. Or, be damned to eternal life. *With sagging boobs.*

Gloria held the pages against her chest and cried herself to sleep. This time when she dreamed, she dreamed of fires burning on the dark horizon, outlining the pine forest beyond her property line in their dancing flames, the shadows of sleek tigers prowling the trees behind her home and the sound of drums in the distance.

Chapter 47

Gloria bolted awake, the pages scattering around her on the bed as she pushed herself up, breathing raggedly, the warm yellow glow of her lamp casting looming shadows in the room.

"Gloria!" she heard him whisper. Henry! She knew she'd heard her name. It's what woke her from her restless dreams.

She knew she wasn't thinking straight but couldn't remember why that was, breaking into a sweat, shrinking from the grasping claws of dementia…knowing it had come for her at last. That dark shadow running wickedly through her family's blood. Perhaps it was psychosomatic, but Henry's story and her own life were beginning to blur together. She had moments where she knew the two timelines merged and ran parallel, with the one being told the story growing weaker as the other grew stronger from telling the tale. But it was all fuzzy now, that thread.

She gathered the pages, compulsively reorganizing them back into a neat stack, fingering the sharp edges of the pages before placing Henry's manuscript on the worn cushion of the reading chair at her bedside. Glancing out the window to ensure Casey's sturdy presence parked beneath her pecan tree (likely sleeping himself), she changed into a fresh night shirt, sliding back to the center of her cold bed, almost immediately falling into another deep and restless slumber.

When her eyes slid open, she saw the blurry outline of a man sitting quietly and calmly in her bedside chair, the chilly light of dawn outlining his red hair gold, his face a blob of pink with a slash of red in the center, her vision still occluded by sleep and farsightedness. Gloria blinked to clear her vision, fear paralyzing her body.

His head lifted, his eyes meeting hers. The young man cleared his throat, holding up a section of Henry's manuscript, the rest laid carefully across his lap. "Well, good morning you!" He greeted her, his lips tipped into a confident, pleasant smile - as if he were walking past her at the bank. He laughed jovially, reading from the page dangling in his fingers with his peculiar accent, his tone mocking, "*I kept thinking I should run. Then, the eternal beating of the tom tom drums and the shouts from the slaves and Indians alike would convince me there was nowhere to run. Now that he'd spoken and told me my fate, Bennett kept up a lively patter of conversation.*" Bringing a hand to his heart, he looked up, his mouth scrunching into a pout, "Aw, can you believe it? He's writing about me! I'm flattered."

Gloria's eyes darted around the room in alarm.

The boy followed her gaze, waving her off with a petulant moan, "Don't worry. I have no current plans to hurt you."

He studied her, his eyes moving over her body as she clutched the sheets futilely under her chin, regarding him with a mixture of stubborn courage and frightened curiosity. Tilting his head as he spoke, his melodic accent filling the room, he went on, "It's not a perfect science."

He placed the excerpted page back onto the stack before suddenly hurling the entire manuscript across the room, the pages exploding against the wall and fluttering down before Gloria's wide eyes. He continued as if he hadn't just lashed out.

"It's not a perfect science, this thing we have inside us. This," he paused, grimacing in distaste, "virus? Maybe? A germ? A seed? It doesn't always take. Or sometimes, it does. But the person is just...too…weak. They have the wrong blood, maybe the wrong genes? I don't know. Henry understands all of that better than I do. And they die. You could die, Gloria. You could still die. Or you could do yourself a favor and kill yourself now, before it's too late."

The boy got up and Gloria noted how unexpectedly tall and gangly he was, seeming so compact while nestled in her reading chair like a viper. He unwound his body and continued while pacing the small room, "It's up to you. I mean, it's really not so bad, this. But you're already old as fuck," he enjoyed a *genuine, hearty laugh here*, "so, I have my reservations - on your behalf. I don't know that *I'd* want to be trapped in that decrepit bag you call a body until the end of days. I don't *think* I would. But hey," he shrugged, coming to stand beside the bed, his gaze almost compassionate as he hovered over her, filling her field of vision with his youthful visage. Gloria opened her mouth to reply though nothing came out as the boy went on, his voice growing stronger, admonishing, "Henry should have thought about that, huh? He's rather selfish, isn't he? This brother of mine. Then to go and run away, leaving you to straighten all this out for him. All this trouble he's gotten himself into. Leaving you like this. F*or her*."

Is that what happened? Gloria didn't correct him.

"There's still a third option, you know. If you want all of this to go away." He let the words hang innocently in the air before explaining, "You could get my knife and kill Henry. That *could* do the trick, if you do it soon. Set you free, back on your boring mortal path to death and decomposition. I bet he hasn't told you that, has he? Well, something to think about."

With that, he stepped back, took a deep breath and bowed courteously in Gloria's direction, "You're still very weak, Gloria. I'll be back when you're stronger. Maybe then you'll feel like telling me where your little boyfriend went." He turned, taking a last glance at the pages scattered across the room, cocking his head and asking snidely, "Did Henry really write that? He couldn't even sign his name when I met him. It's good." Nodding in approval, the young man slipped from the room without a sound.

Gloria blinked, closing her eyes and re-opening them several times to ensure she was truly alone. Her head was fuzzy and pounding with fever, but she managed to push back the covers and throw on her robe.

"Casey," she rapped noisily on his half-opened passenger window. Casey startled, the distinct sound of a fart emanating in the cushioned quiet of dawn, the only other sound the distant cawing of morning birds.

"Whozit?" He mumbled wearily, struggling to push himself up in his seat.

"Casey," Gloria shouted, "did you see him? Wake up!"

"Who?" Casey stumbled out of the cruiser, searching for his gun. "Henry?"

"No," Gloria protested, "There was young man in my room. Just now. He was sitting there when I woke up."

Casey clicked his radio, barking a series of letters and words into it.

"Are you hurt?" Casey demanded brusquely.

"No," she shook her head, "but he about scared me to death."

"What did he do?" Casey pushed, visually scanning the parameters of Gloria's property as he questioned her.

"He…he read to me," Gloria admitted in a feeble voice. Casey paused his search as Gloria went on more confidently, "And he said he was Henry's brother. And…that I was too old to be a vampire."

Casey rocked back on his heels, sucking his teeth while eyeing Gloria critically, "That so? Like one of those stories the kids in your classes write? Like the one you were reading before you fell asleep?" He looked down at her, his expression laced with pity, immediately infuriating Gloria.

"He was just here, Casey. I didn't dream it. And I didn't imagine it."

"Is there any physical proof?"

Several minutes later, as Casey stared dispassionately over the scattered pages of Henry's manuscript, the sheets tossed errantly across the far side of the room, Gloria felt the first trickles of doubt flit through her mind. The room *had* been dark. But he'd been *right there*…talking to her in that strange, melodious voice, his tone dripping in turn with sarcasm and poorly concealed jealousy.

"This it?" Casey lifted his eyebrows in exasperation.

"It's…what I have?" Gloria winced, the steam of her conviction waning.

Casey eyed the disintegration of her bedroom: the pill caddy, sleeping pills, tissues and other detritus of illness littering her personal space where she'd lain delirious, feverish and fitfully dreaming for the better part of the week. It was a dank and depressing place to land, doilies and all, Gloria realized with a start, the general feeling of malaise that had crippled her for weeks lifting like a fog. It was as if she could almost feel the color coming back into her cheeks…and smell the room… which was musty and stale.

Casey spun around to face her, demanding, "Did you call that specialist, Glory? I'm starting to worry about you. I know they said it was just your thyroid, but can *that* do *this*?" Casey headed for the bedroom door, advising gently, "Glor, I think you're having a harder time with this whole situation than you're willing to admit. Perhaps even to yourself."

"I didn't imagine him! There *was* a boy. He was *right here*," she shouted, her voice hoarse and cracking, pointing vehemently to the chair beside her nightstand.

"And yet," Casey tossed a dismissive glance over his shoulder, "he was able to get out without being seen, without a conveyance. No bike, no car, no man on foot," he sighed. "Ah, I see. Vampire, right? Jeez Glory, I'm starting to think you might need to see that specialist sooner rather than later. Has it occurred to you on any level that *this* is starting to sound a lot like one of your stories? I'm starting to *hope* this is real, for your sake."

He left without another glance, slamming Gloria's screen door as he exited. Shortly after, Gloria heard the crunch of his tires on gravel as he returned home…or back to the station…or wherever the Casey's of the world went when they weren't doing their jobs poorly. Gloria's head ached and she wobbled on her feet. Maybe she wasn't feeling better after all. She eyes the pills on the nightstand. Perhaps she had been taking too much?

Her eyes traveled longingly over the scattered pages of Henry's manuscript. She'd never get back to sleep. *She* knew she hadn't imagined Bennet, no matter what Casey thought. She wasn't losing her mind! And if *Bennet* existed, that meant everything Henry had said about his past was true as well. And she was in deep shit.

Too old to be immortal? Now, that stung.

Chapter 48

"I'm so glad you're feeling better," Dee clinked her plastic wine glass into Gloria's. "You are, aren't you? You look better."

"Thanks. I guess?" Gloria winced at the back-handed compliment, "And yes, I do. Definitely. Better than I have in years though I keep getting these waves of exhaustion and fever. I'm pretty sure its malaria." She held the back of her hand dramatically to her forehead.

"Nooooooo," Dee babbled through sips of her pinot, "those doctors did all those tests. They said your recovery could be long and slow. Thyroids are the assholes of the organ world."

Gloria nodded, her eyes filling with unshed tears, though Dee was too busy guzzling to notice her friend's obvious distress. Gloria had struggled with herself greatly since the morning two days prior when she awoke to a phantom lecturing her from her bedside. She'd stopped taking all of her more sedative medications, vigorously cleaning the house while throwing every window open to freshen the air, retracing and replaying the encounter in her mind over and over until she'd convinced herself Bennet was just a hallucination, like Deputy Cash said, still stinging from the pity in Casey's eyes when he realized the true extent of her physical and mental decline.

"I do need to talk to you though, Dee. It's serious. I'm scared." Gloria admitted, pulling Henry's manuscript from her oversized purse.

"Well, you aren't wrong," Dee stated, perusing the pages, squinting an eye to better read, "he is a good writer. So?"

"Dee," Gloria swatted her friend's knee, the hysteria in her voice rising as she proclaimed, "I need your help with this. Talk me back to reality because I'm suddenly dealing with what seems to be some rather unreal shit. And either I'm losing my mind or… Henry's story is…true? It's real, Dee - and, oh my God – I can't believe I'm saying this, I'm going to be one of the undead."

The sting of Dee's palm across the apple of Gloria's cheek startled her from her spiral.

"You feel that?"

"Yes."

"You're not dead." Dee rationalized dryly, pointing to the story, "This. This is a story. A good one, sure, but you're a smart woman, Glory. You have to know this isn't real. Henry is a liar and a most likely a murderer."

"But…I dreamed the same dream about the tiger…"

"Nope!" Dee held her hand up to silence Gloria's rebuttal.

"But I've had the same illne-"

"Nope!" Dee's hand flew up again, palm forward signaling Gloria to stop, "You've been sick and that's all. Very normal."

"But, Bennet-"

"Not a real person. Dream. Cough-medicine dream," Dee crossed her arms across her chest and glared at Gloria, her neck craned dramatically.

As Dee picked up Henry's story to make a point, a stiff envelope fell out from between the back pages of the stack. Gloria reached out to pull it from Dee's lap, but Dee's hand moved faster, pulling the square photo from the envelope with an exaggerated flourish, "Well, well, well, what is this?"

Gloria scrunched her forehead, struggling to recall where she'd gotten it. "I forgot I'd put that…"

"Ah! Ha! Will you look at that," Dee murmured, her eyes

travelling down the glossy reflective photo as she tapped her lip with her forefinger, muttering, "Yesteryear 1961! Where am I?"

Ah! Gloria remembered with a flood of relief. It was just the photo Lenny brought her the day she got sick. She must have scooped it up with the pages from Henry's story, buried by grocery store circulars in the mess of her home.

"Oh, I see *you*. So cute. Let's see. I see Momma Dottie. Gawd, she was so pretty." Dee reached for her purse, "I need to get my magnifier."

Gloria took the opportunity to snatch the photo from Dee, holding it directly in front of her eyes. In the birds-eye shot of Main Street, she quickly located her young self, a rush of nostalgia sweeping over her as she scrutinized the wild curls, the dress and knee socks of her youth. She couldn't have been more than three or four. Standing somewhat alone, brothers nowhere in sight, Dottie, larger than life, standing a good two feet away, one hand shielding her eyes from the sun. Gloria petulantly scanned the parade goers for the outline of her father, as if she might recognize some man in the shot from the blurry picture in her mind.

But Henry…she saw Henry the moment she allowed herself to see him. In the sepia tinged black and white photo - probably one of the first taken for the fledgling newspaper in the fall of 1961 - there he was! Standing directly across the street from her child self, his eyes very clearly pointed in her direction. And her mother…she was looking directly back at him, a smile in her eyes and on her lips.

"Gloria," Dee seemed to say from very far away, a hollow snapping of her fingers, close enough Gloria could feel the reverberations on her cheek, "Gloria, what is it?"

The photo dropped from her fingertips as Gloria slumped into Dee's lap, a blanket of darkness enveloping her. When she came to, it was dark and quiet. There was a sliver of light from Dee's kitchen and the familiar ting-ting-ting of tea being prepared. She'd obviously driven herself too hard after her illness. She pushed herself up, the photo sticking to her hand as she placed it on the couch to steady herself. Remembering everything with a rush of fear, she grabbed the photo, peering down intently. As she thought – there she was, there was Dottie and right there – there was…some guy? Was that Henry? It could have been, she told herself. But then, the photo *was* slightly unfocused as if taken by amateur hands. She had to admit, it could have been anyone upon second glance. She looked again, squinting to soften her gaze. It was Henry, wasn't it?

She felt like she was going mad.

"Teatime!" Dee sang out, entering the room with two steaming mugs that smelled like peppermint. "Rise and shine, my friend! Let's have this sleepy tea and hit the hay. Drive home in the morning. Tonight, you have the most comfortable couch in the world. And you're in luck! Troy's working the night shift. So, you don't even have to share!"

Chapter 49

Gloria thought she would have to cancel her class again. Yet miraculously, her sudden fever and lightheadedness abated after several hours in a cool, dark room, the fan blowing as she took a fitful nap.

"Gloria."

Waking, she heard her name clear as day, bolting upright in the heat of the late afternoon sun, her throat raw and dry from the whooshing fan. The room was empty.

Tears wet her eyes. She was going mad. She heard Henry say her name as if he'd been right there, curled behind her while she slept. And she ached to feel his arms around her again. Sometimes she thought…if he'd just come back, they could go on, never mentioning this strange interlude in life when he was accused of murder, a fugitive at large and a self-proclaimed vampire; or, when she lost her mind, succumbing to post-menopausal madness and paranoia. They could just go on, like they had been before.

Now, her hair a mess, her makeup minimal, her shirt askew, she stood before her disbanded, reassembled and *much smaller* creative writing class, nervously explaining the continued, pervasive health concerns which prevented her from sending so much as a single email during her convalescence. Though everyone here had since heard the truth of it. Their teacher first had sex with a much younger protégé (a fellow student, no less), then helped said protégé (now a suspected serial murderer) flee town and evade the stubby arms of the local law. It was almost more shocking to Gloria there weren't extra students here to experience the spectacle of her return.

"OK, welcome. Let's just pick up exactly where we let off, hopefully everyone has made some headway into their narrative. So…let's get back to business, shall we?"

The door in the back of the musty classroom creaked open. Gloria ignored the late comer, assuming it was the youngish girl with the short, green hair who arrived late every single class, casually requesting, "Who wants to read first?"

"I'd like to take a stab at it, if I may."

Gloria's heart dropped. She could never forget that sing-song accent - the youthful voice dripping with malice - as Bennet went on, leaning out from behind a student in front before standing, revealing himself fully. The other students seemed more curious than leery of this unannounced, new pupil with the balls to not only speak up, but volunteer to read during his very first class.

"I know I'm new to class, but I've read the synopsis. I have a first-person story to read, if you don't mind."

The class watched in quiet amazement as Gloria fell apart and recomposed her expression within the span of half a second,

"And you are?"

"Call me…Ben," Bennet strode to the front of the class in three powerful steps, asserting himself confidently behind the ornate pulpit as Gloria stepped aside. The students were transfixed by the young man pacing in front of them like a caged tiger, his flashing eyes scanning the converted bible school classroom with approval.

He began a slow clap, looking into the eyes of each student as he spoke in his melodic voice, "And everybody, please, a round of applause for our esteemed teacher! I'm sure…you being here to learn from the best…I'm sure you all know who *she* is? The… Gloria…Weidman? A writer the Atlantic Monthly once claimed *gave us the feminist punch in the face we didn't know we needed."*

The class, who had been smiling and nodding as Bennet lauded their respected teacher, grew collectively concerned, the corners of their mouths dropping as his tone turned mocking. Only his unfamiliar accent and odd bearing kept them questioning their own instincts as he continued, his hands slapping together in slow staccato.

"Eh? No one? OK! I'll go on, then. This is…what would you call it? Fan fiction, if you will. A story set in the same universe as *your pal Henry's* tall tale." He paused, winking at Gloria and clearing his throat, shuffling a small stack of typed pages he'd produced from his back pocket, the crease folding them into a vee. He straightened the pages, peering around the room expectantly while the students waited with unbridled anticipation tinged with mounting fear as this harmless looking boy effortlessly took the class captive and began to read.

I smelled honeysuckle first, then the clean scent of the ocean breeze that carried it. Salt and sweat and honeysuckle, mixed with the midday sun. So fresh I could taste her before I ever saw her.

I was surprised then when she broke into the clearing, unaware of my lowly presence, fixed between the trees as I was, invisible as always. I thought from her smell she'd be golden. All spun gold, radiance and feminine lace. Not this sly fox, slinking along the deserted coastline on some hidden errand. The wind picked up, blowing her drab, clenched cloak from her head and I gasped aloud. She must have heard me. I froze as her she tilted her head, her snub tipped nose - sprinkled with freckles - turned up and sniffed the air.

And her hair! The most curious plum colored hair. I was transfixed. She stopped, the air vibrating around her lithe form, balancing gracefully on the ball of one leather clad foot before leaping across the sand, up past the sharp lashes of the cattails into the dark trees lining the beach.

And to think, I'd only meant to find my brother here in this godforsaken scrap of a settlement. Then, to stumble upon this! Her. His. I recognized the scent of honeysuckle from the border of his cabin, I knew that smell already from my surveillance. I just hadn't seen…her. I hadn't known She existed yet. But, I did now. And I couldn't look away if I tried.

I thought I was the hunter. But, when she came to a clearing, a clearing quite obviously used before for her dark purposes - the bones and talismans hanging from the tree, the debased carcass of what was once a cat, the weathered offerings beneath a melted tallow candle - she paused, kneeling beneath the frightening effigy. An alter of sorts. Now, I was in love. What was this slip of a child goading dark gods to do her bidding doing in this place full of buttoned puritans? A viper in a pit of molding bread? Tilting her head, her sharp nose sniffed the air once more before she looked directly at me where I perched in the low branch of a mighty oak.

"I know chou're dere. You can come out now, sir." Her voice, though husky, had a pleasing eastern European lilt to it. I felt it in my toes when she spoke. "And I know full well what ye are so you can dispense wif der niceties."

I landed beside her and suddenly, she was raking me brazenly with her amethyst eyes, which glittered as she surveyed her prey. Who was this magnificent creature and where had she been my whole life? Her cold appraisal made my cock quite hard and that hadn't happened in eons.

"Yer brother has gone and he's nah coming back, I don't think. A coward, he is." She went on, "But, I've seen ye watching him. I've heard of ye.

My slave Birch, her people spoke of you my entire life. The eaters of the world.

The ghosts of Roanoke...who never die? I've been told that yer blood is for sale.

Is that true? Could I trade my soul for a drop?"

And that was it. I was lost in her web, I forgot my reason to be. It was true. I'd stuck around this miserable country for decades. Far longer than I should. Because of him. Because I fancied we'd eventually reunite and make a proper family. I came to this new world with my brother. The only man who ever loved me without brutality. The only man who ever really looked out for me unbidden in my entire life.

We long to be loved. To be captive to someone else in this world. Beholden. Yet, we then hate ourselves for being human. For being weak. That this person's existence now makes us weaker still. We hate that person then, for being our binding. For holding us. We hate what we cannot have and then when we have it, we think it's too easily had. And we hate it anew. Because love should be a struggle, after all. We want it. We get it. We hate it. And we destroy the world trying to free ourselves from its bonds. Like a serpent eating its own tail. Over and over. And now, because of her, we start again.

Bennet finished, bowing his head dramatically before gliding out of the classroom door without another word. Confused and intimidated, the students clapped lightly, their applause tapering to awkward silence. Gloria stood, her eyes glued to Bennett's back until she heard his footfalls down the tile hallway and the clank of the exterior door slamming shut.

“Class, I’d love to hear more. But with that, I think we’re out of time,” she breezed airily, as if ending class early were of no consequence.

“But we haven’t finished-,” one of the long-time students protested.

Her brain had shut down. There was no way she could go on teaching.

“Was that really Henry’s friend?” another chimed in.

“I think we should call the police,” added one of the more mature students.

“Out of time!” Gloria sang out cheerfully, “I’ll see you all next Wednesday. We’ll get to more of you then.”

She waved her hands while the students gathered their belongings, filing out sporting looks of moderate confusion. She needed to get the students away and herself safely to her car, so she could drive straight to the police station to report this. She didn’t know *who* this boy *really* was, but she knew she wasn’t safe now. And Henry wasn’t here to protect her anymore.

Chapter 50

Gloria gathered her papers and notebook, holding her bag tight against her body to exit with the last of the students, mingling innocently in their ranks as they scattered across the small, deserted parking lot for their cars. She tried not to look for Bennet. To do that would show she had something to be afraid of and she wanted to show everyone she wasn't afraid. Bennet said he wouldn't hurt her when he'd appeared at her bedside that night. Or rather, he'd said he wouldn't hurt her, *yet*.

The parking lot *seemed* devoid of vampires. She sped-walked to her car, heart pounding, dredging the bottom of her oversized bag for her pepper spray and keys. *Why* had she parked so far away, convinced the extra steps would do her good. Exhaling audibly as she reached her car, Gloria slid into the cool interior, engaging the locks with shaking hands. She sat for a beat, willing her body to stop trembling. He was gone, for the moment. And, he was just some kid, she reassured herself. Some *friend* of Henry's, up to no good. Someone Henry knew. Or some deranged acquaintance who knew a few things about Henry's story. That was it. This boy was no more immortal than she was. She just needed to get home and call Casey to report this.

She waved as the last of the students pulled onto Main Street, the weak light of the sun shrinking to a line on the horizon, just as her engine turned over and the air conditioner wheezed, air flowing over her sweating skin. The engine coughed, puttered, almost choking, purring back to life as she held her breath, her foot hovering over the gas. There was a thump on the metal hood and in the next moment, glass rained over her in a sparkling shower. It took a second to register the glass came from the windshield; now an open cavity beyond which Bennett perched like a bird on the concave hood of her car, his forearms resting neatly on his thighs as he squatted, peering into the dimly lit interior of Gloria's car with unsettling, cold curiosity.

Gloria struggled from her seat belt, her hands fumbling with the door handle, pushing the door open to flee. The door slammed shut, the force of it pushing her back into the seat, the driver's side window imploding inward. In a flash, his hands were on her neck, pulling her up and out of the side window, her pants ripping as glass raked her skin. He tossed her scratched and bleeding body onto the cracked pavement where she caught herself with her battered palms just before her face struck the ground.

Everything in her body hurt and stung. Gloria shook her head to clear it – a whooshing sound in her ears, her vision narrowing to a small tunnel, her skin numb from shock. She pushed herself into a sitting position from the ground using what little energy she had left to lift her head.

Bennet stood over her sporting a look of vague amusement.

"Where is he?" he whispered, his eyebrows raised.

Gloria pushed herself to stand, ignoring the blood dripping from her legs and arms. She grit her teeth."He's not here."

"Oh, he is," Bennet responded with a knowing smile, glancing up at the sky. When he found what he was looking for he continued, "I can always feel him now. Who do you think that performance was for?" He winked.

"For whom," Gloria corrected him between a wave of stinging pain.

Bennet cocked his head, "What was that?"

"I said…for…whom…do you think…I…performed," Gloria corrected slowly, her eyes boring into Bennet's.

Her head flew back as his hand snaked out, striking her cheek. Somehow, this time, Gloria didn't feel the sting, pausing for a moment before turning back to face Bennet, her eyes steely and focused, a trickle of blood salting her tongue.

Bennet smiled at her defiance. "I usually don't hurt women," he explained with a wave of his hands. "But I find you tedious, Gloria Weidman."

Gloria used his moment of reflection to make a run for her car, still idling nearby. Before she took a second step, Bennet was behind her, pushing her cruelly to the ground, looming over her, his eyes flashing in anger.

"I hope you didn't break a hip," he spat. "Normally, I wouldn't bother. But you've really tested me on this one. I *just* want to know where your little boyfriend *went* with my *wife*."

"Sounds like she was his wife first," Gloria countered, pushing herself to her knees. Bennet stared down dispassionately as Gloria scrambled to her feet. This time, she didn't wobble. And it didn't hurt. Bennet didn't seem to notice, *but Gloria had.* She suddenly felt stronger, as if her mounting fury fed her strength. She stood, meeting Bennet's eyes - her fear dissipating like steam. Her mind solidified. She wasn't afraid now that she could think clearly again.

"I don't know where he is, but if you kill me, you'll never find Liesl," Gloria advised coldly.

"I have no plans to kill you Gloria," Bennet smiled, the sharp needle points of his teeth glistening in the bright moonlight. "But, I do plan on resurrecting you."

Before Gloria could scream, before her brain could order her legs to run, Bennet's hand shot out, his long fingers wrapping around her neck as he taunted her, "I want you to wonder, while you live forever like this," the other hand motioned to Gloria's body, "just *who* you *really* belong to."

As she struggled for air in his firm grasp, her wide eyes on his face, he pushed those sharp, shining white teeth into the pink flesh of his lower lip, the blackish red blood pooling in orbs around the wounds. Gloria could see herself reflected in his blood, a honey hive of her own frightened eyes staring back at her as Bennet lowered his lips to hers.

Suddenly, he wasn't there. He was on the ground some distance away and a small, lithe young woman was there, her brilliant plum hair smooth and flowing, her body encased in tight black leather pants and a matching jacket, wearing black motorcycle boots that gave her unearned stature as she hovered over Bennet's inert form like a pale, vengeful angel.

"Liesl," Gloria croaked, staring up at the young woman in awe.

Liesl gave her a cheeky wink, planting herself firmly over Bennet's prone form, kicking him viciously in greeting. He coughed, springing upright with a twinkle in his eye, his fanged teeth bared in a great smile.

"Aaaaawwww," Bennet exaggerated a frown, shaking grass and leaves from his hair, "looks like we've still got that magic-"

His head flew back as Liesl's fist found his chin with a deafening thwack. Bennet kicked out so rapidly, Gloria never saw his foot before Liesl's body crashed into hers, pushing her back into the moist loam of the dirt and smashing the air from Gloria's body with an oomph.

"I missed you," Bennet crooned, steadying himself on his feet.

Liesl scrambled off Gloria, pushing herself up to block

Gloria from Bennet's eyeline.

Bennet gestured around himself tyrannically, "I'm so glad I finally found you! I've been looking for you. I've been crazy without you, Liebchen. *Look* at all these people you've made me hurt. For you, darling! To find you. To help you."

"Let's be clear, I left on purpose." Liesl countered, centering herself like a boxer, "And *that* - is the language of an abuser."

"It's *been* twenty years," Bennet rolled his eyes.

"The best twenty years of my life," Liesl countered.

The humor fled Bennet's face. The energy between the two immortals crackled with tension. Struggling to steady herself, Gloria backed away on silent feet, her pulse pounding so loud in her ears she thought surely she'd feel Bennet's cold fingers around her neck once again. And this time, she'd never get away.

The sight of her fear-filled eyes reflected back to her in the black blood of Bennet's lips - a witness to her own end - played over and over in her mind. The fear numbed her now, her limbs moving like frozen, unwieldly blocks attached to her breathless torso. She lurched to her car, concentrating on putting one foot in front of the other, her vision narrowing to a tiny point as she went.

"I knew you would come here," she heard Liesl inform Bennet behind her, the tinny vocal fry of her uniquely American voice carrying through the heavy air, "for Henry. I read your whole stupid journal. What a fucking bore. But interesting, because I could have sworn you told me you'd *killed* Henry. And now, I can finally kill *you* for every shitty thing you've done since."

"What?" Bennet held his hand to his heart, feigning outrage. "What did I do to you except give you exactly what you wanted, Liesl? Or don't *you* remember seducing *me*?"

With a scream, Liesl launched herself at Bennet, barreling

forward with the speed of a train. Bennet nimbly sidestepped her, sending her sliding through the rotting leaves littering the ground beneath the trees along the border of the aging parking lot, a deep slash of orange earth appearing behind her half-buried body.

"Oopsie," Bennet cackled, landing with a poof of air beside Liesl's inert form just as her head popped up and she scrambled to her knees, shaking the debris from her hair like a wet dog.

Gloria kept turning back, forcing her eyes from the fantastical conflict, over to her salvation - her car - just a few feet away! She limped back along the grey lip of the asphalt, dragging her mangled left leg behind her, surveying the damage to her sputtering vehicle with a defeated shrug before swinging open the dented car door with an exhausted groan of impatience. Sweeping the glass from the seat before turning back a final time, her eyes strained to see the combatant shadows through the blue twilight, her weak headlights blinding her to the details of their struggle.

She convinced herself to go, to leave Liesl, as her eyes fell to the open glove box, the small pearl-handled pistol Dee pressed into her hands weeks before - peeking out of its street map saddle. "*Take it*," Dee had said then, as Gloria protested. "*Use it if he shows back up.*" Though Dee meant for her to use it on Henry. Armed, Gloria slid over the gear shift to the other side of the car, creeping silently out her passenger side door. Bracing her forearm over the trunk of the car, she squinted. attempting to distinguish between the sparring silhouettes.

Bennet sprang atop Liesl, pinning her shoulders to the ground with his knees as she bucked and struggled. "I didn't want to do this!" Bennet shouted, spittle dripping onto Liesl's face. "I don't want to kill you, my love."

In the blinding full radiance of the setting sun, Gloria couldn't be sure where Bennet ended and Liesl began.

Liesl flinched, stilling beneath him, threatening, "But I would love to kill you, my darling."

"Don't say that, Liesl. I could never hurt you," Bennet's hands tightened around the girl's pale throat. Gloria froze, the bruises around her own neck aching as she watched Liesl struggle, flailing as her small hands pushed and pulled at Bennet's fingers, "I only wanted you to stay with me. I love you, Liesl. You are my wife and my child. You can never be free."

"You…have serious boundary issues," Liesl choked.

Bennet grimaced, his hands going slack as Liesl took a deep, noisy breath of air. Sitting back, he laughed miserably, "I can't hurt you. But I could emotionally devastate you…say, if I killed Henry. Now that you've just reunited…I could do that. I could hurt your tiny black heart."

"No!" Liesl went pale, her body deflating as she realized Bennet's true intent.

"Oh yes," he giggled, "You're just the bait. You always were."

"Let it go," Liesl pled.

"I don't think so," Bennet shook his head. "Now, if you could just tell me where your boyfriend is, I'll be on my way to kill him."

The moon broke through the clouds, clearly revealing Bennet hunched over Liesl's prone form. Before Gloria could think through it, she took a deep breath, aimed - finding Bennet's grinning face – and pulled the trigger. The pistol shook in her hand, smoke rising in a small puff, the comically soft plink of the bullet echoing through the heavy air.

Bennet flinched, pulling his left shoulder back with a twitch, hands falling to his sides. Liesl scrambled from under Bennet, rising to her feet as Bennet sat back on his haunches, rubbing his shoulder.

"Ouch," he muttered, shaking his head in confusion before spying Gloria - armed with an empty pistol - crouched behind her battered car.

Liesl took advantage of the confusion and swung herself behind Bennet, a knife slipping from the folds of her sleeve, the sharp curved blade niftily piercing the flesh of Bennet's throat. Holding the blade to his jugular, her other hand clutching the side of Bennet's cheek in her grip, she whispered, "I know more than you think about this blood. And *I* will end this now."

Before Liesl could pull the blade through his neck, Bennet feinted, slipping from her grasp. He fled through the trees behind them, the outline of his form melting into the encroaching shadows. Liesl glanced over her shoulder at Gloria, her lips pressed together as she exhaled noisily.

Suddenly, there was only silence and Gloria's labored breathing. Her dainty borrowed pistol dangled ineffectually from her hand. She shrank back as Liesl sauntered over, the younger woman straightening her torn clothes and adjusting her hair before pausing several feet away, hands on her hips. Gloria sighed in relief.

"I like that you weren't scared of Bennet," Liesl smiled. "You even tried to save me. Now that's some girl-power shit, right there." She grinned, studying Gloria with a critical eye.

Gloria straightened, staring back at the young woman before her. "Is he with…you?" Gloria dared ask, her voice full of barely concealed hope.

"I figured he might be here," Liesl frowned. "I knew Bennet would be coming after him. Henry took off the minute my back was turned. It was all just to get me away from you. I thought I could save him from Bennet and he'd see…he'd see that I love him. But he didn't want to leave you, Gloria. So, he's put himself in danger for you. Again. Lurking somewhere close, I'm sure. Coward." Liesl motioned to the car, opening the passenger door of the battered vehicle and plopping into the seat with a crunch of glass, gesturing for Gloria to do the same. "I thought…maybe…I could stop them both from ruining your life, too. By killing you, yes. But, to save you." Liesl looked disappointed.

Deflated, Gloria joined her in the car with a distinct crunch, mustering as much dignity as she could with the sharp edges of glass digging through her torn jeans.

"It's a good thing I was here," Liesl motioned to the Community Center behind them.

Gloria raised her eyebrows in question.

"What? I was looking for Henry's manuscript, too. What do you care? I'm obviously too late. You read it, right? He said he left it with Terry…so, too late for everything." Liesl sighed. "Can you do me a favor, Gloria Weidman?"

Gloria nodded, appraising the girl through lowered lashes.

"Give me your phone," Liesl commanded.

Gloria searched the car, finally locating the phone in her book bag, digging it out with shaking hands while Liesl watched patiently.

Liesl grabbed the phone from her hand, punching the screen with practiced thumbs before handing it back to her, explaining, "You have my number now. When Henry shows up, could you… *would you*…call me. If he's in trouble, please. I have to find Bennet now and kill him. Anyway, I guess that was Henry's plan, after all. To lead us both away from you."

Liesl's hand shot out. Gloria flinched, but the girl's touch was surprisingly gentle as she brushed the throbbing bruise above Gloria's right eye, whispering almost to herself, "He hurt *you, too*."

“Which one?” Gloria croaked, her voice raw and small.

“Either?” Liesl shrugged, “Both?”

Gloria nodded sadly, their eyes meeting for a moment of shared pity before Liesl blinked and caught herself. Sitting up straighter, Liesl scanned the dark band of trees on the horizon before kicking open the passenger door and stepping out.

Slamming the door, she sauntered around the back of the car, leaning through the broken driver’s side window with a petulant scowl, admitting, “I wasn’t really a wife to Henry. Our marriage was…not what you think. He only married me to protect me. Though I’d like to think he would have made me his wife one day. But I’m not the child he married anymore. Please tell him that when you see him. I’m a completely different woman now.”

“Did you? Are you? Were you together? When you left with him?” Gloria asked as Liesl surveyed the encroaching shadows of the night.

Liesl shook her head, her shining red hair falling across her shoulders, “No. The plan was just to disappear until this whole thing dies down…look for Bennet. He had no choice *but* to leave with me. Maybe I took advantage of the situation. I mean, I killed Saint in the middle of the Yesteryear Festival, so I had to flee. And I made it look like *he* killed Saint, so Henry *had* to flee. It was convenient to leave together. I’ll admit, I still feel like there’s something there. We talked a lot about our feelings, blech. But hey, it’s been over two hundred years. Do you know what that kind of space does to a relationship, Gloria? It’s beyond complicated.” She tilted her head, straightening before adding, “I hope to never see you again. But…you’re kind of a badass, Gloria Weidman.”

Liesl raised her eyes to the stars as if searching for something, her cheerful tone returning, “I can see why Henry likes you. And you should really think long and hard about what *you want* out of this relationship. There are worse things than eternal life. Anyway, you have more power than you think."

Gloria opened her mouth to ask another question, but Liesl was gone. Only the leaves of the trees directly in front of her car moved as Liesl disappeared into the shadows as the crickets picked their song back up. With that, Gloria clicked on her lights and the air conditioner, the latter of which promptly flowed out the gaping holes where her front and side windows were originally located. With no rearview mirrors, she cautiously, slowly, reversed out of the parking space and drove away without looking back. Only when she pulled onto the quiet two-lane road leading home did she allow herself a stoic cry. She hadn't even bothered to check if she was being followed.

Truthfully, she was stunned. Everything in life had taught her *there were no big mysteries*. People were just awful, awful animals and there was no magic, except maybe in fiction. But this! This proved there *were* still some grand mysteries left in the world. Henry *was* telling the truth. At least, about *this* he had.

And as for the rest, she decided she just needed to gather her strength, pull her shit together and trust her instincts. *For once in her life*. Trust herself. Because she was now both broken *and* stronger than she ever imagined. With or without Henry.

Chapter 51

The bathwater was pink with her blood. Gloria shivered, pulling her knees as close to her chest as she could, which somehow made her feel a bit more pitiful. Her legs were a map of scrapes, bruises and ruined skin. Every breath she took hurt a different part of her lungs. But…part of her…part of her vibrated with a new energy. She closed her eyes and leaned back, humming tunelessly, something she'd done to comfort herself for as long as she could remember. She should be dead. Yet somehow, she'd walked away. Well, driven really. How was it possible she'd survived?

But didn't she know, already? Wasn't it something she'd not allowed herself to see? Like so many things she'd hidden from herself throughout her life. Doubt and fear, doubt and fear - this was how she'd grown so small. But now, she was strong. Stronger than she'd ever been. Only her doubt kept her weak this long.

"Beautiful," the melodic voice sighed.

Gloria didn't open her eyes because she didn't want to face the empty spot beside her. Then suddenly, suddenly his hands brushed her back, the washcloth dipping into the soapy pink water before gently dabbing the aching rows of disrupted flesh canvassing her skin. She knew she looked anything but beautiful, but it was so good to hear his voice.

"Lean forward," he commanded.

She obeyed, a small smile on her lips, her eyes firmly closed. Henry's fingers ran down Gloria's flayed back, gently tracing the cuts of her torn skin, the bloody furrows where the glass raked her body, traveling up the crease of her neck to caress her face. He bent over her, his lips brushing hers. A torrent of emotions swirled deep within her, though she longed to feel his touch, to be his and for him to be hers for just one more moment.

Her hands shot up, grasping the collar of his shirt, his hair tangled in her grasp. Their lips met somewhere in between, finding each other, her hands dancing along his back. Henry lifted her effortlessly from the water, pulling her slick skin to his, his body closing the space between them, ignoring his damp clothes as they knelt together on the squeaky floor. Forgetting her wounds, Gloria pushed Henry down and threw her leg over his hips to straddle him - her lips finding his again. And again. Desperately. Deeply.

Henry bucked his hips, his hands grasping her hips as she moved over him, her hands pushing at his clothes. She sank into him, groaning in ecstasy as they moved in perfect rhythm - his sharp white teeth nipping at her shoulders, his hands gripping her shoulders, pulling her hips down to his, sliding over her breasts. She could feel him *everywhere*. Together, they reached the axis of their passion, arching and folding into one another, sighing as they slipped into each other's arms and slid further down the linoleum floor with entwined, sweaty limbs to hold each other as if they could lose the other in the dim light.

She felt Henry's gentle touch, his fingers grazing the raised welts on her back and closed her eyes, fighting off her mounting paranoia.

"I'm so sorry Bennet did this to you, Gloria. I came as fast as I could."

"Were you there? Like Liesl said?"

It came out as an accusation. Henry ignored it. Gloria shivered, feeling the phantom grip of Bennet's hands tightening around her throat – seeing her scared eyes again and again, reflected in the orbs of his black blood.

"I couldn't have stopped what was happening. And I knew you would be alright," Henry's hands stilled as he rationalized, "Gloria. You can always be this strong. Stronger. I know you can feel it." He searched her face, his hands gripping her upper arms.

"Henry, I don't want this. *Why* would I want to be like *this* forever. Would you want to be forever...old? Feeble?"

"Do you feel old?"

"No"

"Do you feel feeble?"

"No. But, Henry," Gloria shivered, pulling herself from his embrace, reaching for a towel, "I don't want to die."

"None of us really do," Henry confirmed, following her to her feet.

"Do I still have a choice?" she reached for her robe, her fingers hovering over it as she waited for his answer.

"Yes," he confirmed after a long moment. "You can continue to get stronger. Or you could…die, I guess, if you chose. But I won't help you with that. I'm not sure I know how."

Gloria wrinkled her nose in frustration though he didn't notice as he stood, sauntering to the small window above the sink and peering out.

"Henry, is there a third option? A way for me to remain… me?" She asked, remembering Bennet's dubious instructions.

He paused a bit too long before responding, "I don't know." She bit her lip to keep from crying as Henry went on, oblivious, "Where's your shadow tonight? He wasn't at the station."

"Oh, he's here less and less. Should I call him?" She taunted, her concern for Casey mounting with Henry's casual knowledge of the deputy's whereabouts.

Henry's eyes flashed with anger, quickly concealed. "Gloria, you will have to decide what you want. Soon." He looked up at the dark night sky, searching, his body relaxing as he spied the weak, red streak of a falling star to the west. Gloria followed his gaze with an exasperated huff. She saw nothing.

"I think I need some time, Henry. This is all too much to process. What I've seen…what I've done. You've made me feel crazy and I don't know what I believe or what I want when I *do decide* what I believe. I'm old and I'm confused. And I don't like what you've done to me. Now, I'd appreciate it if you would get out."

"Gloria," Henry reached for her. She slapped his hands away as he tried to appeal to her, "you need me. You won't understand what is happening and until Bennet is truly gone, we're all in danger. Don't you see? He's not well. He won't stop coming after you, trying to ensnare you in some convoluted prank. He's just…bored. And evil."

"I can see that. And I'm starting to think he's not the only one playing games. Go. Now! I need some time to think."

"But you knew. Didn't you?" he pressed. "Part of you had to."

Had she? She didn't know anymore. Had she known what Henry was doing to her when it was happening, deep down inside? Or was that just how *he* remembered it? She knew she had loved him, had trusted him, once. But that was before.

"Gloria," his voice broke as he pled, "I have always been a coward. I probably always will. And I know I've given you no reason to trust me. To believe I've only done what I've done for love. I only ever wanted forever. For both of us." His hands dropped. He nodded in resignation, leaving Gloria to finish dressing.

When she emerged some time later, the ends of her hair still damp, Henry was gone. A stack of typed pages lay on her mantle. Atop this was Bennet's knife, the identification tag and evidence number from the local police station still attached to the bone handle. The house was silent and dark. Empty.

She eyed the manuscript. She knew she had to finish reading it. It would tell her everything she wanted to know - in what seemed to be the only way Henry could express it. But first, she needed to see her mother.

Chapter 52

Dottie's eyes slid open, blinking rapidly to focus.

"Whozit? Wade?" she asked in a small, hopeful voice.

Gloria's heart sank. She'd been too slow to evade Beverly Kent in the dining hall several weeks before, being pulled into the adjacent hallway where the harried director confided Dottie had grown more agitated of late, her memory slipping more often, struggling to place people in the correct context, it seemed. Time was catching up quickly now - decisions would *need* to be made.

"No, Mother. It's Gloria. It's your daughter." She grabbed her mother's cold hands in her own, but Dottie pulled her fingers from Gloria's clutches with a determined, annoyed shrug.

She couldn't explain why – but she couldn't bring herself to read the final pages in her hand after Henry left, hugging them to her chest as her thoughts raced. In the end, she grabbed her mother's keys from the junk drawer and came here, to her bedside. Things kept getting stranger and stranger, obviously. She needed to know that her mother was still safe.

"Gloria, you scared me to death."

"Just visiting," Gloria shrugged.

"Why is your hair wet? What time is it?" Dottie raised her head, adjusting her pillow.

"It's almost eleven. Sorry it's so late. I know you stay up reading, sometimes."

"You look like hell. Why are you driving at night?" Dottie sat up, exasperated, "who died?"

"No one died," Gloria shook her head.

"Doubtful," Dottie cast her eyes suspiciously to the door and the spaces beyond.

"Mom," Gloria slumped over, resting her forehead on the cool linen of Dottie's freshly laundered sheets. She'd almost convinced herself everything happening had a rational, if not sad, explanation - that it wasn't real. That she was losing her mind. She felt her mother's hand on her head and tears sprang from the corner of each eye. She dabbed them as she straightened.

"Why are you really here, mouse?" Dottie stared into her eyes, the halcyon glow of a bedside lamp painting her mother golden, lifting years from her face as she cocked her head.

"Henry," Gloria sniffed.

"Hmmmm," Dottie harrumphed, "what did that old man do now?"

Gloria caught her breath, her Mother's eyes were clear and focused.

"You knew?" Gloria demanded.

"I've always known. I mean, not exactly *what*. But I *knew* the second time I met him he wasn't just a man. He hadn't aged. And my grandmother told me the same. Every generation, he'd show up to visit. But he never stayed. Until now."

"Mama…were you? Did you…love him?"

Dottie guffawed, waving Gloria's horrified expression away, "Not in the way you're thinking. Of course not. He was always and will always be a friend to our family. But for you…it's different, I know."

"But what if loving him isn't enough? I'm not sure I can ever forgive him. I don't know if I care to know what happened to make him this way. I'm more concerned about myself! Is that wrong?" Gloria confided in a rush. "How in the world could you do this to someone you love. How could he involve me in this madness if he loved me?"

Dottie smiled and went on, "I'm sure Henry has a plan. He's had a very long time to think about these things. But he's a man of few words. Have you noticed? I think that's why he writes. It's why he chose to write his story. For you. You two are alike that way. You are both made of words. Maybe *writing* is your love language."

Gloria didn't know how to answer.

After a comfortable moment of silence, Dottie went on, pulling her covers to her chin contentedly, yawning, "What mother wouldn't want their child to live forever, Gloria?"

"But at what cost? Did you think of that? I think I can still stop this, mama," Gloria raised her voice, gently trying to rouse Dottie while she was lucid. "I think I can reverse it all. I can still be myself. If…I kill…Henry."

Dottie closed her eyes for a moment, then blinked, scrunching her nose in disapproval, "Gloria! Have you lost your mind? Why in the world would you kill one of your students."

"So, I don't transform. Mother…are you-" Noting her confusion, Gloria realized Dottie had lost the thread of the conversation.

"We are always, all of us, on our way to and from somewhere we've never been before in time and space. Never forget that." Gloria felt her mother's cold hand cover hers and squeeze before advising cheerily, "Your whole life is one great transformation, Gloria. Don't be afraid of the metamorphosis."

With that, Dottie snuggled back into her comforter and promptly began to snore. Gloria sat for a moment longer, watching her mother while she slept. Then, she drove her mother's rusting Cadillac home, casting a sad glance at her own ruined car as she pulled in front of the house.

She felt like a stranger again today. A stranger in her own life. Inside, she eyed Henry’s new manuscript on the mantle, hands trembling as she reached for it.

Chapter 53

If his written words were Henry's love language, what was he telling her with the last part of his story? Her mother's words ringing in her ears, Gloria pulled the pages to her chest and settled on the couch, tucking one foot under her body. Taking a single, calming breath, she smoothed the bowed stack of paper on her lap and began to read Henry's…confession.

In the aftermath of my terrors, I did what all madmen eventually do, I fled for the forests and buried my newfound peculiarities in the savage chaos of nature. I moved inland, to climes devoid of man.

Like many in those tragic tales, I didn't understand my own strength, my new speed, my darkness. Did it come from me, or had Bennet truly infected me with his unrelenting poison at last? Was I destined to be like him now?

Would I enjoy the hunt as well?

Instead, I became an herbivore in defiance of the heat coursing through me - this new sensation of power beneath my skin, this desire to claim my dominance. I was alone, as I always feared. I had no one to face now but myself. And, I had let it all happen with my inability to act, even in the face of mortal danger. I decided one fine morning to end it all. Taking the tatters of my longabused shirt, I wove a fine rope with which to hang myself in a favored pine tree - one I'd often nested beside as I slept.

I hung myself without preamble, tying the rope about my neck in a noose and slipping wistfully from where I perched on the lowest suitable branch. Thrice I tried, hearing the bones of my neck crack while I waited for the resulting asphyxiation to no avail. I tried six more times before a small birdcall startled me from my Sisyphean task.

I'd never been so relieved to see a wild Indian in all my life. But, as Wamenu stood there, appraising me silently, bow drawn with an arrow notched, pointing only slightly left of my red and straining face, I realized he'd shifted the arrow ever so slightly back on me.

As my bare feet struggled to find purchase on the leaves beneath my swinging corpse, Wamenu let go, the arrow singing through the wavy spaces between us, sliding with a sppphhhthunk into my eye. Four more arrows followed in short order before the rope around my neck was cut, dropping my limp body to a bloody pile on the leaves beneath my hangman's tree.

I felt a light kick of leather clad feet on my torso, another on my haunch before Wamenu leaned down, putting his face directly in front of my own. "It's too late, Henry. You're already dead now." Standing over me, Wamenu shook his head regretfully, his shadow engulfing my bleeding, prone body.

"And yet, I cannot seem to die," I bit out, glancing with curiosity at the feathers protruding from the arrows embedded in my neck, thigh, torso and ribs.

"I see that," Wamenu assessed, searching the dense walls of forest around us.

I sat up, tugging unsuccessfully at the wood between my ribs until firm hands gripped it from both sides, breaking the shaft of the arrow before pulling the other half from between my bones with a dramatic squirt of bright blood. I had never been good with blood and grew faint, requiring Wamenu to lower me back to the forest floor lest I fall to further bodily ruin. I won't even go into detail as to what happened when Wamenu ripped the arrow from what had been my eye; though suffice to say, it ended with me back on the ground, staring into the hot afternoon sun overhead with one eye - the other a cavity to be swathed in spiderwebs and rotting bracken, secured with willow bark and a strip of thin rawhide.

Ironically, I was a sight to see as I trudged back to Wamenu's small camp - myself shirtless, bleeding profusely and full of holes. A summer hunting camp with about twenty small leantos and four small longhouses lay in a half ring nearby...closer to me than I thought. Turns out, just beyond the expansive forest where I'd fled and imagined myself alone, I was never far from others. Never isolated as I'd imagined. The Indians simply allowed me my privacy to... well, I'm not sure exactly what they'd expected me to do, but they'd allowed my presence. They politely waited to see what I would become, Wamenu informed me on the short walk. A suicidal sad sack, it was revealed. Yet, rather indestructible by their estimation.

Wamenu, however, was all too eager to explore these newfound talents on my behalf, his naturally agile mind quite thrilled by the resulting mysteries. In addition to arrows, he allowed me to rehang myself, providing sturdier tools: to impale myself in all fashions: to immolate myself in a rather more public spectacle than I'd planned as others offered poisonous toads, serpents, a variety of deadly wildlife and metal knives traded for throughout the southern lands, each sharper than the last.

With each recovery, my confidence grew - as if I would indeed live forever as Bennett predicted. That kind of power is intoxicating. Thank goodness I've never been an ambitious man. Or brave. The combination could have been deadly, even for me.

I realized as the months wore on that each injury, each death, did not weaken me but instead, the opposite - I was strengthened. My rate of healing and regeneration increased in speed. Hundreds of years later and further up the coast, with help from a local scientist, I would find that there was a medical explanation. My viral load doubled with each experiment, my white blood cells doubling - my blood enriching, muscles growing at an accelerated pace. Each time I died, I became faster, stronger – more. But then, this was all miraculously new. And I had been reborn. I had…transformed.

Things continued like this for some time and I grew complacent, even enjoying my light captivity. I'd quite convinced myself that I had nothing to fear. Then, one clear summer morning, I rolled over on my sleeping furs and jumped as my arm slid over the rough skin of tree bark laid beside me. It was a rather advanced carving on the smooth side of the wooden plaque which fell from my shaking hands as I studied it. A snake eating its own tail. I glanced around, hoping it was a gift from one of the children - most too shy to even look directly at me; but, the camp moved along beside me as it always had. I was just a visitor.

The next day, there was another. I hid them in shame, knowing then Bennet was still close though he never answered as I screamed his name into the far corners of the forest until I could no longer speak. He never stepped from the shadows but continued to taunt me with carved imagery appearing at random where I slept, knowing I couldn't read. Making it known he was watching me. Violent pictographs displaying the basest of his nature. Instructions for me, as it were, evolving into multipaneled masterpieces of tigers eating men, men eating tigers, men eating men and finally, men tearing other men - and tigers - apart with their hands.

After a matter of months, even Bennet grew bored with my ennui - my obvious lack of bloodlust, my cowardice - of coaching me from afar. But this cowardice was the characteristic I chose to nurture instead. I moved with the tribe to the larger winter camp. In my abject fear, it never even crossed my mind that I might endanger others with my mere presence. How confident I'd been in my ability to control my own baser urges. I tried and almost succeeded in forgetting the chaos that followed me.

Once there, over the course of several weeks, five of the natives went missing while gathering food or wood away from camp. Only one body was found - days later - assumed to have been mauled by animals in his advanced state of decomposition, though I quietly noted he was missing his head. My paranoia grew. I thought, cravenly, of slinking off in the middle of the night, disappearing to nobly lead my monster away. But I stayed. And he found me.

One new trait I was overly fond of was my keen hearing, using it in times of boredom to listen to the rhythm of the tribe, unobserved. I slowly learned their language through pure osmosis, so I could eavesdrop somewhat passably. The voices carried because of the silence of the winter night. It was crisp and still with only a few grey wisps of clouds scuttling through the black skies. One of these voices was Wamenu's. And he sounded angry.

I couldn't help myself, I've always been nosy – ever the watcher. I knew I shouldn't, but something compelled me to rise and find out who or what angered my friend. Perching in a nearby tree, I concentrated on listening to their voices across the distance, slowly able to pull some phrases from their rapid hand signs and hushed dueling dialects.

"Only then..." I heard a scratchy, female voice reply in the dark. Their languages were similar, guttural, but not wholly the same.

Wamenu shook his head as she finished, gesturing back to the camp and then to the moon in the sky. "We must kill them both.

And burn them until they are dust," he argued.

A wooden staff taller than its owner shook in his direction, silencing his barks with a harsh rejoinder in his own language. Whatever she said seemed to mollify him. It was said too quickly for me to catch.

"He is weak and small," she spat, shaking the clinking staff in the village's direction. The berobed figure seemed to hear something, cocking her head and turning it in the shaft of moonlight so I could just see her wrinkled face from my spot in the oak. I was far enough away they shouldn't have been able to detect me. But her sightless, milky eye snapped in my direction as she spoke. "I have cousins on the water," she turned her other eye back to Wamenu, "I will go and get more memories – and then we will know how to kill it."

I suppressed my urge to gasp! It was the Sassafras Crone! I was told later she was an aunt, of sorts - a distant relation functioning more like a travelling medical ministry - spreading rumors, cures and spiritual instruction to the infirm of the tribes, arriving only when summoned.

"Find answers and return," Wamenu agreed cautiously, looking around the shadows of the night forest and failing to spot me glaring down at him. "Or I will find a way to kill this one myself."

"No!" the crone hissed, "I want the old one for my own. This one is his child. We need him. No other way."

My heart sank. I'd thought Wamenu my friend. Would I ever learn? I'd been right to be paranoid. I didn't even bother returning to camp to gather my things and tromp theatrically away. I just ran. As fast and as far as I could. This time, I made sure I was alone. And I stayed that way for the better part of two years. I've never known loneliness like that...separation from the world.

Winters choking by a fire in a cave, buried in the snow. It destroys you if you like to chat now and then.

And then one day while I hunted far from my caves, I heard voices. English voices in the trees around me. English muskets being fired. Oh, it was so tempting to run straight into that English camp and declare my name and rank, joining my countrymen once more. But I didn't. I lingered. I watched a bit. Ultimately, I returned to my hermit's lair and to my existence outside of humanity. In exchange - or in fear - for theirs.

For months, I kept my distance. But one day, whether by accident or subconscious design, I stumbled across them. There was a small detachment sent from their rapidly built enclosure, quite far from our original fort, in an area I was less familiar with than the dense inland forests I now called my own. A horse had been lamed by a falling tree, an emergency made worse by cold and snow - shouts and yells for assistance from their own people nullified by sheer distance. But I heard. I only meant to watch, not stride forward and offer help to a group of stunned onlookers staring as if a ghost appeared in native costume.

I held my hands palm forward so they could see I wasn't armed and continued disarming them by greeting them in proper English and asking from where they haled?

The stoutest lad of the quad stepped forward as soon as I spoke, taking care to avoid staring rudely, thrusting out a soft, slick hand. "I'm Edmund," he announced.

"Of course you are," I laughed, because of course he was.

"And I," I took a breath, it had been so long since I said, "I am Henry. Henry Wynter. From England!"

The three men and one woman exchanged incredulous looks, trading them with each other during a long, awkward silence that hung in the weak rays of the afternoon sun until

Edmund spoke again, his eyebrows raised in astonishment, "And yet, your Edmund has found us, too. How can it be? It's a miracle! Henry Wynter? I've heard the name a thousand times from him. He will never believe this! We must away and reunite the two of you as soon as possible."

Chapter 54

Edmund? My old friend Edmund, who I thought long dead? How in the world had he managed to survive on his own so long. He must be greatly changed, I thought. I had hope for the first time in years. I barely recognized the odd sensation.

"He found us the week after we landed," Edmund explained in response. "He said he was on a supply run with that last group of unfortunates, and had grown ill and disoriented one eve, somehow managing to get himself deucedly lost in the forests, only emerging ashore as the ship home crested the horizon. In a hurricane, no less. Damn sad tale we've always said. But this will cheer him so! His dear friend, Henry! He will be amazed."

I was embraced and carried back to camp atop the one hale horse, surrounded by stares and questions as we rode through the raw, wooden gates like victorious warriors returning from battle. What were the odds? Edmund! We had both been saved! I savored that joy as I searched the small, straggly group of strangers' faces for Edmund with naïve cheer.

"Edmund!" This Edmund called out, questioning a nearby woman, "Edmund?"

"He's gone out with the trading party. But I imagine them back any day!" she supplied with a nervous smile.

Edmund bobbed his head, turning to me with an apologetic wink, "As luck would have it."

The settlement was less populated than I'd thought at first glance, I reflected later while nestled on a tic mattress beside the fire. There were far too many crude huts for the rough count of settlers I'd made upon my arrival. And yet, they were quick to explain their leader, a John White, had already made his way back to England for assistance when the site wasn't quite all they'd been led to believe. It sounded a familiar enough tale.

I found the remaining Englishmen suffered many of the same tragedies as our ignorant crew and their numbers continued to dwindle unchecked since their arrival with several having gone missing just the past few weeks. It seemed their decaying relations with the local natives was to be blamed. My heart dropped further as I heard this tidbit over a savory porridge by the central campfire the next day, a filthy blonde-haired woman recounting the details with an air of Christian resignation.

It seems Edmund, my long-lost friend, had been an absolute godsend, wandering into their midst mere days after White's departure home for supplies. Edmund had been instrumental in protecting them from the local Indians and a huge help in identifying edible flora and fauna. True, their numbers continued to fall even with this Angel watching over them, but his appearance alone had been seen as a sign from the Almighty. My mouth was dry with anxiety as she finished, meandering away after I failed to answer a question I hadn't heard.

A victorious ring of cheers disrupted my paranoid ruminations, a cascade of noises heralding the return of the traders, my Edmund presumably amongst them. It would be good to put my hands on his shoulders and assure myself of his safety. Assure myself of mine.

The group that returned to us - from what I heard murmured as they rode into camp - was not the same party that rode slowly out their listing, ineffectual gates ten days before. This silent octet led nine horses with sixteen packs. A pack for each man who'd left camp. Several settlers cried in distress as their loved ones failed to reappear.

And then, I saw him. Edmund. He winked as he went by, his face otherwise dirty, downcast and obscured by the scarf looped about his head in place of a hat. Other than his costume, Bennet Chappell seemed to be thriving, once again. There were surprised cries and wails of grief upon the announcement that these eight were all that was left of an original party of sixteen, the natives striking them cruelly and repeatedly.

It was a tragic tale told over the fire and porridge that morning. He remained silent, as I'd heard Edmund was wont to do, while the others told in faltering voices of the series of tragedies befalling them on their expedition. I felt his eyes upon me as they spoke, daring me to expose him – to expose us both.

It seemed the savages, unseen, picked the settlers off one by one - only appearing during a violent, afternoon gale to taunt them from the trees, carrying their brethren off into the dark forest, one by one, as they struggled to reach home. I realized then he'd never stop. Bennet would destroy everyone I ever cared for. Every time. This was a game to him. He'd been alive so long he no longer valued life itself. And he envied me mine…my naïve hope.

"That's not Edmund!" I shouted abruptly. The orators fell silent in their tale. Everyone turned to face me. "That is Bennet Chappell and he is death incarnate. He killed the real Edmund, I'm quite sure. And now, he's killing you!"

I caught the exchange of several knowing glances in my side-eye as I pushed myself away from Bennet, to the other side of the lean-to, shaking his cold hands from my shoulder while he shrugged apologetically on my behalf.

"I was worried this would happen," Bennet supplied quietly, smoothly, going on with a helpless headshake. "He was quite mad the last time I saw him. I hesitated to say, but I thought

I'd never see him again."

More murmurs around the fire and funny looks, as if Bennet had been building this narrative for a good portion of his time here. He'd already poisoned the well, it seemed. I was restrained - for my own good, they told me - as I railed at them with quarter-strength, careful not to toss them from me like dolls, aware if I lost control, Bennet would surely follow suit and I'd be responsible for a full massacre. I knew then I had to kill him. Or he must kill me. And I had to find the courage to accept either.

It was quiet. The nearby fire had dwindled in the light wind to ashes, thin tendrils of smoke drifting between the soaring trees. It had been quieter than normal with another small, desperate hunting party gone from camp for the week, but I'd enjoyed the solitude of my captivity. I had been dreaming of the very thing I was doing - lazing about. Usually, in the near distance, there were the sounds of leather clad footsteps on the soft, leafy loam of the ground - the noise of cooking, working together to string drying meats, the shouts of joy when happy, the screams of men and women over the crack of falling trees they chopped in teams from the perimeters of camp. The screams of men and women…I heard the distant screams. And then silence. Just silence and the bird calls from the forest around the camp. Was it children playing? But there was just the one little girl here (a silent child, her mother long dead), her father gone from fever, they'd said. It didn't sound right. Nothing did. Even the vacuum of sound drifting across the village with an advancing, shadow-casting bank of clouds seemed misplaced.

My heart raced as I bolted from my nest, running as I hit the ground, pushing through the ineffectual crossbolt securing the thatch door. My anxieties peaking, I raced through camp, my heart dropping further as I realized the settlement was quite empty. Not a single industrious soul about in the afternoon warmth, just a birdcall in the distance, a rumble from the clouds on the horizon. Deadly silence. I slowed, caution directing me as I passed through the web of log cabins and wood and skin huts to the center fire of the camp. There should have been scores of people working together, passing through, reigning their horses, hauling their stores from the frozen pits on the edges of camp.

It took me several moments of shock to realize what I was looking at. The great stack of lumber in the center of camp, the pile of trash beside it: a large and ever burgeoning pile of refuse. But the pile of refuse…was bodies. Stacks of people, the last of Bennet's victims still bleeding and broken atop the pile. Bennet smiled, his legs dangling over the side of this monstrosity, a mischievous grin on his pink lips.

"Henry!" he gasped, holding his hands to his heart. "What have you done?"

My first instinct was to fly at him, to tear his limbs from his body and throw him on the pile of bodies where he sat like an ogre, numb to the carnage beneath him. It was - and remains - the single worst thing I've seen in my long life. Nothing I can ever forget. It haunts me still.

"Nooooooo," I roared.

"I mean…yes?" he finished with a shrug, hopping down, wiping his hands across his cambric pants.

Only then did I realize my ultimate folly, my total and utter ruin. I'd been so caught up in my own transformation, I had never even mentioned Bennet's name to these people before he returned to the settlement, never warned them of the possibility. Never thought to prepare them for a thing. Because I had been afraid. This was all my fault. And now, it was too late. My cowardice was their end.

"This will happen again and again," Bennett announced confidently. "You did this, Henry. You killed all these people."

"I didn't." I heard myself protest weakly.

"You were already halfway done when I got here!" Bennett lied. "Are you sure you're feeling alright?"

Had I? I had been sleeping, I was locked in, jailed. I was only dreaming of the settlers screaming, wasn't I? And yet, my hands were covered in blood when I looked down. I was covered in someone else's blood. What had I done?

"You've been busy," I stated hollowly, surveying the carnage.

"I'm not sure if you're cut out for this after all, Henry," Bennett sighed, wistfully kicking the foot of a nearby corpse.

"I know I'm not," I felt myself go numb, my legs crumpling beneath me.

"Well," Bennett answered cheerfully, hovering over me with a sneer, "This power I've given you, its not always the same. You could just die – still. And stay dead. Sometimes my friends get very sick and die when this happens."

He stated this as if it would cheer me, smiling when I glanced up with a hopeful frown.

"It's true," he nodded sagely. "Or you could do yourself a favor and kill yourself now."

I knew then he hadn't witnessed that very thing and the failed results of it years ago, but I didn't enlighten him to my contrary findings. Or maybe he did know what happened and mocked me still. Maybe it made him stronger, too, each time I died. I looked down at my hands, tears carving white tracks down my blood-caked face.

Bennett turned as if to leave, spinning back around, "There's one other thing you could do, Henry, if you weren't such an all-encompassing coward. You could take this knife of yours and kill me. But you have to do it now or it will never work. If you do that, you might become...well, weak, again...but you would be back to yourself."

Bennet didn't speak again, cocking an eyebrow and shrugging whilst dramatically backlit by the roaring infernos of several cabins, his destructive pattern complete. He held the knife up, the curved blade winking in the firelight before hefting it in his left hand, catching it flat on his palm before holding the weapon out to me invitingly. I thought I'd left that wicked knife behind at the fort.

"Ah, Henry. If you can't love me back, at least put me out of my misery..." he pleaded disingenuously, balancing the knife on his palm level to my eyeline, pushing the deadly blade ever closer to me, "You know you want to!"

I snatched the knife from his palm, testing the weight in my right hand before facing Bennet's steady gaze one last time.

"If you do this – you can be free," he shouted over the din. "But you'll be weak again. You'll die one day, just like everyone you've ever known." He studied me as he made this proclamation, "But you must do it now. If you wait - even one more day - it won't work." He'd already lied over and over. What were the chances this wasn't just another ruse?

"If I leave – you'll never see me again," Bennett warned, turning his back to me. "I'm going home, Henry. I'll leave you here with these savages for the rest of time so you can think about things." Here, he turned back and paused, arms raised at his sides like a religious statue. I froze as he leaned forward, closing his eyes while lifting his chest to me in offering. I knew what I should do. But I couldn't. I couldn't make myself move. He frowned, his eyes snapping open as he sighed in disappointment. And then he

left. Just like that. Two steps forward before zipping away, crossing into the wall of snow tipped trees lying forever in every direction.

The knife drooped in the loose grip of my hand as I assessed the senseless massacre before me, vowing then and there, the next time I saw Bennett, I would be brave instead. But for now...now I ran.

It was fully dark when I reached the beach, the rhythmic lull of the shoreline pulling me to the sand where a crisp north wind battered the choppy waves of the cove. I thought it a wild animal at first, crouched by the water, its antlers visible in the moonlight between the sea and the clouds above. The animal stood erect, its antlers seeming to stretch clean up to the sky: a giant beast with the fur of many, the black and white stripes of raccoon and badger creating a tasseled fringe sweeping a semi-circle in the sand around the creature's knee-high moccasins.

The beast pointed at me with its claw, its red eyes burning into mine. And then I heard her voice - the scratchy echo of the Sassafras Crone - the clicking bear claws sewn to the staff at her side shaking before my parted lips, as I fell to my knees and awaited her killing blow. The wind howled as the waves picked up, thunder cracking overhead, followed by an electric streak of lightning travelling across the horizon. The crone put a finger to her mouth as if to silence me – a burst of lightning behind her head. I bowed my own, accepting my fate.

I looked up into her wild eye, raising my arms at my side, opening my heart to her. She lifted her staff, her mouth forming a circle as if to scream. I closed my eyes. But it was only the wind howling - whipping the clouds past the moon, the waves slapping against the beach. I knelt, my arms akimbo, offering my life in exchange for my lack of courage. Yet nothing happened. I cracked one eye open and then the other as the Crone stepped back, her staff raised. I noticed the black outlines of several silent witnesses around a distant, small fire lit in anticipation of my visit. Eight dark eyes winking in the moonlight. Wamenu held his right hand up as he approached, palm forward in peace like our first meeting aboard ship. Words failed me as I stood to take his hand in mine.

"No, Henry," he stopped me. "This is not for you, but for my ancestors and for those that come next."

The Sassafras Crone stepped closer, her staff clinking with each footfall on the sand it steadied. I pulled Bennet's knife from my waistband, my hand shaking under its deceptive weight, offering it to her.

"Cursed boy," she hissed in perfectly accented Queen's English - clear as glass - pushing the knife back in my hand with an impatient grunt. "You cannot kill what will not rot. No matter what you do - that devil will not die. His fathers, your grandfathers, are older than the mountains themselves. They walked this land while our people still crawled in the dirt." A claw-like hand flew out, gripping my neck with surprising strength, that dead eye fixed directly to my face.

"How do we stop him?" I heard myself choke out, spots dancing before my eyes.

"It will take more than that blade, boy," she shook her staff towards me with her other hand, gesturing to the knife in mine before adding, "that alone is not enough."

That was interesting, because Bennet seemed sure that it was.

"Just kill him while we have him," Wamenu pled.

"Silence," she let go of my throat, raising her hand to shush him, her clear eye fixed on mine. "You must find your courage, Henry. You alone are not enough. You need at least three of your strength to even wound him. He will never die but he can

be stopped. For as long as his body, his heart and his head are kept separate. Only then...and, not forever. You must find your people. You must find family for this to work. Do you understand? They must have your blood. His blood. The tainted blood running through your tree." Family?

I nodded mutely. Wamenu's hatchet caught my attention from the corner of my eye, just as it flashed overhead, striking my neck with a startling crack. And the world disappeared in a wink. Regardless, my last conscious thought was a warm one. Family.

There was a short, handwritten note in Henry's recognizable scrawl at the bottom of the final typed page, though Gloria's eyes filled with tears as she tried to finish it, blurring the spidery lines of his postscript. She wept. Her heart broken open for all of them.

Henry wanted family. Needed family. His blood. And hers. That's what he'd been trying to tell her earlier. But how did she use this to help him now? Was it possible Bennet didn't know of that secret meeting with Wamenu and the Sassafras Crone, all these years later? Could she even trust Henry after everything he'd done? And finally, did she use this information to help Henry or to save herself? Could she find a way to do both?

Chapter 55

Having read the final piece of Henry's story, she was conflicted about many things. But she knew she was still in love with Henry Wynter. She would always love him, though she didn't trust him anymore. She didn't like what he'd done to her in the name of family. She despised the chaos he'd invited into her soft, easy and finite life. But most of all, she was disappointed. How could Henry think his wants *for* her somehow superseded her wants for herself? You would think at almost five hundred years old, he'd be a bit more enlightened. But he *was* just a man.

When her phone rang the following afternoon, Gloria almost cried in relief. Surely this was Henry calling. And she'd tell him…she almost understood. *Almost*. Her initial reaction was one of relief - relief he'd called so she didn't have to make the choice to reach out to *him*. Which is why it took a moment to understand the caller's muffled voice.

"Gl…ma…smee….Ted," the crying, sniffling voice whispered, "Carroll."

Gloria's stomach dropped, "Ted?"

He was alive! Wait. Why would he call her and not his wife, or the police? She parted the window blinds searching for Casey's car, but he wasn't at his watchful post, having been there less and less as the stakeout stretched from weeks to months.

Gloria raised her voice, "Ted? Is that you? Where are you? I'm calling the police now."

"No police," Ted moaned in a strained whisper, followed

by the transient muffle of a hand over the mouthpiece of the phone, "you can't call the police. I can get out while he's gone tonight. Meet me at the park swings at midnight. And bring the dagger. It's the only way you can stop him. Stop all of this."

"Ted, where *are* you?"

"I don't know," he whispered. "You have to help me. He never leaves for long. Someone has to stop him. You have to-" There were garbled noises and clicking, "Bring the dagger. Do you understand. It…only…way."

"Who?" Gloria probed, expecting to hear Bennet's name.

"It's Henry, Gloria. Henry's the killer. He killed them all."

Gloria dropped the phone, her hands lead blocks in her lap as her vision narrowed to tiny points. Henry?

Chapter 56

Real life is always stupider and sloppier than those shiny, cozy mystery novels you read at the hotel on your beachside vacation. Your actual time on Earth is generally a monotonous series of compromises until you reach a state not quite of your own doing. A swampy bog filled with tax returns, dishes, visits to the dentist, inflation, laundry and general human sufferings.

And yet, even with the mind-numbing monotony of life, it went against every self-preservative instinct Gloria had to show up tonight. As apathetic about things as she had become before meeting Henry, she found now - in the end - she desperately wanted to live, one way or another. She was still so curious about how everything ended. And this smelled like a trap. She *knew* it was a trap. But *she* was walking into this trap with several of her own.

Parking up the road, she turned her lights off before stopping the car, cruising dangerously blind past the almost deserted police station, like Anne Delancey on a covert stakeout. From the bushes rimming the chain-link fence marking the border of the park, Gloria peered into the inky shadows wrapping the giant ash tree in the center of the open green space. She adjusted her oversized purse, patting the curved blade of Henry's knife in the side pocket reassuringly.

"Pssst."

Gloria heard him before she saw him. Ted, slinking into view, skirting the shadows rimming the chain-link fence. He limped toward her, his eyes darting from Gloria to the dark landscape behind him. From this distance, he resembled a molting parakeet.

"Stop right there," Gloria commanded.

He froze, peering around, searching beyond her with deceptively alert eyes, his carefully constructed visage of helplessness suddenly replaced by an inscrutable, frightening mask of arrogance.

"Jesus, Ted," Gloria whistled appreciatively, "you look like shit."

"But I feel great," he trilled, a slight lisp in his song, his thin lips curling unnaturally over freshly grown incisors. Patches of his skin peeled from his face, his complexion light green under an oily sheen of sweat. He seemed to cramp suddenly, grimacing as he bent over with a hand on his stomach, straightening with a stiff smile on his chapped lips. "Did you bring the knife? We'll need it for the cerem-"

"Bennet," Gloria cut Ted off, "you might as well come on out."

Malicious cackling dripped down from the highest perch overhead where Bennet squatted like a gargoyle on a sturdy branch in the moonlight, the whites of his eyes glowing bright, ordering, "That's enough, Ted."

Bennet dropped down, the air pushing against Gloria with puff of kinetic wind. She had the urge to applaud his showmanship.

"I came to finish what I started," he confided with a shy smile.

"And what futile fuckery might that be?" Gloria chided him.

Without uttering a word, Bennet stepped behind an oblivious Ted, taking hold of both sides of his head with his long, white fingers and snapping his neck, twisting Ted's spine one hundred and eighty degrees before easily plucking his head from his shoulders like a overripe grape. Ted's body crumpled into the grass, the head landing with a thud at Gloria feet where Bennet tossed it, an elated expression still glued to his face.

"He was broken anyway," Bennet shrugged. "I told you that happens sometimes. Where's your boyfriend tonight? He still writing his silly stories? He lies, you know. I know you know."

Gloria's blood ran cold. She fought to stay calm, countering, "He's always been honest with me."

"I find that hard to believe," Bennet snorted, "he's rarely even honest with himself. He *said* he loved Liesl. But he couldn't change her, so he left. He'll do anything to erase his past as a coward."

He looked up, black eyes winking in the dark like a flame. Gloria knew she should run but stood her ground, trying to remind herself *who she was now*. She was *Gloria fucking Weidman* and *she* had superpowers, that's who.

"It's too late, Bennet," she shook her head pityingly, "I'm a different woman than I was before. *I* am a woman transformed. Surely you can see." It was a hollow threat. Gloria was quite aware Bennet's strength exceeded any paltry strength she'd acquired in the past two days.

"Doesn't matter," Bennet shrugged, nudging Ted's corpse with his boot, prodding a belching fart from the body in the process. "I can still kill you. You *are* just a baby. An *old*, *ugly* baby. But weak, like all children."

Fury caused Gloria's voice to shake, "I told Henry to leave. He told me everything. *I* know how to hurt you now Bennet, even if *I'm* the weak one."

Bennet raised his eyebrows, "I really don't care what you think you know. You are nothing to me but Henry's ridiculous grandmother complex coming to an unenviable head. I don't care anything about you."

"You may not. But I do." A familiar voice carried across the square green of the park.

Bennet threw his head back, laughing heartily, "Ah, there he is! Henry, join us."

Henry emerged from the darkness, his pale, determined face wreathed in the weak light of the moon and Gloria fought the urge to run to him and embrace him, despite it all. His gaze went immediately to Gloria. She could see relief wash over his rigid posture, his shoulders dropping as his chin rose.

"Glad you could finally stop lurking about," Bennet's eyes raked Henry hungrily. "Good to see you, brother."

While his attention was on Henry, Gloria slipped a shaking hand into the pocket of her oversized purse, fishing for the handle of the sharp, Damascus blade. Her hand brushed the bone hilt, grasping it, ready to strike.

"Are you alright, Gloria?" Henry asked.

"Yes," she assured him, "I knew you'd come."

Henry turned to Bennet, taunting, "You always want what I have, Bennet. Why can't you find your own people?"

"Who says I haven't, Henry?" Bennet's mouth tightened, his eyes flashing dangerously. "You understand now. You see it. When it's your blood in there, you can smell it a mile away. How do you think I found you?"

Bennet paused, giving his cold revelation greater effect. "Never thought about that one, did you?" Bennet giggled. "If you can find *your* progeny, then surely in a tiny world with seven billion less people, *I* could find *mine*. Wouldn't you think? You always thought your fate was an accident? There are no accidents like this," he roared. "All that bullshit about choosing *your* family.

Well, guess what, Henry. *Your* family chose *you*!"

"*You* are not my family," Henry stated with a sad smile. "I could never be like you."

"A killer?" Bennet shrugged. "I bet a stack of corpses you are. Indirectly and...directly, if I recall? Even recently, eh? What did Rusty Fry ever do to you, Henry? So, he had a few photos of you nosing around, so what? You could have just taken the files."

Gloria froze.

Bennet turned to Gloria, noting her look of repulsion, taunting, "Oh, you didn't think he was one of those good vampires, did you? Awwwwww." He laughed, his features lighting with glee, "I've been watching him since I turned him. He's a coward, our Henry. He doesn't know what it means to fight for love. And I hate to burst your bubble, Gloria Weidman - I've seen him kill a score of times. And he enjoyed *every one*. Didn't you, Henry?"

Henry rocked back on his heels, stunned, shaking his head in disbelief. He turned to Gloria, noting the horror in her eyes.

"I never...," he protested, stuttering, "I mean, only if I... had to...but I had no idea how easily I could lose control, how fragile..."

Bennet materialized in front of Henry. One moment he was in front of Gloria and the next - the next moment she saw his fingers coiling around Henry's neck before Henry even registered his presence before him.

"Tell her the truth," Bennet roared, loosening his grip on Henry's neck only when Henry spoke, his voice so hoarse and quiet Gloria strained to hear.

"It's all true," Henry admitted, looking beyond Bennet's shoulder to find Gloria, his eyes filling with tears. "The first person I killed was a native who tried to help me after Roanoke. I killed him and then I killed his wife. I killed the priest that saved me next…I killed Rusty Fry. I had too. He was onto me, and I was so close to getting to you. I thought he worked for Bennet. I promise I didn't know about Liesl. I would have told you, Gloria. I would have told you everything when I thought you were ready. When you could understand it all better."

"Tell her you were *there* the other night," Bennet commanded, "watching." Henry wilted as Bennet went on, "Tell her you were willing to let her die."

Gloria felt dizzy as the words sank in.

"No," Henry protested, his eyes fixed on hers. "It was too late to help. Liesl was there. And I knew…I knew if you died, we would *both* be stronger to fight Bennet."

A proud smile stretched across Bennett's pudgy face – the face of a proud father, his hands falling slack to his side. Henry scrambled from his grasp with a resentful glare.

"I'm not sure what I believe anymore," Gloria admitted weakly, her voice catching in her throat. She was so angry and hurt she forgot to be afraid for a moment. The hand secreted in her purse tightened on the handle of the blade reassuringly.

"I would have told you everything," Henry pleaded, "Eventually. I tried."

"It was a beautiful story," she agreed with an imperceptible nod. "But I should have seen the plot twist coming."

Henry smiled ruefully, winking at Gloria, rubbing his neck, "Not that original, huh?"

As Bennet shifted his attention back to Henry, Gloria took a deep breath, yanking the blade free of her purse pocket with a distinct rip of fabric. Two wadded tissues, four crumpled receipts and three rogue mints flew from their confines with the knife as Gloria launched herself forward into an imbalanced lunge, the toe of her shoe catching a patch of grass. She lost her balance. Instead of victoriously plunging the knife into Bennet's heart, she tumbled to the ground with an "oomph", Bennet feinting around her so quickly she missed him entirely. The blade was simply *gone*, lost in the dark carpet of grass beyond her outstretched fingertips.

Bennet launched himself at Henry, all the pain and loneliness of his tortured life pouring into his primal scream, his head and shoulders crashing into Henry's ribs as both men slid violently into the base of the park's oldest maple tree which heaved and split, it's twisted trunk decimated in an explosion of wood chips and wet, rotting leaves. Wood shrapnel rained down over her, stinging Gloria's skin as she frantically brushed the detritus from her shoulders. She struggled to her feet desperately scanning the ground for Henry's dagger. Scratching in the grass blindly, her hand brushed something that felt like polished stone, her fingers finding and wrapping around the bone hilt of the knife.

"You think I won't rip your heart out and choke her with it?" Bennet smiled before flying into Henry chest, pinning his shoulders to the ground with his knees, his hands at Henry's neck again, "This won't hurt *me*."

"I'll take you to her," Gloria cried, desperately scrambling to her feet, Henry's knife secreted behind her back.

Bennet's hands froze. He cocked his head.

"I'll take you to Liesl. I know where she's hiding," Gloria offered.

"No, Gloria, no," Henry moaned.

"Go on," Bennet prodded, his chin jutting out stubbornly. He loosened his fierce grip on Henry's throat, allowing him to writhe uncomfortably beneath his weight.

"She doesn't know where Liesl is," Henry managed to choke out.

"Tell me," Bennet commanded as Gloria stalled, catching a

glint of movement in her peripheral vision.

"She doesn't know," Henry struggled, bucking ineffectually against Bennet's hold, "Gloria, save yourself. Run!"

Gloria grasped the handle of the knife, pulling it forward and holding it aloft, commanding, "Stop this right now. Both of you get up. Put your hands in the air."

Bennet sat back on his heels, staring up at her with an amused frown before raising himself from his predatory squat. He motioned to Henry who struggled to his feet, hands at his neck.

"I'm clearly transforming, Henry. *You* did this to me," Gloria announced, the knife shaking in his direction.

"I know," he sighed.

Gloria shifted her gaze to Bennet, "In Henry's story, *Bennet…* you…said he…*you*…killed your maker. But you're still immortal? Why didn't you die?"

"We aren't the same, Gloria Weidman," Bennet spat derisively. "*I* was much stronger by the time I killed my maker. By then, I was already hundreds of years old. Now give me back my knife, if you're such a coward. And I'll help *you* by killing you both. Or you can use it, just kill Henry and free yourself."

"Do it," Henry shouted. "Do it. I love you. You *should* kill me and free yourself. It has to be family, Gloria. I know you know."

"Kill him," Bennet coached, tilting his head to the knife in her hand. "Don't be a *coward*."

"Do it, Gloria. Kill me." Henry offered softly, throwing his arms out to his side like a religious figure, opening his heart to her, "It's okay. Set yourself free."

She'd had enough!

"Oh! My! God!" Gloria roared, "If one more *man* tells me *what* to do or *how* to do it. Or *how to feel* when I'm doing it…I'm going to murder us all."

Gloria was startled to feel the cold steel of the blade she'd been holding suddenly on her own neck - her right hand still lifted, empty - as Bennet's pubescent voice snarled in her ear, "What was it you were saying?"

From the corner of her eye, Gloria caught a streak of plum hair as Liesl stepped silently from the shadows behind a line of large trees along the back of the park, Henry's nameless Rottweiler from the lake prancing happily at her side.

"Sing it, sister," Liesl added in a cheerful tone.

"Liesl!" Gloria cried in relief.

"Liesl!" Bennet cried with joy.

"I'm only here because Gloria called. And *she* wanted help getting rid of *you*!" Liesl corrected him.

Bennet, stricken by her betrayal, his mouth an angry slash, pushed the tip of his blade further into the flesh of Gloria's neck, blood staining the front of her shirt as he threatened, "Then she won't need so much help the next time!"

He raised the curved blade over Gloria's heart. Time froze.

There was a low growl, then the blur of brown and tan. The Rottweiler leapt forward, streaking past Gloria's wide eyes, barreling through the trees like a growling wraith, hurtling towards Bennet's outstretched hand where his great row of sharp teeth latched, ripping the arm from Bennet's body with a crunch, the knife still gripped in Bennet's detached hand. A torrent of black blood poured from Bennet's body, back into the Earth around him. He clawed at the gaping wound, his eyes blinking in disbelief as he stared down at his missing appendage, staggering a few uneven steps back.

The dog circled back to Liesl, his teeth firmly clamped around the bloody stump of Bennet's arm, which the dog dropped at Liesl's feet. Liesl bent over, retrieving the knife from Bennet's clenched hand, tucking it into her own waistband. She bent, giving the dog's chin an affectionate scratch as reward, the nub of his tail wiggling victoriously over his bloody trophy.

Choking and covered in gore, Gloria fell, scrambling back like a crab, wiping at her face with the back of her hands. Before she could clear her vision, Bennet took hold of her hair with his remaining hand, dragging her across the grass. She struggled to rise to her feet, falling as she fought to loosen his grip.

Liesl rushed forward - pushing Henry back from his trajectory to rescue Gloria - yanking the knife from her waistband as Gloria screamed, arms raised protectively in front of her face, hearing the zip of the blade and feeling the steel swish past her ear.

There was a blur of bodies connecting.

Bennet staggered back, the curved Damascus blade protruding from his chest, his eyes wide and focused on the shiny bone hilt of the weapon. Blood poured from the wound, staining his path as he staggered to his knees, his mouth open in shock. He clawed at the knife with his one hand as he sat back, sitting with his legs splayed before him on the ground, looking decidedly child-like.

"How could you?" Bennet looked from Liesl to his bleeding wound.

"You were right when you said I could never kill you, my love," Liesl crooned. "But I have Dodge here now and he will do anything I ask because he is mine, forever. *He* is my family *now*."

Henry's eyes met Bennett's. Gloria could see the connection. It was palpable and electric. Bennett lifted his arm, reaching for Henry then seemed to crumble, the outstretched hand falling to his side, his body limp.

Everything went quiet. There was only the noise of the

night and their heavy breaths in the vacuum. Liesl's hands shook as she wiped at her eyes, tears coursing down her cheeks. She held her hands before her face, clenching her fists before stretching her neck and tilting her head in each direction with a small sniff.

"He lied," Liesl confirmed sadly, meeting Gloria's questioning gaze. "I'm no more human than I was a day ago. Fucker." She kicked his boot and angrily stomped away, snapping her fingers for the dog to follow. "Good thing we talked about this."

Wiping the last of his blood from her eyes, Gloria didn't notice Bennet's body rise behind her – his eyes fixed on her, his hand clawing at the knife, pulling it from his chest to raise overhead. She heard Liesl and Henry call her name just as she felt Bennet lunging toward her.

Liesl clicked her tongue twice and Dodge leapt through the air with a feral growl, clamping his great jaws over Bennet's head and muffling an indignant scream with a tremendous crunch, ripping it from the neck with a wet pop. He loped back to Liesl, dropping the head like a ball beside his master before sitting like a good boy. Liesl pet the dog's forehead tenderly, gazing down at the mutilated head at her feet with a sigh.

Gloria thought of the Sassafras Crone's words to Henry - the very words she used when calling Liesl for help earlier tonight: *You alone are not enough. You need at least three of your strength to even truly wound him. He will never die but he can be stunned. You must find family for this to work.*

Henry and Liesl's eyes met. Without words, they seemed to agree on what needed to happen next, moving in unison to Bennet's still body as Liesl dramatically transferred the knife to Henry's outstretched hand with a pointed look.

Gloria averted her gaze as Liesl placed the bloodied head

into a large paper bag she found in a nearby trashcan. Henry crouched over Bennet's headless corpse, ribs breaking with a sickening crack as he worked, lifting the knife and setting it at his feet before placing Bennet's dripping heart into a plastic grocery bag Liesl provided with a wet plop. He remained staring down at Bennet's headless corpse, his shoulders rising and falling with his ragged breaths. Gloria found herself drawn to his side to comfort him.

Liesl, however, having had enough, clicked her tongue twice, disappearing into the trees at her back after a brief nod in Gloria's direction, her immortal pet trotting obediently behind her into the shadows, her gory souvenir staining the paper bag in her hand red. Earlier, Liesl agreed to take Bennet's head to an undisclosed location where she would bury it, promising to never reveal the location to anyone, including Henry and Gloria. Henry would do the same with Bennet's heart. Beyond that, nothing had been decided in their haste.

In the near distance, there was the audible clank of a car door. The sudden flood of headlights temporarily blinded Henry and Gloria.

"Stop right there," Casey shouted, his hands shaking visibly as he drew his gun. "Don't move, Henry," he ordered, balancing the pistol on his forearm.

What followed seemed to happen in both slow motion and fast forward, as if it all took place at once. Gloria saw Casey's gun swing toward Henry, still crouched over Bennet's body, rising as he turned, his hands lifted in surrender. His mouth opened to speak, the bloody knife still in one hand, the other raised in surrender.

Henry! No!

"Don't hurt her—," she heard Henry shout.

Gloria didn't think. She rushed forward, throwing herself in front of Henry as the gunshot echoed through the air, hanging for just a moment in the ether, followed by the soft pling of the bullet hitting flesh, the recoil of the pistol throwing Casey off balance. Gloria's body arched, a shock of the pain ripping through her back and chest. She fell into Henry's outstretched arms.

"Noooooooooooo!" Henry howled, catching Gloria as she fell, lowering her to the ground, her head cradled in his hands. She struggled to sit up, unsuccessfully, her blood pooling rapidly beneath her.

"You must… run, Henry," she tried to say, though the words were coming out wrong. "I love you."

"Gloria, you'll be ok," he whispered as she struggled to answer. "This will only make you stronger." Her vision narrowed to small points, her breath coming in great gasps.

Henry put his lips to her ear, "I'm glad you called for help. And I love you, too. Do you hear me? *I* will *always* love you. *We are* family. No matter what."

She heard the scrape of Henry's shoes as he rose, his footsteps moving further away. She could hear Casey's panicked aspirations in the near distance, running to her side as he puffed, muttering, "No, no, no, no, no, no, no, no, no, no."

She struggled to sit up, but her limbs wouldn't move. She could feel her blood flowing from her wounds with each slow beat of her heart. As Gloria floated somewhere between the plush green expanse of the city park, the dark grey clouds and the distant hum of insects singing in the night, she could see a pink slash in the corner of the inky sky, a ribbon of red light she'd never noticed before. She saw it now, she thought dreamily. She saw it *all* now. Struggling to catch a full breath, Gloria's eyes slid closed.

With a grunt, Casey tumbled into to the cool grass beside her, panting from his wild run, pulling Gloria into his lap. She cried out, a sharp pain radiating from beneath her ribs, bringing her back into her body. His shiny face hovered over her own, lips twisting in apology, his tears wetting her face, though she couldn't seem to form the words to tell him it was all going to be okay, she'd enjoyed her metamorphosis and tried to say as much.

"Yeah, go Mets," Casey humored her slurry attempts to form those very words.

He held one of her cold hands as the distant wail of an ambulance grew louder and louder, cradling her head while applying his torn shirt to her chest wound, talking a mile a minute to try and keep her alert, "Now that note you left me sure was *something*. I'm glad you told me…about Henry and Bennet. I mean…I still don't think I believe all that malarkey, but I'm sure it will help me process what I've seen here. We'll get to Ted Carroll in a moment, don't you worry. Questions will be asked, of course. Your boyfriend's run away. And I mean *run*. I saw it this time. Boy, they'll have my hide for this one. If I don't lose my job for shooting you. But don't you worry about a thing. I'm calling Dee and Terry. Everyone will meet us at the hospital. And I'm not going anywhere. I've got you. Just hold on there, Glory. Hold on…"

Gloria tried to smile. Liesl and Henry had escaped. And Bennet had been stopped. For now.

Only then. And not forever. You must find your people.

Her last thought as she lost her hold on her center, before she faded into a snug blanket of silence and peace, was a warm one. *Family.*

Chapter 57

Coughing, Gloria hugged the pillow tightly to her chest alleviating the very slight ping of resulting pain. The doctor said her discomfort would fade but her lungs had been significantly bruised for someone without a chronic respiratory disorder. Yet another one of Gloria's little medical miracles. Luckily, the local physician was a uniquely uninquisitive soul. She'd heard, "if it wasn't for your zipper," after being shot enough times to trademark it.

"And could you walk me through what happened next?" The investigator coached softly, remembering after a moment to click the button on her small recorder, shuffling it nervously around Gloria's cluttered coffee table.

"I don't remember," Gloria shook her head regrettably, looking over the brown ponytail of the suited woman in front of her to Casey's reassuring thumb's up.

"She told ya'll all a'this," Dee broke in protectively. "What more do you want?"

"There is the matter of the-" the investigator glanced at her notes, "the third suspect? A young woman? Did she leave with the second suspect, Henry Wynter? Or was she *taken*? Think carefully."

Casey offered a small, subtle shake of his head before Gloria answered, "I'm certain I saw her leave. I think she had a dog with her? One of the victim's dogs? Is that right? She just left. I didn't get her name."

"Was she traveling with the killer, Bennet Chappell?"

"I'm not sure. No? Maybe?" Gloria struggled to recall, stating for the record the entire night was a blur, adding she couldn't believe the details herself when she'd been informed later, post amnesia.

"When did you last see Henry Wynter?"

"Yesteryear, I think?" Gloria answered, scrunching her forehead in concentration.

"Was Henry Wynter at the park the night of Ted Carroll's murder?"

"I don't…know. No. I don't remember him being there. I?" Gloria looked over to Dee for reassurance. Dee nodded approvingly.

"I think she's worn out, Stella. Can we maybe finish this another time?" Casey broke in impatiently, shooting Gloria a small wink over the woman's head.

"Yeah," Dee added, patting Gloria's knee protectively from her perch beside her friend on the couch.

"Just one more question." Stella held a hand up as if to pause Casey, "Gloria, do you know what happened to the bodies? The body of the victim, Ted Carroll? Or the accused suspect, Bennet Chappell? Did you see *any* wild animals in the vicinity after Deputy Cash shot the suspect?"

"No," Gloria frowned, "I'm sorry, I know this doesn't help find the bodies."

"We found…*some* of Mr. Carroll's personal effects. As well as…as an arm," the detective confirmed before clamping her mouth closed, embarrassed to gossip about the case at hand.

"All I know for sure is they said there was a shooting. And I got in between Casey and…the *real* Lakeside Slayer…that he killed Ted in front of me. But I don't…I can't…," Gloria felt her face flush, unshed tears of frustration shining in her eyes.

Detective Stella clicked the recorder off with an audible sigh of resignation, "Ok. We can do this another time." Spinning around in the dining table chair where she sat, she glared at Casey. "I was just doing my job, Deputy Cash. You know it's highly unorthodox for you to be here," she added sourly, gathering her notebook and recorder into a leather book bag.

Casey shrugged naively, escorting her out.

"How many more times you gonna have to do that, ya think?" Dee commiserated, flitting around Gloria to adjust the pillows enveloping her.

"I guess until they are satisfied I truly don't remember what happened that night," Gloria realized with a sad shake of her head.

Dee plopped down, pulling a rogue TV Guide from under her as she adjusted to a more comfortable position on the couch beside Gloria. Staring at her oldest and best friend, Dee squinted her eyes suspiciously, prodding, "You don't, *do you*? You really don't remember anything that happened? Nothing at all?"

"Just that call from Ted," Gloria sighed. She'd answered this line of questioning from Dee several times, with several variations of approaches, to no avail. Covering a small smile, she turned stiffly to look her friend in the eyes, taking Dee's hands in her own. "You know I'll always protect you. Because I love you, right? And if that means I forgot something I should probably remember…well then, I forget because I care. We're family, Dee."

She squeezed Dee's hands before releasing them, then grabbed the remote from the coffee table. Dee smiled approvingly as Gloria clicked on the opening montage to a previously recorded Fashion Boat.

Later that evening, Gloria sat alone at the old dining room table, the back door of her house open to the cacophony of nature outside, a crisp breeze and the distant rumble of thunder on the horizon. She glanced down at the fan of old photos, clippings and her scribbled pages of notes, sighing. It was all here. Everything. Henry was gone, but the rest of her was here. She caressed the worn creases of the pages of his story, her eyes traveling to his last handwritten note to her. The one where he'd been honest. And brave. And gave her a choice.

Gloria,

Bennet will tell you many things. Most of them are lies, but some of them are true. In my life, I've been a savage, a killer, a monster and a coward. I've killed when I had to - to protect myself, to protect my family. I killed Rusty Fry. I'm sorry I didn't trust you enough to tell you the truth.

You should know my sins before you make your choices. And, if you have the courage, use this knife and set yourself free. I beseech you to follow your heart.

I always thought...the next time, if I was brave, I would find my people. And then I could face anything. But the choice, ultimately, is yours. I love you, Gloria. No matter what, my thoughts of us will always be a warm one. Family.

Eternally yours, Henry

For the first time in a long time, Gloria was *excited.* She had hope. She almost didn't recognize the sensation. Her fingers hovered over the keyboard of her laptop for a moment, practically vibrating before she began to tap the keys.

Prologue

Dean took a deep breath of the crisp morning air. He got up every morning at exactly six and made his breakfast. After a quick, dry piece of toast, coffee in hand, he'd amble down the sloped back lawn and step onto his boat dock in his slippers and robe, staring out at the rising mist from the lake. There was rarely anyone else up and about at this time of day – the solitude suited him. He noticed the grass was getting a bit high. Maybe that chunky kid from down the street would offer to mow for him again. He was getting older and the stigma of being a widower made him the target of sudden kindnesses. A casserole here, a lawn mown there. Nothing he wouldn't have done himself in better times.

He glanced at his watch, the frail hands of it barely visible in the sepia light of dawn. Almost six thirty, and it was Sunday. For a number of years, at exactly six thirty in the morning, every Sunday, Rusty Fry would buzz past Dean's dock, burning fuel and oxygen as he sped by in his cigarette boat – breaking several laws, including the speed limit – spraying Dean in a misty rainbow of exhausted lake water laced with oil. The first time it happened, Dean suspected it was a miscalculation, a drunken lark. But instead of screaming curses, Dean simply raised his coffee cup and shouted, "See ya later, ya slick bastard."

Three years later, it was practically a comedy routine, perfected by years of mutual cooperation. Dean noodled over various insults to shout to his elusive neighbor this morning. *Something* cocksucker - maybe *dumb* or *stupid* - was high on the list of potential candidates. Outside of this bizarre weekly ritual, Dean had no contact with Rusty, who was quite a few years younger. Who wasn't, these days? The receded hairline and pot belly of his nemesis put him at maybe late fifties, sixty, tops? He knew Rusty worked in a neighboring town, a bigger one, not this small one on the lake. Was it Tyler? Or Longview? Did something with taxidermy, or was it bail bonds? Something lucrative. The cherry red boat was a beauty.

Normally, as the semi-stranger passed, he'd speed up and whip the tail of the long speedboat around, slicing it perfectly to the southeast, narrowly avoiding a collision with the dock. Rusty would finish by pumping the engine, stirring up several large waves, lifting what appeared to be a permanent beer from his lap as a salutation, punch the gas and speed off until the next Sunday. Not the classiest of exchanges. But it was something to do, some routine, not too up close and personal, yet *somewhat social*, and that amount of contact suited 'em both just fine.

Dean heard a distant buzz and scrunched his eyes, peering into the fog over the water. There he was, like clockwork. The red of the sleek, shiny fiberglass boat appeared on the water line, drawing closer, faster and faster. The boat rushed forward, moving out of the fog, weaving a bit unsteadily as it accelerated. Dean stood, transfixed on the dock, watching the speedboat move faster and faster, the space between the dock and boat shrinking exponentially with time. Dean thought, as the boat failed to arc into a slice upon its approach and smashed into the pier, *he should really slow down.* The speedboat launched into the air, careening sideways as it went airborne, sailing past Dean's wide eyes as he remained rooted to the spot, remarkably unscathed by the explosion of decking and fiberglass.

He saw Rusty's hands clasping the steering wheel - the ever present, silver can wedged between his generous thighs - sunglasses still dangling from the stub of his neck. There was no head! The boat sailed like an unwieldy dart into the aluminum siding of Dean's boat house with a crunch, forcing its front end through a weak piece of metal which groaned as it was pierced and collapsed, the mangled red boat slowly sinking into the bashed frame of Dean's weathered pontoon.

Stupid cocksucker it was.

www.ingramcontent.com/pod-product-compliance
Lightning Source LLC
LaVergne TN
LVHW010641110826
845149LV00014B/2921

* 9 7 9 8 9 8 8 4 5 9 4 1 5 *